# Marshal Warrix

by

Nathan Wright

Nathan Wright

This is a work of fiction. All of the characters, organizations and events portrayed in this book are either products of the author's imagination or are used fictitiously.

If a man had the ability to choose the day of his death he would probably rather not put that ability to use, at least that would be the desire of most men. To know would take the spirit, and the mystery, out of life. But, if a man could choose the day of the week for his passing that might be a different story. A Sunday sounds pleasant enough, at least compared to the other six days. As an example, who would want to die on a Wednesday? Nope, a Sunday just sounds better. All in all, it would take a rather morbid sort to think of such things.

Joshua Warrix wasn't of the type one would consider morbid, but on this day, as he leaned against a big cottonwood, these thoughts were front and center in his mind. It happened to be a Sunday and not one of those other, lesser, days of the week. The reason Warrix considered his own mortality on this particular day was because earlier that morning he'd experienced an unfortunate mishap. As he crossed a fast moving stream he'd lost his footing and fell from the carcass of an old fallen tree that spanned the water from bank to bank.

Upon first seeing the fallen tree, Warrix considered it to be a blessing. That blessing would now prove his downfall, pun intended. When he fell his left leg had caught on a broken limb, a sharp limb. He had managed to impale his leg and for a moment he hung there, upside down, with his head under water, cold water.

After what seemed like forever, but was closer to only a few seconds, the remainder of the limb gave way and both it, and Warrix, fell into the fast moving water. The pain of the injury, and the shock of being submerged in ice cold water, gave Warrix a momentary rush of adrenaline. Warrix wasn't thinking of such things as adrenaline and had probably never heard of such a word. He only had one thought in mind, escape the stream and its icy water before it killed him. He fought his way to the bank and then clawed his way out of the water and into the nearby tree line.

As he leaned against a tree and tried to regain his breath, or catch it as he'd often heard, he realized that nearly drowning in ice cold water was exhilarating. He almost laughed as he realized that *exhilarating* and *terrifying* were interchangeable, especially in his current situation.

Nearly all he owned had been lost to the fast moving stream. Most of his belongings were in an old army knapsack and a pair of worn-out saddlebags. What remained of his meager belongings was what he carried in his coat and pants pockets. He did have the old Army Colt and his gun belt, now soaked and probably useless. The weight of the Colt had tried to pull him under but once he realized the water was only waist deep he gave less thought to his gun trying to drown him and more thought to the opposite bank.

Now a man might think this was an unfortunate series of events, which it was, but it also wasn't the first time a man had fallen from a natural made bridge and gotten impaled by a limb. There was a story in the high country of a trapper finding the skeleton of another man draped over the carcass of such a bridge. The body hadn't been completely eaten away by predators, at least not yet. What was left was a gruesome sight.

In that part of the country an injury, even a slight one, could prove fatal. Warrix had thought of that story while making for the bank. It's funny how a story a man had heard many years prior would suddenly show up at this particular time. He'd liked that story all those years ago but never dreamed he'd be living it.

No sooner had he made it to the trees than the pain of his injury made itself known. He looked down at his leg and noticed the blood oozing from a tear in his raggedy pants. The cold water must have numbed the pain a little because until he made it to the trees he really didn't think he was hurt all that bad. Now though, the pain was there and becoming more evident with each passing minute.

Warrix needed to get back to the water and retrieve his belongings but doubted he could make it very far with his injured leg. He also needed to stop the bleeding. His first thought was to take his gun belt and use it as a tourniquet. He quickly put that fatal thought away. To stop the flow of blood would soon invite gangrene, best to bleed to death here and now than suffer that horrible fate. He had heard of men in the war who had died of gangrene poisoning, the stories made him shiver.

If a tourniquet wasn't the solution then slowing the bleeding was. He took his jacket, one that was soaked, and tied it around his leg using the two arms to make the knot. As he sat there and considered his situation he emptied his pockets. Inside was a folding pocket knife and a bandanna. No money resided in those pockets, the last having vacated the premises days earlier.

He made the decision to remove the coat and try to patch his wound using the bandanna. Too bad it wasn't clean but at the moment such things didn't matter much. Ten minutes later and the wound was patched. He would examine it more carefully later in the evening. His main concern now was to make it back to the water's edge and see what might have become of his belongings.

When Warrix tried to stand he knew immediately that his leg wouldn't support his weight. He also knew that any hope of retrieving his belongings depended on making it back to the stream as quickly as possible. With that thought in mind he began to crawl as best as he could, dragging his injured leg as he went. Luckily, if it could be called luck, the distance back to the edge of the water wasn't that far.

Warrix propped himself up on one elbow and scanned the stream, he saw nothing. When he looked back to the fallen tree he was pleasantly surprised to see his saddlebags draped over the trunk. When he slipped and fell, the saddlebags, which he carried over his shoulder, must have landed perfectly on the tree. There they were, safe and sound, and also dry, hanging about five feet above the water.

The sight of the saddlebags was a bit of luck in a day that had shown very little so far. Now the problem was getting the bags off the tree. Warrix scanned the clear water; he could see the bottom of the stream. It looked to be maybe two feet deep on this side but much deeper on the other. At the spot where the saddlebags were the current was steady. Farther over toward the center of the stream it became much faster. His clothes were still soaked so he decided to just wade over and retrieve the bags. He was already cold and knew he needed to warm up quick. His matches were in those bags and the thought of a blazing fire prompted him to simply slide into the water as best as he could and ease over to where the saddlebags were.

His leg hurt but the thought of a fire made that pain tolerable. A few minutes later he had the bags and was back at the same spot where he had applied the bandanna. He looked inside the saddlebags and found what he wanted, matches.

Twenty minutes later he had a fire going and it wasn't a minute too soon. He had begun to shiver almost uncontrollably. Without the fire he felt he wouldn't have survived the day. Now though, as he warmed he began to wish he had a coffee pot, and a coffee cup, and maybe some coffee. The thought almost made him laugh.

As Warrix sat by his fire he took stock of his situation. He was injured and alone. He had nothing in the way of food except a little jerky, no flour, no tobacco, no coffee. His injury seemed to be less serious than he had originally thought but that didn't mean he could just walk his way out of here. The leg would need to be rested often if he intended to walk and walking was exactly what he needed to do if he expected to get out of the mess he now found himself in.

Warrix owned a good horse, strong, lean, capable of long days on nothing more than late grass. The only problem with the horse was that it was dead. He'd lost that horse earlier that morning, shot by some no goods he'd been tracking for a heinous crime they'd committed. A crime that would see the four hung if they could ever be brought to justice.

The four somehow suspected they were being followed and decided to set up an ambush. The ambush almost worked but instead of killing Warrix they missed and hit his horse. He really liked that horse.

Having to leave his horse was bad, having to leave his saddle was worse. Warrix knew that on foot he was several days away from the nearest town. In this situation, and trying to carry a saddle that far, was about as impractical a thing for a man to try as he could think of. Nope, he left that saddle lying right there beside his dead horse. All he had was an old canvas sack and his two saddlebags.

After the better part of a day he suspected the men he'd been chasing, the ones that had killed his horse, were long gone. He still used caution just in case they were now hunting him but as the hours went by he became more convinced he was alone. Probably not another soul around for fifty miles. Now he thought about the time he'd be forced to waste while trying to walk out of here on a busted leg. All he'd accomplished so far was nothing, and for what? A dead horse and nothing much else to show for his efforts. All this even before his accident with the footbridge that might still manage to kill him.

The whole thing started the previous day, a day that held promise, same as every other day. But even before the first rays of light reached the ground events would unfold that would tear his world apart.

Joshua Warrix was a lawman. He'd been one for five or six years and enjoyed the work, up until today. Warrix was doing something that went against his better judgement. More than one of the townsfolk said it wasn't smart to take off after four men that were known killers. The four proved that when they killed a bank teller and a patron of the only bank in Dakota City while attempting to clean out the safe. They hadn't completely cleaned the bank out of all its money, but they had come pretty damn close. Twenty-five thousand dollars in cash and gold would put that bank out of business if it wasn't returned.

Most folks in Dakota City wanted their money back with little consideration for the two souls that had been killed during the robbery. Warrix didn't care about that, if the money was never recovered then so be it. What did matter to Warrix was the two murders the bandits committed during the robbery and two more that were used to lure him from town so the bank, and the rest of the town for that matter, would be unguarded.

The hardest part to accept for Warrix was that the bank teller was his sister. His only surviving family member had been taken all because someone wanted money from the bank where she worked. They killed her and then rode away. Men like that needed to be hunted, they needed to be killed. Warrix had now made it his sole mission in life, find those who had brought death to Dakota City.

On the night before the bank robbery took place the three robbers held up and killed two miners that were working about three miles outside of town. There had actually been three miners, but the plan was to let one go about two hours before first light. It was assumed the man would hurry to Dakota City and report the crime to the town's marshal, and that's exactly what he did. There was a fourth member of the gang, he'd been stationed in Dakota City as a lookout. Warrix considered this man just as much a killer as the others. If the opportunity presented itself then the marshal would kill that man, same as the other three.

Warrix had been at the jail early that morning looking through some wanted posters. He had seen a couple of men at the saloon the previous evening and the more he thought about it the more he thought he'd recognized at least one of the men. When he came to the dodger he was looking for he had to admit, the appearance of the line drawing was very similar to one of the men's faces from the saloon. He was about to head over and talk to the man that ran the place, if he could roust the man at such an early hour, when the front door to the jail burst open.

"Marshal, I'm glad to find you here. Something terrible has happened out at the mine. They killed Jess and Sonny," James Hayes said as he tried to catch his breath, something he seemed to be failing at.

James Hayes was a down on his luck silver miner. The two dead men he spoke of were his partners, or at least they used to be. The three had been prospecting for the better part of a year and had nearly starved to death for all their troubles. Now two were dead and Hayes was nearly there, having ran most of the three miles to town without stopping. The old miner went to a chair and sat down, more like fell down, as he tried to rest himself.

Warrix stood and went to the stove. He grabbed a tin cup from a nearby shelf and filled it with strong coffee. "Here you go, James, drink this. It's hot so be careful."

As the miner sipped the coffee his breathing slowly came under control. A moment earlier it looked like a heart attack was coming on and coming on hard.

"What do you plan to do, Marshal? I can't go back to that mine and bury my friends as long as those bandits are there. If I do then there might be three graves needing dug instead of two."

Warrix looked out the front window into the dark street. Daylight was still a good thirty minutes away. He needed to ride over to the mine and investigate but didn't want to leave the old miner at the jail by himself. He decided to not speak for a minute or two so the old man could calm a bit. As he looked out the window he suspected the sky was filled with clouds, clouds that wanted nothing more than to start spitting snow. He couldn't see the sky, but he'd lived here long enough to know when bad weather was snooping around.

"I reckon I'll be heading that way as soon as it gets good and light outside. Before I go I'll need to see if Beasley can come in early today. He stayed here late last night so I doubt he'll walk in anytime soon without me going over to his place and banging on the door."

The deputy, Ray Beasley, liked to work evenings and nights, usually till the last saloon closed. It was a schedule he liked because it kept his mind busy and that's the way he wanted it since his wife of five years had up and left town. The wife he still grieved over had actually decided being in the Dakota City was a little too far west and way too far north to suit her refined ways. She waited until her husband went to work one evening around two o'clock and then took their buckboard over to Fenton. It was the nearest town that had a railroad depot.

Sally Beasley had planned her escape with clockwork precision. She made it to the depot only minutes before the seven-thirty train was scheduled to depart. She tied the old horse, a very tired old horse at the moment, to a hitch rail and hurried to buy a ticket and board the train. As the train pulled away from the loading platform the woman didn't even look out the window. She was forgetting the last five years as fast as she could. Her husband would spend the night pacing the floor worried about the whereabouts of his wife.

Sally might not have given a second thought about leaving her husband, or the way she went about it. Even if she cared to wonder what effect this might have on the man, it was her decision to never look back.

Someone came for Beasley the next day; they had recognized the horse and buckboard and figured the deputy might want it back. The deputy borrowed two dollars from Warrix and then rode to Fenton. It wasn't really a sad trip because Beasley still didn't know what was going on. Once there he asked around about the whereabouts of his wife, a woman he had to describe because neither she nor her husband had been to Fenton in nearly two years. The ticket agent knew the description as being that of the woman that left the previous evening.

"So, you say she parked that buckboard right there and then bought a ticket heading east. Can you tell me the destination of the ticket?" Beasley asked the man.

"I'm not allowed to give out any information on the passenger's destinations, Deputy. All I can say is that she was heading east. Probably going to buy another ticket at the next stop. I can only ticket to the adjoining towns. Any continued travel requires a different ticket. Sorry I can't be of more help." After he said this the man turned and walked away leaving the deputy standing there. The ticket agent had managed to create more questions without answering anything.

Knowing what little he did, and suspecting much more, all Beasley could do was go to the livery and pick up his buckboard. He figured his horse wouldn't be left out on the street all night and suspecting this he figured there would be the price of room and board for the animal. There was a fee of fifty cents paid to the friendly old hostler. The deputy got a break because everyone in town had heard the story. It was the story of a woman leaving the harshness of the west and heading to what she knew, eastern cities and eastern ways.

This wasn't the first time a woman had left on a late train never to return. It wasn't all that common, but it did happen. Every time it did there was usually a husband left behind and sooner or later he would come looking for answers. Deputy Ray Beasley was no different. He came looking for answers but left with only his buckboard.

Warrix made sure the old miner had calmed before heading out to see if he could roust Beasley. James Hayes was tired, and he was upset. Who wouldn't be after experiencing what the man had gone through the night before. He was now the sole owner of a money losing silver mine. He had watched as his two partners were gunned down at the hands of bandits. If he never saw that mine again it would be too soon. But he knew he would see the mine again, if for nothing else he had to go there to bury Jess and Sonny. Now that would be a sad day.

After leaving the jail Warrix headed for a back street where his deputy rented a room. Back when times were good, Beasley and his wife had a small home with an adjoining barn and corral but after her abandonment he just couldn't bring himself to stay there any longer. He gave away nearly everything he and his wife owned and rented a single room for himself closer to town. His bed was a horse blanket on the floor and his table was an upturned wooden barrel. He had one chair and not much else. This arrangement suited him just fine. He didn't want anything that might stir old memories. Different men have different ways to cope, Beasley had found his.

Beasley could afford the house he and his wife lived in before her abandonment. He not only worked as a deputy, but he also bred and sold horses. He did odd jobs for folks around town, anything to earn the money to afford the things he thought his wife wanted. What she really wanted was to take what money she and her husband had in the bank and leave town. After what happened Beasley stopped taking on extra work, he also got rid of his horses. He survived on his deputy's pay and nothing else. His money was so tight he didn't even buy his own coffee, choosing instead to wait until he was at the jail and drink coffee for free.

Warrix made it to the side street where his deputy lived and knocked on the door. He had to knock twice before he heard any noise.

"You in there, Deputy? I need to have a word."

Finally the door swung open, and Beasley stepped out. He was unshaven and hollow eyed as any man might be after being up half the night and then awakened at first light.

"Morning, Marshal. Anything wrong?" Beasley asked as he looked around.

"I got James Hayes over at the office. He says some men rode into their camp last night, said they killed Jess and Sonny."

If the deputy hadn't been fully awake when he opened the door, then the news he just heard cleared the cobwebs from his head real quick.

"Killed you say? Now who would do something like that?"

"I don't know but I plan on heading that way as soon as you make it to the jail. I don't want to leave James there all alone. From what I gather he nearly ran the three miles from the mine to town. After watching his two partners get murdered I'd say he did the right thing," Warrix said.

"Give me a few minutes to get woke up and I'll be there. You think we should get someone else to sit with old man Hayes so I can go with you, Marshal?"

"I thought of that, but I hate to leave town and not have anyone here wearing a badge with three killers on the loose. Hurry on over, I need to get back and check on James," Warrix said.

When the marshal got back to the jail he found James Hayes sitting right where he'd left him. He looked none the worse for wear, he actually looked better than he did when he first arrived at the jail. A hot cup of coffee can lift most men's spirits, especially in October.

"Glad you're back, Marshal. A stranger came in a few minutes ago but not before peeking in the window first. He wanted to know where you and the deputy were. I told him you'd both be here soon. When I told him that he turned and left, didn't say another word."

"You say you've never seen the man before?"

"Never, but I don't get to town that often, maybe once a month to turn in our silver and buy a few beans and coffee. Might be somebody that lives right here on main street, but I couldn't rightly say."

Just then a horse and rider went by. It was now light enough to make out anyone on the street, so Warrix went to the door to take a look. Hayes could see from where he sat that it was the same man.

"That's him, Marshal."

Warrix continued to watch the rider. The man hadn't seen him yet but that was only momentary. When he turned in the saddle to take another look at the jail he saw the marshal standing in the doorway. The marshal was looking at him. The man touched spurs and his horse picked up the pace. It wasn't quite a run, but it was a fast trot.

"You recognize him, Marshal? I wouldn't be interested but something about the man told me he's trouble. Maybe it's just the imaginings of an old man who just witnessed the killing of his two friends," Hayes said as he turned his attention back to his coffee cup.

"I didn't recognize him, or his horse for that matter. I tried to see if the horse was wearing a brand but couldn't make one out." Warrix turned and closed the door behind him. "You say that man looks like trouble to you?"

"He does and I really can't tell why he strikes me as trouble, but he does. Might be that gun of his and the way he wore it. The day of wearing sidearms I thought was nearing an end. Five years ago every man wore a gun and even some of the women folk. Now though, it's becoming a little less common. Then again, if it'd been five years ago Jess and Sonny would have been wearing guns and them three that came into camp last night might have thought twice about what they planned to do." Hayes looked down into his coffee cup as he thought about his two dead friends.

Just then Beasley came in rubbing his hands together. The man wasn't wearing gloves and his coat looked a little threadbare for a man to be wearing this far north and this late in the year.

"Got here as fast as I could, Marshal. I really hope you got some coffee left, I ain't had a bite to eat or a drink of nothing since I got up," Beasley said and then added. "Which was about ten minutes ago."

"Well James, the deputy is here so I'll be heading out to that claim of yours. Why don't you spend the morning here instead of heading back to the mine. Wait until I make it back. The men you spoke of might still be about. I believe the deputy was about to stir up some flapjacks. We make them with flour and water, it's all we got here at the jail but after eating so many of 'em I think they're pretty good fixed that way. We even got a little maple syrup in the back room, stays good and cool back there," Warrix said. He knew Beasley would be hungry and hoped Hayes was too. Anything to keep the man here until he inspected the claim. The one thing he didn't need was a prospector tagging along.

The miner agreed. He was more than content to sit in the front office of the jail and sip coffee. The room was warm, and the coffee was free, and the deputy was going to make flapjacks. Hayes suddenly realized he was hungry.

Warrix went to the livery and saddled Dusty, his three year old horse, named such because of his light tan color. Dusty wasn't too happy about getting saddled this time of day. The big horse knew it was early, he knew it was cold outside and he also knew he hadn't had his oats this morning.

After leading Dusty from the barn Warrix headed toward the claim. He knew about where it was but had actually never been there before. As he rode he pulled the collar of his coat up and then pulled his hat low. For this to be the latter part of October it was surely cold, and looked to be getting colder.

The trail the marshal used wasn't that well-traveled. He checked for sign and not long after leaving he found some of the stumbling tracks Hayes had left as he headed for town. Warrix was a good enough tracker to see that the man was trying to move fast, not a walk but not a run either. The way Hayes moved caused the toe of his boots to rake the front of his footprints. A sure sign a man was going faster than just a walk.

As he got closer to the claim Warrix decided to veer off the slightly used trail and into the timber. No way did he want to come into full view of the three men Hayes said killed his partners. This would allow the marshal to approach slowly and hopefully, unseen.

The claim was about where Hayes had described. Warrix sat his horse as he took in his surroundings, he was in a good stand of timber and well hidden. After about thirty minutes he decided no one was around. The best thing to do at this point was to tie Dusty to a tree behind cover and investigate on foot.

Warrix pulled the Winchester from the scabbard and then gave Dusty a pat on the forehead. The big horse didn't like the gun. He wasn't afraid of it but the noise it made was something he could do without, especially this early in the morning.

It was a good two-hundred yards to the entrance of the mine. Warrix tried to stay in cover and did a pretty good job of it due to the roughness of where the claim was located. After a few minutes he was within twenty yards. He knelt on one knee and listened. He listened for a good five-minutes but heard nothing. When he stood he stepped into the open and approached. There, not more than ten feet from a well-used fire pit were the two bodies of the miners.

Warrix looked over his surroundings, caution being his main concern. Again he assured himself that what had happened here was over, the men that did this were long gone.

The two miners hadn't been touched by a predator. This meant the men that did the killing were probably here until very recently. Now though, with no one around, the wolves might make an appearance. If any had been close then the bodies would have shown signs. As it was, the camp looked to have been vacated in the last hour or so. The fire pit had been covered with a little dirt but the stones around it were still warm, real warm.

Suddenly there was movement over to the left. Warrix spun in that direction, bringing the Winchester up as he did. There, standing about thirty yards away was a wolf, a big wolf. This must have been the first one to smell the blood in the air and then track the scent this far, arriving only ten minutes after Warrix.

The marshal lowered his Winchester. He wasn't afraid of a single wolf, but that might change at any moment. He'd seen packs of as many as a dozen and knew if food was scarce the packs would be larger than that. Food wasn't that scarce in October. Most of the animals that went to den wouldn't do that for another month at least.

He knew wolves traveled a large territory. This one must have either been a ways off when it smelled the blood or waited until the three killers rode away. Either way, the marshal now had another problem. He had to bury the two men and then use a top cover of rock and logs to keep the predators out. He'd hoped to send someone from town as soon as he got back but by that time both men's bodies might be totally consumed if the rest of that wolfpack came along. This was a very real possibility.

Warrix didn't have a shovel but figured the prospectors would have one nearby. He actually found four shovels, all well-worn, along with a pick. With two dead bodies and one wolf nearby he decided to bring Dusty in. The big horse would find no trouble at all dealing with a single wolf but if several more showed up he would have to either fight, or run. Tied to a tree the way he was meant he would fight.

Now a horse is a powerful animal and can do about as much damage with its hooves as a man can do with a gun. Warrix had even heard a tale once about a horse that killed a bear with a lucky kick. He didn't know if that story was true but who knows, stranger things had been told out here in the wilderness.

Anyway, it was time to bring Dusty in. The big horse was glad to see the marshal. He looked nervous, something Warrix knew could mean more than just one wolf was about. He tied the horse near camp, not more than fifteen feet from where he intended to dig the graves.

The big wolf was still standing in the same spot. It hadn't made an attempt to investigate the two bodies even though

Warrix had been gone to get his horse. Now that was strange. He figured in the little time it took him to get Dusty the wolf would have come into camp and began investigating the meal left lying there on the ground, it didn't.

This led the marshal to do something he knew better than to do. He dug into a saddlebag and got out a piece of jerky, the wolf watching his every move. He took a step toward the animal expecting it to run away, it didn't. He took another step; the wolf closely watched him but again made no effort to run. After three steps Warrix tossed the jerky in the wolf's direction. This too didn't startle or anger the wolf.

The marshal retreated a couple of steps and waited. The wolf took some very slow cautious steps toward the jerky and sniffed. After that it raised its head and looked Warrix over. Men in this part of the territory both shot and poisoned wolves. This particular animal wasn't afraid of the rifle Warrix held but was cautious about the jerky, it wouldn't touch it.

The marshal went back to the saddle bag and pulled out another piece of jerky and then stood facing the wolf. He slowly took a bite and chewed. The wolf eased its head back down and grabbed the piece of jerky that had been offered. In one quick bite it was gone. Warrix studied the animal. Surely this wolf wasn't that smart. Did it eat the jerky only after seeing that it was truly edible. If so then this was one smart wolf, and a big male wolf at that.

After finishing the jerky the wolf did something else that wasn't expected. It stretched out and put its head on top of its two outstretched front legs. Within a minute it was dozing off. In all his years Warrix had never seen a wolf come into a camp and take a nap. As a matter of fact he couldn't remember seeing a sleeping wolf before.

Well, enough attention on the wolf, there were two graves to dig. With pick in hand he selected a spot near the camp that he hoped old man Hayes would approve of. If he didn't then he was more than welcome to dig the two up and relocate their bodies. He seriously doubted that would happen. Once buried he doubted they would be moved, one spot for a grave was as good as any other he thought.

Once both holes were dug he decided to empty the men's pockets and place the contents where Hayes could recover them. This was a job the marshal would rather not do, but he did it anyway since no one else was around to volunteer. The pockets contained what he expected, a few coins, a couple of dollars in paper money, matches and the makings for a smoke. Warrix put the items in a paper sack he found in the men's rough tarpaulin covered half dugout, half tent.

Once the bodies were placed in the graves he quickly covered both with two ground covers he found in the tent and then quickly covered both with the freshly dug dirt. He topped each grave with rock and logs he found nearby, not an easy job for a man used to doing marshal work, not undertaker work.

When finished he drove two crude crosses at the head of both graves and then took off his hat.

"Two miners lay here, both good men I suppose. May they rest in peace." Warrix put his hat back on. He figured a real preacher would find his words lacking in so many ways. A preacher wasn't anywhere near, the words would have to do.

Warrix took one last look around the camp. He had already determined the direction the three horses were headed when the men left the claim. He wanted to think of them as murderers but refrained. He always thought of men like these as suspects, or accused, or even outlaws, but not murderers. That was a designation he would gladly allow a jury to determine. Now if he actually witnessed the crime then he could say for sure these men were murderers, until then they were suspects.

A judge once told him that the easiest way to come to any conclusion was to build all the evidence with one thought in mind, the outcome you wanted. Try to take everything you discovered and twist it to fit that outcome. As he stood and looked the claim over he tried to see if there might be any other way to view the evidence, there was.

What if three men stopped by the claim for coffee and conversation before riding on out. After leaving, James Hayes could have murdered his two partners and blamed it on three men that were only guilty of stopping at the wrong camp to rest a moment and warm by the fire. He could then walk, or run, to Dakota City and claim three men had killed the two. Adding this scenario to the one told by Hayes earlier made for two different, but completely plausible, explanations for what had happened. It was time to head back to town, the marshal's head was starting to hurt.

Dusty was standing there looking at the marshal, the marshal was standing there trying to think of different outcomes to the same problem. The big horse didn't know why the man was still hanging around here looking all stupid, and he didn't want to know. What he did want was to ride back to his nice warm stall in what he considered his barn and have a little breakfast, he was hungry. While waiting on the marshal he had nibbled on a few late hanging leaves, a little grass, a little bark off a tasty looking tree and damn near anything else within reach. It was time to go.

Warrix decided he had seen enough. He knew which direction the three men had rode when they left. It didn't look like they had robbed the camp, it didn't even look like they had entered the prospector's tent. That would lead more to Hayes being guilty than anyone else. Again, Warrix was being cautious not to lead the evidence at hand in any particular direction. It would require more thought though.

22

When he climbed into the saddle he noticed the wolf, it hadn't moved from its spot the whole time he had been digging the two graves and doing the burial. It hadn't moved as he inspected the camp one last time. It had raised its head a time or two to see what Warrix was doing but made no threatening sounds or movements, it had just laid there.

No sooner had Warrix turned Dusty toward the trail than the wolf stood. It was then that he noticed something he hadn't seen, or paid attention to earlier, this animal was damn near starved to death. As big as it was he really didn't think about its condition before, big meant big. But now, upon closer inspection, he could see the washboard sides of its ribs and its sunken stomach.

Warrix felt a bit of sympathy for the animal. He stepped from the saddle and dug into a saddlebag. Dusty turned his head and just looked at the man, now what, he thought. There were six or eight strips of deer jerky and of this, he decided to grab it all.

"Here you go," the marshal said as he tossed a piece over.

The wolf didn't hesitate, he grabbed the jerky and began chewing, but only for a second. It didn't take an animal that malnourished very long to chew and then swallow whatever it found to eat.

Warrix tossed each piece to the wolf, but one at a time. He didn't want him to get choked by trying to devour all of it at once. When finished the wolf did something else the marshal wasn't expecting. He took a couple of steps closer and then laid back down. This was one strange animal. Maybe far from tame but not totally feral. It was as if it had been around folks before. At any rate, the marshal had to go, before heading out he looked back at the animal.

"Doubt we'll cross paths again. You take care," he said as he started toward town.

Warrix wondered why the wolf looked so undernourished. As he rode away something suddenly dawned on him, that particular wolf was a nomad. It was traveling through this territory trying to find a spot it could call its own. Either it had been abandoned while young, and then rejected by the rest of the pack, or someone had killed all the other members of his clan. Probably the latter. That would explain the fact that it was underfed. Wolves are pack hunters. No pack meant no food, or at least very little food.

Knowing the men that killed Jess and Sonny were headed north meant Warrix would need to provision back at Dakota City and gather a few willing men if he wanted to go after the three. As he rode he was making a mental list of who he would ask to join his posse. From time to time he turned in the saddle to check on the wolf he had left behind. It wouldn't be hard to identify from other wolves in the area. One thing that made it unique was its emaciated condition, no other wolves he'd seen in the area were half as ill fed as that critter.

Another thing that made him unique was a scar on his right front shoulder where the coat didn't grow back. It was a place maybe five inches long and not wide at all, maybe a quarter inch. This normally would have been hard to see from fifteen or twenty feet but the fact that the scar was there meant the animals coat took on a part such as you might see on a well-groomed head of hair on a schoolchild. The rest of the wolf's coat was thick and unbroken, except at the scar. Warrix decided he better tend to the job at hand and forget about a homeless wolf.

It was not more than a mile from town when he spotted the tracks of three horses coming out of the timber. He wondered if this might be the tracks of the same three riders that had killed the two miners, couldn't be, those men had ridden north.

As Warrix tried to consider the implication of this new set of tracks it dawned on him. This bunch had killed Jess and Sonny and then held James Hayes in camp the rest of the night. According to James they released him a couple of hours before first light.

They wanted him to make his way to town and tell his story. If that were the case then they hoped the marshal and deputy would take off to the camp and try to capture the killers. And then there was the man riding past the jail, the one that had stuck his head in earlier looking for the marshal and his deputy. If that were the case then there were four men working together and they had managed to get the marshal to ride out of town. 'These three riders had taken a side road not wanting to meet me and Beasley as we went to the mine to investigate,' Warrix thought to himself, he actually said it out loud.

Warrix touched spurs to Dusty and the big horse responded with a burst of speed. It was a good mile to town, three minutes. Warrix was mad at himself for being tricked out of Dakota City. Moments later Dusty made the corner of Main Street and barreled toward the jail.

Warrix could tell trouble had visited Dakota City in his absence. Two men, merchants that ran the Mercantile, were standing on the boardwalk in front of the store, each holding a shotgun. A few more men were on the street, he noticed they were wearing guns and Warrix knew for a fact that these men never wore guns. These men must be on the street to prevent someone from returning. Someone that had caused trouble.

Warrix slid Dusty to a stop in front of the jail. As he tied the horse to the hitch rail he noticed two bullet holes in the front of the jail and another in the awning post. He rushed inside to find out what had happened and was met by James Hayes. The old prospector was holding one of the old Winchesters from the jail's gunrack. He could tell the gun belonged to the jail, it was old and rugged looking, just like all the extra guns the jail had.

"Where's Beasley?" Warrix asked.

"A couple of men carried him over to doc's place. He's alright I think, took a bullet in the leg," Hayes said.

Warrix stepped back onto the boardwalk and looked the town over. "Anyone else get hurt?"

Hayes stepped outside, he was still holding the Winchester and didn't intend to let go. "I can't really say, Marshal. As much shooting as I heard I figure there might be. Do you want to go check? I'll stay here and look after the jail. One more thing, Marshal, I recognized three of the riders as the ones that killed Jess and Sonny. And that one that rode by this morning, well, he's the one that ambushed the deputy."

Any doubts Warrix had about the story Hayes told earlier were now put to rest. The man had told the truth and in doing so it had prompted the marshal to leave town to investigate. Now his deputy was wounded, or maybe even dead. Warrix had to put those thoughts out of his head. With the information he had this morning all he could do was exactly what he had done, go to the mine and investigate. Now he regretted it.

"Alright James, you stay here and keep lookout. If you see any of the men that did this then get back inside and lock the door. I'm going to check on the rest of the town and see what I can find out," Warrix told the man.

As he started for the center of town he heard the door close. Before getting to far from the jail he went back to Dusty and grabbed his Winchester. When he walked up he noticed the big horse standing three legged. Now what was that all about, it wasn't nap time. Whatever was ailing him, now wasn't the time to check. As he walked he noticed a couple of men looking down one of the side streets, it happened to be the same street Beasley lived on.

"Marshal, where have you been?" a man named Kelso Blair asked. Kelso was holding a shotgun, something about as old as the Winchester James Hayes was using.

"Out to check on a couple of killings. What happened here, Kelso?"

"It was bad, Marshal. Three men came riding in here a couple of hours ago. They went straight to the bank. I think someone in there got shot. I don't know all the details. The deputy has every able-bodied man that owns a gun out on the street in case they come back," Kelso said.

The bank was where the marshal's sister worked as a teller. He took off at a run, scanning for trouble as he went. Here and there he saw bullet holes, either from the men that had invaded town or the townsfolk firing back.

When Warrix got within sight of the bank he knew the story Kelso told was true. There were two men out front, each with a gun in hand. He also saw Doc Reynolds coming out the front door. He was carrying a leather bag and had a very dejected look on his face. There was also blood on his shirt and trousers.

"Doc, what happened?" Warrix asked as he approached.

Reynolds looked up, "It's bad, Marshal. They shot John McCloud, he's dead."

"They killed John?" Warrix asked. McCloud was the bank president.

"That's not all, I'm afraid, Mae, got shot too. I hate to be the one to tell you that, Marshal."

Mae Fuller was the marshal's sister. Her husband was a man by the name of Claude Fuller. The two hadn't been married more than a year.

"Is she alright?"

Reynolds looked the marshal in the eye. He didn't speak, just a slow nod. The marshal's sister was dead. Warrix slowly stepped to the door of the bank, there were ten or twelve people inside. The place was a mess, papers strewn everywhere, chairs knocked over and then he saw evidence of the brutality of the men that had done this. There, lying in the floor, was the body of John McCloud.

Warrix stepped inside the bank and took in more. As he did he felt a heaviness in his chest. A weight had been placed on him, something he couldn't explain. His eyes were watery, his hands shook. He went to one of the teller windows and looked in, there on the floor was his sister. Kneeling beside her was her husband, he was holding Mae's hand, he was sobbing.

Warrix couldn't explain what happened next. He didn't go around the teller windows to be closer to his sister. He left the bank. He stood out front looking at the town, now armed and ready to do battle. There were men outside who in his entire life he had never seen carry a gun, they were carrying them now. This had shook the townsfolk, they were scared.

The marshal sat down on the steps; his knees were weak. As he sat there he wondered what he was going to do. Dakota City was a small town, only one town marshal and one deputy. He had been tricked, outsmarted by some men dead set on robbing and killing. Now his sister was dead, she was the only sibling he had. His mother and father had died years earlier. He was now alone in the world. For all the sadness he felt for the loss of his sister he began to notice something, it could only be described as rage.

Warrix stood and took off his hat. Although it was cold outside he noticed he was sweating. He took a handkerchief from his coat pocket and mopped his forehead. As much as he wanted to go back inside the bank and spend a few last minutes with Mae he knew there was something else he needed to do. Finish seeing to the needs of the town in this time of crisis, and then hunt down and kill the men that had done this.

The best thing to do at the moment was go and check on Beasley. He needed to walk, he needed to walk away from the bank because if he went back inside he might just give up. The only family he had left in the world had just been taken from him. After he found the men who did this he would either bring them to justice, or kill them, then he could give up. Then he could sit down and grieve for his loss. That would be for a day in the future. Today was not that day.

Warrix put his hat back on and looked toward the doctor's office. There were people there, standing on the porch. He walked that way.

"Marshal, I heard what happened. I'm so sorry for your loss. Mae was such a sweet girl. She didn't deserve what happened," a woman said as Warrix walked by. He looked at her and nodded, he didn't speak, only a slight nod. His heart was heavy, and he knew if he tried to talk his voice might break. Hearing the first words of sympathy for Mae hit hard. As much as he wanted to, he couldn't stop and talk to the woman.

The marshal kept walking. As he walked he realized that, even now, the men that did this were speeding away. They had formulated a plan to lure him out of town and then rob the bank. That plan had worked, now his sister and three other men were dead. He had thought killers to not be smart, just men that reacted violently to a situation they found themselves in. This wasn't the case here; these men had worked out a plan and then methodically carried it out. This was premeditated, this was brutal.

The doctor for the town was Elroy Reynolds. He lived on a side street down from the bank. There were several people already there, most on the porch, some standing in the small front yard. Warrix went inside, no one spoke to the marshal as he entered. Most just didn't know what to say.

Warrix went to the kitchen, hoping to find Reynolds there but the room was empty. He went down the hall but before he got to the end Reynolds stepped from a side room

"Hello, Marshal, I guess you're here to check on Beasley?" After leaving the bank Reynolds had hurried back to his office, people there needed him.

"I am, and I got a few questions if you can spare the time," Warrix said.

Just as the two turned to enter the room Beasley stepped out. "I heard about Mae. I'm real sorry, Marshal, she was a fine person and highly regarded by all that knew her," the deputy said. The deputy was wearing a bandage on his upper right thigh. His pant leg had been cut off above that.

"You're up. I figured you were...well I don't know what I figured. All I heard was you had been shot," Warrix said.

"He was shot but not as bad as I first thought. The bullet that did the damage must have hit something else first because it only went in the leg about an inch. I dug it out and then sewed him back up. He'll need to stay off it as much as possible," Reynolds said.

"Ah, it ain't nothin,' Doc. I can walk just fine with this crutch you gave me. I won't be running no races anytime soon, but I can still do my job. Marshal, I heard what happened. Are me and you going after 'em?" Beasley asked. Warrix was impressed with the spunk his deputy was showing.

"I'm going, you're staying here so the doc can keep an eye on that leg. You think you can stay at the jail for a few days? Maybe sleep there in the back room. I think the town folk will sleep better knowing someone's there while I'm gone," Warrix asked.

"I can do that but I'm telling you, Marshal, I can ride. You can't just go off on your own after them bandits. You need somebody to back you up."

There were several people standing within hearing distance and the marshal didn't want to talk particulars in front of them. "You think you can make it to the jail, I need to talk to you, find out what went on this morning?" Warrix asked.

Beasley looked down at his bandaged leg. "I might if I had a pair of pants. The doc done cut one leg clean off," Beasley said as he gave Reynolds a sour look.

"I had to cut that leg off, I didn't know how bad you were shot," Reynolds said, maybe a little too loud.

A woman standing in the front room heard what the doctor said. She immediately passed out. Others in the room rushed to her.

"Maybe me and you better quit arguing about those trousers of yours. Folks are starting to think I really did cut your leg off. Now get out of here while I see to Ms. Carter," Reynolds said. That was all Beasley needed to hear, he was free to go. But the doc wasn't quite finished. "And one more thing, Deputy. Next time you get shot maybe I'll sew that mouth of yours up too." Reynolds turned and went back down the hall mumbling to himself as he went.

The deputy got along pretty well with the wooden crutch the doc had loaned him. He got the hang of it pretty quick. As he and the marshal approached the jail they both noticed Dusty standing in front of the hitch rail. He was still favoring his right leg, holding the left up slightly. He wasn't applying any weight to that leg, this meant trouble.

"Looks like Dusty might have gone lame on you, Marshal. The way he's holding that left leg don't look good at all," Beasley said.

They were met at the door by James Hayes, he was still holding the old Winchester. "Looks like the doc got you fixed up real good, Beasley. I found where that bullet came from that got you. Take a look at that awning post."

Warrix and the deputy looked at the post Hayes was pointing at. There was a hole drilled right through the center. The exit point was splintered out, it looked nasty.

"Well I guess that explains why my leg wasn't shot clean through. The bullet was slowed some by that post. If not for that it would have blown my leg off," Beasley said as he leaned over to look through the hole. It was then that Hayes noticed the man was missing a pant leg. He also noticed the bandage the doc had applied.

"Last time I seen a leg like that it was on a turkey," Hayes said.

Beasley looked down at his leg. "Now what kind of thing is that to say? I've been shot."

"I meant no harm, Deputy. You might want to find another pair of trousers though, don't want folks to think you're proud of that leg," Hayes said. Beasley wasn't getting any sympathy from anyone it seemed.

The men stepped inside. Warrix knew the best thing for him was to stay busy, put the murder of his sister out of his mind until he brought the culprits to justice. He decided he would do just that, concentrate on the crime and deal with the personal aspects of the situation later.

"James, I made it to the claim and found things just the way you described. While I was there a big wolf came into camp. He wasn't acting menacing, but he was acting hungry. Because of the wolf I went ahead and took the time to bury Jess and Sonny. I put markers on both graves. If you're standing at the foot of the graves, Jess is on the right and Sonny's on the left. Maybe you can make better markers with their names on 'em when you get a chance," Warrix said.

"Well, old Dakota didn't get killed by them three bandits after all," Hayes said.

Warrix looked at the man. "You know that animal?"

"I do, that big wolf came into our camp about a month ago. He's running I believe. Other wolves that claim that patch of territory want his hide, and they'll get it too. He's weak from lack of food, not a lot of fight left in an animal half-starved like he is," Hayes said.

"You named him?" Beasley asked as he stoked the fire and checked on the coffeepot.

"We did, we call him Dakota. It's an Indian word, means friend. After he hung around that first week we figured he wasn't a threat. When the other wolves would be working through that area we would know it because of their howls. We also noticed the closer they got the closer Dakota got to our camp. He's an outsider and if that pack catches him in the right spot they'll kill him."

"Dakota, a wolf named Dakota. How do you know it's the same wolf," Warrix asked.

"Dakota has a scar on his right front shoulder. Not a big scar but it makes the coat look funny. He's real big ain't he, Marshal?' Hayes asked.

Warrix thought about the wolf and his appearance. "He's big, that's for sure. I wonder how much he would weigh if properly fed?"

"Biggest wolf ever killed was about a hundred and seventy-five pounds. That was a monster. I done some checking a few years back before coming to the claim. I wanted to know what I'd be up against. As long as there's plentiful game they'll leave humans alone. A bad winter, or drought, makes them dangerous. If they can't find food then we begin to start looking like big rabbits to 'em.

"I doubt this one will last the winter though, and it's not a problem with game, the other wolves are after him which means he can't hunt. If the other wolves don't get him then he'll die of starvation. I believe he's too weak to move on out of the territory but smart enough to know the other wolves are in the area. He might catch the occasional rabbit, or field mouse, but that ain't gonna' to do," Hayes said.

"Did he come to the camp begging for food, looking for a handout?" Beasley asked.

"I don't think so, wolves don't come begging. He came to the camp for protection. As long as we had a fire he felt safe. We did toss him some scraps from time to time but mostly what the three of us ate was beans and biscuits or maybe cornbread. When one of us killed game to eat we gave Dakota what was left after we cleaned it. He'd gobble it up like it was a treasure of a meal. I feel bad that we didn't do more for that critter," Hayes said.

After some thought he added. "When I make it back to that claim I'm making Dakota a full partner. He'll eat three meals a day and I'll make sure he's protected to boot. I plan on nursing him back to health. Maybe then when a pack of lesser wolves makes a show he can give the bastards their money's worth." Hayes smiled as he said this. The old man suddenly had a new purpose. He was going back to his mine, and he was going to have company in the form of a gigantic wolf. The thought seemed comforting to the old miner.

As the men talked Warrix gathered what he needed for his trip. He intended to hunt until he found the men that killed his sister and robbed the bank. The other three deaths mattered too, but when he found them it was his sister he planned to avenge. Either capture, or kill, that was his plan for every last one of 'em. If he only did one thing for the rest of his life, this was going to be it.

Beasley went to the coffeepot and lifted the lid. "You gather your stuff, Marshal, and as soon as you're finished I'll get my gear."

"You ain't going with that busted leg of yours. Anyway, somebody needs to stay here in town," Warrix told the deputy.

Beasley didn't like that one bit. "You can't go riding off alone after three or four killers. That ain't any different than suicide."

"I don't care, the men that did this will be brought to justice either at the end of a rope or my gun. Plus, I'll have an advantage. They expect the town to put together a posse. Dakota City don't have enough able bodied men to ride a posse. Our town might be young, but our residents are mostly old. They won't expect a lone rider to be after them," Warrix said.

Beasley thought the marshal's thinking was sound. Sound for a lunatic. "Alright, Marshal, I'll stay but I want it to be known that I'm against your plan. And another thing, I can ride a saddle better than I can walk these streets. You sure I need to stay here?"

"You're staying. I plan on riding as far as Ralph Bishop's place today. That's the same general direction the four took when they headed out of here according to what some of the witnesses said. If Bishop can spare a couple of hands maybe he can send them to town to help out until I get back. A good portion of the money that was stolen was his I reckon."

"You figure they only headed north to throw you off their trail. They probably changed direction once they got out of town," the deputy said.

"I thought of that. These men are smart, they planned this robbery down to the last detail. My guess is they planned their escape from town the same way. Head north thinking it was just to throw me off, I'd go south. But they wouldn't turn south, just keep going north. That's where I plan to head. I'll be checking for sign along the way. They were probably riding hard, four horses at speed leave good sign," Warrix said.

"What about Dusty? He didn't look up to a trip right now if you ask me," Beasley said.

Now that was something the marshal had completely forgotten about. He'd need to have the horse looked at before he left. He couldn't head out on a three or four day trip riding a three legged horse.

"If you don't mind, Beasley, gather some ammunition for my Winchester and Colt. Maybe fifty rounds of Winchester and a full box of Colt cartridges. I'll walk Dusty up to the livery and have Sanders take a look at him." With that Warrix headed out the door.

As he walked his horse he knew Dusty wasn't going to make the trip. The big horse had a limp, no denying that. Hopefully it wasn't anything serious. Maybe Sanders could tell him more. If the town of Dakota City had anything even close to an animal doctor it was Sanders.

"Well, Marshal, might be a stone bruise. When did this start anyway?" Sanders asked after Warrix brought Dusty in.

"This morning, we were riding hard trying to get to town and nothing seemed out of the ordinary. After I tied him up he began favoring that foot. You think it's really a hoof bruise or stone bruise?"

Sanders looked again but his opinion remained the same. "His leg seems fine, if you were riding hard when this happened then he just hit something that made his foot tender.

I'll know more tomorrow, there might be a little bruising and that will tell the tale. What do you want to do?" Sanders asked.

"I need a horse. It needs to be hardy and suited to long days and night grazing," Warrix said.

Sanders thought a minute. He had a horse in mind, but did he really want to do that to the marshal? This horse was a demon wearing a saddle.

"You know of Pulpit don't you, Marshal?"

"Pulpit, I've heard of him, and I've heard of his temperament. He's about the meanest horse to ever stop by Dakota City. Surely that ain't all you got? I could do with his size and strength, but that horse is downright feisty."

"He is feisty I'll have to admit, but he's got spirit and he's smart. He might be a couple years past his prime but that don't take away from his abilities. He can get you out of a bind if the need arises," Sanders said.

"Show him," was all Warrix said.

Sanders led the marshal to the side corral. There, standing with his head in a bucket was Pulpit. He was about the same size as Dusty but several years older. "How old you reckon he is?"

"I know exactly how old he is, he's fourteen. The man I bought him from had a good set of papers. I wouldn't let you take him if he was any older. This might be his last adventure. I think every horse needs a last adventure," Sanders said. The man talked of horses like some folks talked of kin.

"I still got some stuff to do before I can leave. Can you have him ready in an hour? Use my saddle and gear," Warrix said as he turned to leave.

"I'll have him ready. While you're gone I'll see to Dusty," Sanders said. "He's headed for a stall and some hay. Maybe a little grain might cheer him up too. When he sees you ride out of here on Pulpit he might kick a hole in his stall."

Warrix went back to the jail, waiting on him was Will Farley. Farley was the mayor of Dakota City. He wasn't exactly a friend of the marshal's, or the jail for that matter. He kept their funds at the end of a short leash and their pay at a level that prevented the two men from enjoying even the basics of life.

"Marshal, what do you plan on doing about the money stolen from the bank this morning. I just left there; the initial tabulation is those outlaws got away with somewhere north of twenty-thousand dollars. The bank will go under unless that money is returned," Farley said.

Warrix stopped what he was doing and just looked at the man. The mayor hadn't mentioned the two deaths at the bank, probably didn't know about the two dead miners either. The marshal wanted to knock some sense into the mayor, probably an impossible task for a politician. Good sense didn't seem to stick to small town office holders.

"I plan on hunting down the men that killed my sister and three other men. If you're worried about the bank going under then get your horse and a gun and go with me," Warrix said. He was taunting the man and didn't care how he liked it.

"That's not my job, Marshal, it's yours. Now I say you do your job before..."

Warrix did what he'd wanted to do ever since the mayor was elected, he grabbed a handful of the man's shirt and backed him up against a wall. "Now you listen to me, Farley. I just lost my sister. I'm in the mood to kill someone right now and if you don't shut your mouth I might just give you that honor. Piece of advice, think real hard before you say another word." He roughly released the man's shirt as he took a step back trying hard to regain his composure. As bad as he wanted to hit the mayor he knew he had problems much more important than Will Farley.

Farley took in a breath as he straightened his collar. "I meant no disrespect, Marshal. I now realize I was out of line. I also want to express my sympathy for the loss of, Mae. She was a lovely girl and didn't deserve what happened, no one did."

Now this wasn't like the mayor at all. Warrix didn't need, or want, the man's sympathy. He figured Farley had gone back to being a politician. "In answer to your previous question, I plan on heading out within the hour. Beasley will be here at the jail while I'm gone but it might be a good idea to keep some of the townsfolk on the street with guns. I'm going to see if Ralph Bishop can send a couple of men over to help the deputy until I get back. If he agrees it's still a day and a half before they get here."

"Ralph Bishop, that's good. I think most of the money that got stolen was his anyway. I'll see to a couple of guards on the street until they show up. How many days do you think you'll be gone?" Farley asked.

"Three or four, but if Bishop can spare two men then I might be gone two or three weeks. I plan on finishing this, one way or another."

The mayor realized Warrix was a man with backbone. He also realized the man was taking very little in the way of food. "I saw Quint and Maxwell standing in front of their store while on my way over here. I'll see to some proper trail food. If you're going to be gone weeks I expect you're taking a pack animal?" The men he mentioned were Quint and Maxwell Wilson, two brothers that owned and ran the general store.

Warrix just looked at the man. This was the first generosity the mayor had ever shown to the marshal. "No pack animal. I plan on traveling fast and light."

"Alright then, that gives me something to go on. I'll be back in a few minutes," Farley said as he headed out the door.

Beasley looked at the marshal, surprise plastered all over his unshaven face. "Is that the same mayor, or did we get a new one lately?"

"My guess would be a new one if I hadn't seen it with my own eyes. I'm glad though, I was going to have to shoot a rabbit or two to finish this job," Warrix said.

"Marshal, I know how you feel, or at least I'm trying to imagine how you feel after what happened at the bank but are you doing the right thing going after them four by yourself. Another thing, once you're five miles from town that badge ceases to have any authority. The sheriff takes up the reins at the five mile mark," the deputy said.

"By the time we get word to the sheriff, and he gets a posse together, it'll be too late. The outlaws will be long gone, probably clean out of the territory. I'm still going, at the five mile mark I guess I'm just a vigilante looking to carry out justice. I'll still be wearing the badge, but it won't mean much."

Ten minutes later the mayor was back. He was carrying two cloth sacks, both looked fairly full but not unhandy for a man on a horse. "Here you go, Marshal. I told the Wilson's what you were going to do, and they fixed up these two sacks. Said they hoped you were successful. I didn't tell them you were going alone; I was afraid word might get out."

Warrix was surprised. Keeping his number a secret was a good idea. "Thanks," was all the marshal said as he took the two sacks.

"One more thing, Marshal, after you leave town you'll be leaving your jurisdiction and that badge loses its steam. I put some thought into that while waiting for the Wilson brothers to gather your stuff. I wrote out a letter that explains what happened here and why you're working far from town. There is a useful statute in the Territory's charter that says a lawman chasing lawbreakers can continue the chase even past his jurisdiction. I actually came across it while researching my powers as a small town mayor. You take this letter; you can go as far as you please in pursuit of the men that did the killing. Here, I've got something else you'll need."

Farley reached into a jacket pocket and pulled out a hundred dollars in twenty dollar bills. "Take this Marshal. I don't know how long this trip will take but the supplies in those sacks won't last more than a week or ten days. You can replenish at the first town you come to." With that Farley turned and headed for the street.

The three men in the room didn't speak for a few minutes. Finally Beasley said, "That is not our mayor."

"You said it, Deputy," Warrix said as he stuffed the money in his pocket. He considered it town money; his money was in the negative due to some unpaid bills and a couple of IOU's. The two sacks and the hundred dollars meant he could range as far as needed in his search for the killers. He now thought of them as killers, not bank robbers. He didn't give a damn about the money they took.

There was still the problem of the original two killings. With the four killers on the loose it would be a bad idea for James Hayes to go back to the claim.

"James, what do you plan to do?" Warrix asked.

"I believe I'll stay here at the jail if that's alright with you. The deputy here is all broken down from that gunshot wound and I figure to stay right here and guard this coffeepot."

This suited the marshal; it probably suited the deputy too. He wasn't going to be running any races anytime soon. Hayes had proved himself steady under pressure and his presence at the jail would go a long way in making sure things went smoothly. If nothing else he could keep Beasley supplied with hot coffee.

Warrix left the deputy and Hayes at the jail. He headed for the livery hoping he could make it to Ralph Bishop's place by nightfall or shortly after. Sanders had Pulpit all saddled up and ready to go.

"Looks like you plan on being gone for more than a day or two, Marshal," Sanders said when he saw the two sacks.

"I do at that, but I'd like that to be known by as few people as possible. Say, would you have an extra ground cover lying around somewhere? I got one but in this kind of weather I probably need a spare," Warrix said. What the marshal didn't say was that he wouldn't be using a fire after nightfall when he camped, and the extra ground cover would actually work as a top cover. He could even make a small tent if rain or snow looked imminent.

"Got a brand new one, Marshal. Let me get you a hank of rope to go with it, just in case," Sanders said. The hank wasn't actually rope but heavy twine. This would come in real handy for the marshal. The liveryman wasn't fooled by the marshal's story of extra ground cover. He knew the man was after some pretty bad characters and probably would be spending his time in cold camps. Sanders wasn't born yesterday, more like fifty years ago, plus a yesterday.

"Got it, Marshal. Let's get it tied on behind the saddle along with them two sacks. Might cover the saddle bags but that shouldn't be a problem. As the sacks empty out you can save them for the next store you come across. I've traveled the rough and tumble back in my younger days. Hard to carry much on a horse you're riding. Pack horse would have solved that, and you could have taken a little grain along. If Pulpit is going to live off grazing then he might start to slow a little after a few days. He's well fed but he's also a stable horse. All and all, he'll do fine though."

The marshal thanked Sanders and then headed out. Pulpit didn't like the way things were looking, the big horse was smart enough to know that a couple of extra sacks tied on his back usually meant a trip. This time of year he really wanted to stay in his stall and the corral next door. Then again, it had been some time since he'd been on a trip. Maybe this would be alright after all. Pulpit decided he was ready for an adventure, as long as he was back before the snow started piling up, time would tell.

Warrix left town heading in the same direction the outlaws had taken. He kept a close eye on the tracks, not really expecting the four riders to head either east or west. North was his guess and the farther he went the more convinced he was that they hadn't tricked him again.

The day was cloudy, not a ray of sunshine could be seen anywhere. The trail he traveled was not much of a trail at all, more like an old buffalo run that had been crowded back to nothing by trees and brush. The tracks were easy to find and follow though. It was almost like the four didn't think they would be pursued.

Two hours after leaving Dakota City the marshal found where the men had watered their horses and then tied them out. By the look of things the men had been in that spot for at least an hour. It looked like they even built a small fire, undoubtedly for coffee. With a little looking around he found where they had dumped the coffee grounds and then where a man had gone to the stream to wash the pot. These four weren't concerned in the least about being followed.

As smart as the men had planned the bank heist they were now being pretty stupid. Not more than ten miles out of town and they were leaving sign a blind man could follow. Warrix mounted back up and continued. Pulpit was actually glad to be in some strange country. He was almost excited to be on a trip. That would change if the snow started in, or if he started craving something other than graze.

Sam Aldrich was a sorry cuss on a good day. On a bad day he was mean and hard to be around. This was not one of the bad days and still the man had managed to rob a bank and kill the bank's president. The other three men he rode with didn't know why he'd shot the man? He had done as told and emptied not only the safe, but also the trays of the four tellers. Three of the tellers hadn't been at the bank this morning, they usually came to work an hour after it opened. The four tellers rotated opening hours, the teller at the bank that fateful morning was Mae Fuller, it was her day to be there at open, an unlucky day.

"You want to tell any of us why you shot that woman, Bryson? Buford Fenton asked.

Heith Bryson rode on in silence. He was trying to remember why he had killed her and then it came to him. "I'd never killed a woman before; thought I'd give it a try."

"Well that was a plain stupid thing to do. You shoot a man or two doing a job and the town wants justice, and that can take a while. You kill a woman, and they hang you as soon as they find you. I'm surprised we ain't being hounded by a posse already," Fenton said as the four rode.

"We done scouted that town, ain't more than two or three men there that are capable of riding posse. That whole town is old if you ask me. Folks just stay there until they die I guess. We done hurried two of 'em up if you ask me," Marcus Rowley said.

"Yep, and don't forget them two miners. We done lowered the population of that town by a fair amount," Aldrich said. Of the four riders, Aldrich had proven on more than one occasion that he had the least amount of brains. Sometimes the other three wondered if he had brains at all?

"How about the three of you riding quiet for a while. I doubt a posse is after us, but you never can tell," Heith Bryson said. Heith was the leader of this bunch, a leader by his own account anyway. The men knew they had hit the bank hard. They knew when the most money would be there, and their timing was perfect. Bryson hadn't figured this out on his own, he was being instructed.

These four had legitimate jobs that would hopefully provide an alibi if needed. The man they worked for ran a substantial operation. He owned the largest ranch in the Dakota's. Where other men had failed in trying to raise cattle this far north Ralph Bishop had succeeded. Now these four might have worked for Bishop, but that didn't mean Bishop was an outlaw. Bishop, for all intents and purposes, was an honest man. The four that rode from the town they'd just shot up worked for the man as hired hands, not bank robbers and killers. They normally spent their days riding line and herding cattle.

Bishop had sent the four south to one of his line shacks to round up strays and get them gathered in for the winter. This wasn't usually what Bishop did with his southern stock, he let them range far and wide during the winter. But this winter was shaping up to be different, cold with lots of snow. Bishop had no more evidence of this than the next man, he just had a hunch.

So far when Bishop had a hunch he was usually right. He had grown his ranch by playing hunches. Probably the worst bit of luck, and there was no way of knowing this yet, was his hiring of Heith Bryson and the other three men that rode in with him. The four were wanted, both in the south and the east, so they came to the Dakota Territory and found a job.

The ranch Bishop had built was a good day's ride north of Dakota City, but his property ran within five miles of the town, it was a big ranch. Trying to raise cattle this far north was a fool's errand, at least until Bishop came along. Most other men that'd tried had failed, and in doing so had lost their stake.

Bishop had the brains and the money to try things his way. He knew cattle and he knew terrain. He got the land cheap because no one else wanted it. Before bringing in the first head of stock he built his ranch house and the support buildings his operation would need. He also built ten line shacks on the periphery of his property. He had good water and adequate grazing. The grazing would be improved as his herd grew.

What made Bishop confident he could succeed where so many had failed was his deep pockets. He'd made his fortune back east as a banker. He'd known banking in his former life, but he knew ranching in this life. He loved what he did, and he loved where he was. The winters were harsh but the other three seasons made up for it.

He ran a crew of anywhere from forty to sixty men depending on the time of year. But if anyone cared to count, as big as the ranch was, you'd think there wasn't more than four or five hands to the whole spread. That's because you never found more than four or five in the same spot at the same time. Bishop managed his men like he managed his ranch, no wasted effort, every move carefully calculated. To make money in cattle this far north could only be done if everything worked smoothly. This had been Bishop's goal and it was now a reality. That was until he hired Heith Bryson and his bunch.

"Those men you got on the south boundary; you think it was wise to send those four there? They ain't been with us very long and I got my doubts," Windell Toler asked.

Toler was the foreman for Ralph Bishop. He was another reason Bishop's operation had succeeded. Toler was a man that got things done. He was weatherworn and tough. The man had literally been in the saddle his entire life, at least since the age of seven. Bishop had learned to trust the judgement of Toler. So far the man hadn't given the ranch owner any reason to doubt that judgement.

"I got to thinking a couple days ago about that very matter. I sent a man down there and told the four to relocate to the north. The line cabin there hasn't been used since summer. I was a little concerned about leaving those four that close to Dakota City. The temptation of a saloon is too much for some men. Until I learn otherwise I plan on keeping that bunch working the north boundaries. You were doing a head count out west of here when I made the decision," Bishop said.

"I believe that's the best move, boss. The four don't impress me and until they do I'd just as soon they be put somewhere away from Dakota City. The north line shack will do," Toler said.

"How did the count go yesterday?" Bishop asked.

"Good, real good. Branded about a hundred. Our estimate might have been off a couple of hundred head. We're not short, we're over by two hundred," Toler said as he looked at his boss.

"Two hundred over, that will just about balance out what we lost in that flood back in August. I swear, between drought, and flood, and snowdrifts up to their bellies, that herd has survived better than I could have hoped. You still planning on going to Dakota City this week?" Bishop asked.

"Leaving tomorrow at first light. How many men you want me to take?" Toler asked.

Bishop thought it over. His payment from Chicago was at the bank in Dakota City. The herd his men had taken to the railhead eight weeks prior had made it to Chicago and payment was now waiting in the bank in Dakota City. City Trust Bank was where Bishop had all his money, except for a few thousand he kept in a big safe in his office. He considered this his emergency money.

"Take three, each of you take one of the 1873 Winchesters and extra ammunition. I want two of you to have an extra Greener, the ones we had tooled down to eighteen inches. Use the new scabbards we got a while back," Bishop said. Toler liked the idea; he was the one that talked Bishop into buying the coach guns in the first place.

Cattle in 1886 Dakota territory were going for seven to ten dollars a head. Bishop was a better business man than to accept such an amount. He had his men drive the stock to the railhead at Butte City and then loaded onto cattle cars. He had an agent contracted in Chicago that made the deals with brokers there.

The cattle were sent east as far away as New York and Boston. Easterners had taken a liking to western beef. The taste and texture of cold weather stock seemed to be well regarded and as such it brought top dollar. What sold for around seven dollars a head in the Dakota Territory went for four or five times that much back east.

Bishop shipped his cattle in four-hundred head lots. The drive took a week to ten days, the railhead was only eighty miles. Covering ten to twelve miles a day, and depending on the weather, eight days was about the best time made. That was another thing the ranch foreman had implemented, never push the herd more than twelve miles in a single day. Ten miles was optimal and twelve was the high side of what he wanted. There were good spots along the way where the herd could water and graze. This kept weight loss to a minimum. A fat cow was a money making cow.

The last herd Bishop sent to Butte City was four-hundred head. Toler liked to push that many because a dozen men could control the pace and direction just fine. They had tried five-hundred and fifty once and had problems. Four-hundred suited Toler just fine.

Another problem was cattle cars. A typical car could hold twenty to twenty-five head. At twenty-five it would take sixteen cars to haul Bishop's herd to Chicago. Coordination with the railroad was critical. The cattle cars were usually there two or three days before the promised delivery of the herd. Toler always made his appointed time at the yards where the herd was allowed one days rest before being loaded. Timetables were always worked out in advance. Careful coordination made sure train and cattle met at the right time. If a train sat waiting on the herd then Bishop paid a steep penalty, so far that hadn't happened.

The payment for that last herd had been slightly better than previous contracts. The price per pound was up and of the four hundred only eleven had been lost due to accident or other problems. Slightly more than fourteen thousand dollars had been deposited in City Trust Bank three days prior. Thursday, October 21st, the bank received the money, and the balance sheet of Ralph Bishop was increased ten-fold. The money wasn't a windfall though, wages and taxes had to be paid. Upkeep and supplies for the ranch also came out of the proceeds. It was a never ending process, money in, money out.

All in all though Bishop was making money, good money. The herds were driven to the railhead four times a year. He was staying ahead of his creditors and planned on keeping it that way. He had a small cushion if things went wrong, maybe a month's wages could be scrapped together if something out of the ordinary happened. Something wasn't going to happen; Bishop was too shrewd a businessman to make mistakes.

Where he'd once had deep pockets of cash he now had more, but not cash. His wealth had increased but it was in cattle and land. To be rich in cash was a waste Bishop had always told himself. To be rich in assets was to be truly rich. Assets make money, cash just sits there. For this reason he had lots of assets, but cash was always tight. Not a problem, one step ahead of the creditors that had advanced him the money to buy four times more land than he could initially afford made for a large venture, and Bishop felt it kept him sharp.

Bernard Rumford was the cattle agent Bishop used for his shipments. This had been the fifth lot handled by Rumford and to this point, everything had gone according to plan. What

Bishop didn't know was that his cattle were bringing five more dollars a head than being reported back to the ranch. The agent was skimming two-thousand dollars on each herd, and this was only from one rancher. There were two more and he had worked those clients much longer than Bishop.

Rumford had been envious of the land Bishop owned in the Dakota Territory ever since his first dealings with the man. The ranch was called the Double R, named after the first initials of Ralph and Rhonda Bishop. Rhonda had passed two years prior, but the name stayed the same, at least for the first year after Rhonda's death. It was now called the Box W Ranch. The name held no particular meaning, that was the reason Bishop picked it.

The Box W had fifty thousand acres of rough land. Maybe half suitable for cattle but good water anywhere you looked. The sixty or so men that worked the ranch were responsible for seventy square miles of land and cattle. The line shacks, of which there were a dozen were placed along the boundaries. Most were used by a single rider whose job it was to see that any cattle drifting toward the boundary were headed deeper into Box W territory. Not all the line shacks were used depending on where the herds were. A few of the shacks housed as many as five wranglers depending on where most of the cattle were at the time.

Rumford had a plan; it was something he had been working on for the last two years. The money he'd been skimming was safely tucked away in a safety deposit box at a bank down the street from his apartment in Chicago. He now had over thirty-eight thousand dollars tucked away, that was a lot but not enough for a man like Rumford. He needed sixty-seven thousand five hundred. This was for the Box W Ranch, forty-five thousand acres at a dollar and a half an acre.

Rumford was nearly thirty thousand dollars short, but this was a shortage he could overcome. As good as Bishop and Toler were at running the Box W, Rumford was just as good at theft and deception. He had a plan, and it wasn't something he had just arrived at, he'd been putting the wheels in motion for two years.

"Where we heading anyway, we been riding for the better part of the day and all we're doing is following this trail. A destination might be nice to know," Marcus Rowley asked. Marcus had taken orders from Heith Bryson for years; it was probably because he wasn't smart enough to come up with any plans of his own.

"You got someplace you need to be?" Bryson asked as he led the way.

"No place in particular, but a destination would be nice to know."

"Destination, I didn't know you could use a word that long. Maybe you ain't as slow as we think," Bryson told the man. The boss wasn't above being a smartass and the other three men knew it.

"Anyone that's been on a train knows what destination means. Now where are we going?"

"I got word yesterday to head to that northern line shack. One of Bishop's men headed me off while I was scouting these trails looking the ground over in case we got into trouble. He spotted me and came over. He knew we were checking for strays and thought nothing of me being where I was. He gave me the message and then headed on into Dakota City. He was leading a packhorse and was going into town to pick up mail and tobacco. Seems that bunch ran out of the makings before the next supply run. Bishop always resupplies after picking up his pay from the last herd he sends to the railhead. The money we got in the saddlebags was what he was going to use to pay all the hands and buy supplies. Hope the man's got good credit," Bryson said as he laughed.

"Are we headed back to the ranch?" another of the four asked. His name was Buford Fenton. Fenton was a solid guy that had fallen in with the wrong crowd. Bryson had convinced the man to come along when the other three went to the Box W looking for work. He was in over his head now though. He hadn't killed any of the four victims, but he was guilty by association. If found out and caught all would be tried and hung, probably from the same tree.

"We're doing what I was told to do yesterday. We're heading to that northernmost line cabin and riding the boundaries. We'll hide the money until I get word from the man back east."

"Well I got an idea. You said each of us would get three hundred dollars for the bank job. Now don't get me wrong, that's a lot of money. More money than I've ever had before. But what if we just kept going and kept it all?" Sam Aldrich asked.

Bryson stopped his horse and looked at the man. "I reckon if you would steal from the man that put this job together then you might decide to kill the three of us and just keep it all for yourself." Bryson had his hand on the butt of his gun; this wasn't lost on Aldrich.

"That's not what I'm saying at all. We all took a chance doing this job and if we're caught it's us that'll get hung. The man that put this all together won't face charges, he won't even be implicated in them murders," Aldrich told Bryson. As he said this he didn't take his eyes off the gun.

Bryson eased his hand away from the Colt and continued riding. The other three knew very little about the man from Chicago that was calling the shots. They also didn't know the type of friends the man had. Each would be hunted down and killed in a gruesome fashion if they did what Aldrich had just mentioned. Didn't matter, the three weren't going to live that long anyway.

Warrix had been tracking the four men for most of the day. He figured he wasn't gaining on them, but he wasn't falling behind either. The trail they left behind as they rode told the marshal two things. They weren't afraid of a posse, and they weren't trying to hide their tracks. Both meant they were either reckless or dumb. The way the robbery had been planned meant they weren't dumb, so that only left reckless.

As the marshal rode he kept trying to figure out the reckless part. If what the mayor said was true then they were carrying a sizable amount of money. Men in a situation like that would take precautions, yet these four weren't. It just didn't figure.

The marshal stopped a couple of hours before dark to let Pulpit drink. The stream looked clear and cold. Going ten feet upstream he filled his canteen. His plan had been to head for the Box W and see if Ralph Bishop could send a couple of hands to Dakota City to help out. The trail the outlaws were using was swinging wide of the ranch and Warrix didn't want to leave it for fear of not being able to reacquire it the next day. He'd stay with the trail. Hopefully Beasley and the mayor could arrange a schedule for a few men to patrol the streets. There was probably no need to worry, the outlaws were getting farther from town with each passing hour.

Figuring the four men he was chasing would stop a good hour before dark to make camp, Warrix pushed on until almost dusk. He hoped the forty-five minutes or so might help diminish the gap. With the light of day vanishing fast the marshal quickly built a small fire hoping it was barely light enough to not reveal where he was and dark enough to hide the smoke. It only took fifteen minutes to boil a pot of coffee and fry a little bacon. Once finished he quickly put out the fire.

Pulpit had been watching the whole time and hoped there was a little grain, or maybe some oats, in one of those two sacks. After a few minutes he decided there wasn't, so he started cropping a little grass. What kind of a man would forget oats? Pulpit figured then and there that Warrix was a dumbass.

After finishing supper the marshal washed the small frying pan and even smaller coffeepot. He wasn't complaining though, the mayor and the two store keeps had done him good. He figured the contents of the two small sacks would do him a good week, maybe longer if need be. After cleaning up the camp as best as he could he grabbed Pulpit's reins and led the big horse away. He wanted to walk at least a half mile to get away from where he'd built the fire, just in case someone came looking. It wasn't just the fire but also the smell of bacon and coffee, it travelled.

He'd spotted a place as they rode in and knew pretty much where it was. Didn't take more than ten minutes to get there in the dark. There was water nearby and late graze for Pulpit. He staked the big horse out and then spread his ground cover. He had both the Winchester and the Colt under the blankets as he stretched out. It was then that the memory of his sister hit hard. Sleep didn't take hold for quite a while, but it wasn't a problem, grief took its place.

Dawn came on just as dawn always does this time of year, cold and a little late. It had company in the form of a light dusting of snow. Snow could be good and bad for the marshal. It could mask the previous days trail but once found it would identify the route the killers were taking. If Warrix was lucky enough to find the trail, and find it early then he could move faster. Fresh tracks in the snow would make his job easier.

After saddling Pulpit he quickly gathered his gear and then mounted up. He didn't even think about breakfast, this light snow might prove to be an opportunity. Ten minutes after first light he was on the hunt. He wasn't tracking outlaws, he was hunting them, all the way to the gates of Hell if that's what it took.

The going was slow at first, all ground sign from the previous day was hidden. Warrix was a better tracker than most and now his skills were being put to the test. He looked for disturbed limbs or small branches. He looked for the tossed quirlies the men smoked and then absentmindedly tossed on the ground. He doubted any of the bunch smoked store bought cigarettes. In all his life he never knew a man that smoked store bought cigarettes. A good way to get laughed at he thought.

Just when he figured he'd lost the trail he found a sign. A hand rolled smoke that had been tossed to the ground. It had continued to smolder and left a recognizable stitch in the thin covering of snow. This bunch might have had a good plan, and managed to carry it out, but they were leaving a trail any white man could follow. White man meaning, non-Indian.

By ten that morning Warrix knew he was gaining ground on the four. It was still snowing, but lightly. As he rode he started making out faint tracks covered with a little snow.

Before long he could make out more tracks, they weren't under the snow, they were in it. They were maybe an hour ahead, not much more than that.

An hour later and he knew he was getting close. He was in timber; the terrain had grown much more rugged. He figured he was still on Box W land but didn't know exactly where. He might even be off the ranch by now. This was territory he was unfamiliar with. The streams in the area were running fast, not deep, but not shallow either. The elevation had changed, moving higher. He could tell by the change in the vegetation and trees.

He was going to need to use more caution, not wise to get caught in an ambush. No sooner had this thought gone through his mind than there was a gunshot. Pulpit jerked and then went down. The bullet meant for Warrix had hit his horse.

As the horse fell Warrix tried to pull free of the stirrups, he wasn't successful. His left boot was under the horse, but not far. He yanked hard and pulled his foot free, but not his boot, it was still under the horse.

The marshal saw where the bullet had struck Pulpit and realized the shooter had him dead in his sights, but the shot went low. There could be two possible reasons for this, well three if you considered the shooter just missed, but he doubted that was the case. Shooting uphill will cause a man to shoot low or, the distance was greater than allowed for. At any rate Warrix knew from what direction the bullet had come from.

Luckily the scabbard was on the right and all he had to do was reach up and pull his rifle out. No sooner had he yanked the Winchester free than there was another shot. Again the bullet struck Pulpit. The big horse didn't move, he was already dead.

So the shooter had seen the marshal's hand as he grabbed the gun. If he stuck his head up then he was probably dead.

Lying behind the body of his horse gave him an idea; he removed his hat and waited. When he felt the time was right he put the hat on the barrel of the Winchester and eased it above Pulpit's body.

Another shot, this one a little high. It was what Warrix had wanted. As soon as he heard the shot he took his left hand and batted the Winchester's barrel causing his hat to fly a foot or so in the air. He really didn't think that would work but had heard a story once of just such a stunt, he figured he'd give it a try.

"Did you see that, Bryson, I hit the bastard," Marcus Rowley said. He was the best shot of the four and it was decided to let him kill the marshal from a distance.

"I did at that. He raised his head up and you put that bullet through his face," Bryson said. Of course none of the men had seen the face, or the bullet, but they could imagine.

"The way his hat shot up you must have taken the top of his head off. That was a damn good shot, and you know how I hate to brag on you, Marcus," Buford Fenton said. All four men were impressed with the resolution of a problem they had expected all day. Marshal Joshua Warrix was dead, ambushed while he rushed to serve justice. The four didn't set much in the way of marshals, a dead marshal was their kind of lawman.

"We better ride, no use in waiting around to see if he was traveling alone or not. If there was a posse then by the time they find his body and give him a burial, we'll be miles from here," Bryson said.

"Doubt that town would have sent a posse. Warrix was just stubborn enough to come after us on his own. I know the type, small town marshal that thinks he can take on the world. When they pin a badge on a man he suddenly becomes ten feet tall, at least he thinks he is," Rowley said.

The four went into the timber and retrieved their horses. After leading them out on the other side where they could pick up the trail again without being seen they mounted up and rode off. Each convinced the marshal, and his horse, were dead.

Warrix held still and waited, if they came his way he had the advantage of being the defender of his position. They would need to come to him and thus be exposed. He had to give the shooter credit though, he was good. The only mistake the man made was not allowing for elevation and distance. The mistake was the reason Warrix was still alive.

After ten minutes the marshal eased back from Pulpit's body and then moved left ten yards. He found a spot where the cover was rock and scrub. He eased forward and peered through the scattered vegetation. What he saw was four men heading into the timber. They were leaving.

Fifteen more minutes of waiting convinced him that they were gone. At first he thought they might ride up to investigate but this was a confident bunch. They had killed the marshal and now had places to go. Warrix eased back to Pulpit and checked the horse. He'd been shot twice, the first was fatal, judging by the impact point. He patted the big horse's neck and spoke a last word to him. Some men can lose a horse and never think twice. Warrix was a bit more sentimental than that. Pulpit had gone on one last adventure, at least that was something.

With some work he managed to free his boot. One of the two sacks was securely under the horse and there wasn't any way to get it out. He salvaged his saddlebags though, of all wonders. The worst luck, other than losing his horse, was that the box of ammunition was in the sack that he couldn't get to. What ammunition his Winchester held was all he had. His Colt was fully loaded, and he had maybe a third of his belt loops filled. If he'd had more time, and a little money, he would've bought an extra box of .44 ammunition for the Colt. What he had would just have to do.

After crawling back to his previous lookout position he scanned the area the four had taken, no movement. He was convinced they had left him for dead, it had almost been the case. All he had now in the way of supplies was his saddlebags and one of the sacks. Even his two groundcovers were wedged firmly under the horse. They must have shifted as he went down and landed under, rather than away, from Pulpit. As bad as it was though, it could have been much worse.

Warrix decided to keep to the timber, his preferred path would take him higher and away from the four gunman. He doubted they would use any of the high up trails that the area was filled with. Over the hundreds, hell, the thousands of years, larger game had made trails through the mountains. It was these trails the marshal intended to use to stay away from the men he sought. Now wasn't this a confusing situation. Stay away from the men he sought; it almost made him laugh.

He figured it to be around noon, if he could make three miles an hour then he could travel maybe fifteen miles before it got dark. In those fifteen miles he hoped to find a trapper's cabin or a small ranch where he might be able to borrow a horse. It wasn't much of a plan, but it was a plan just the same. One thing he did know, if he made it fifteen miles on foot today then he was going to be one tired bastard. Before leaving he took one last look at Pulpit, damn.

"You reckon that marshal was alone?" Aldrich asked.

Bryson had been wondering that very same thing. He figured if there had been more than one then the others would have come riding hell bent for leather to see if the marshal had found their quarry. In the fifteen minutes or so they had waited there hadn't been anyone else around, the marshal was alone.

"I believe he was. Now why would a man head out after the four of us by himself? I can't say as I know a single lawman that would have done such a fool thing. And it ain't like he didn't know there were four of us, everyone in town could count to four I reckon," Bryson said.

The four rode on in silence for a while. It was around three in the afternoon when Marcus Rowley realized they were heading east rather than north.

"Say, I thought we were heading to that line shack on the northern boundary. I'd say we're at least ten miles off our track."

Fenton and Aldrich looked at the sky, the sun was hidden by heavy cloud cover. "I think your compass is off Marcus. How in hell can you tell which is north and which is east in this kind of weather?" Aldrich asked.

All three looked at Bryson. He knew this land better than any of them. "We might have steered off our course a mite. Won't matter, we're still heading away from Dakota City."

"But you told us we're expected at that line shack. The sooner we get there the better our story holds that we weren't in Dakota City when that bank got robbed," Aldrich said.

Bryson reined up and thought things over. "This is pretty rough country, not many folks ever come through here. I just figured we would do well to stay away from some of the more used trails. Tell you what, Aldrich, you head over to that rise and see if there's water. The horses could use a rest and my canteen is nearly empty."

The three wondered what that was all about, they knew for a fact that Bryson's canteen was nearly full, he'd not taken a sip since morning. Aldrich did as he was told and headed for the other side of the crest. As soon as he was out of sight Bryson pulled his Colt and shot Marcus Rowley in the back. As Buford Fenton turned to see what the shooting was about he drew his gun, he was too late. Bryson shot the man dead center of his chest. He too fell to the ground, same as Rowley.

Aldrich heard the shots, he spurred his horse and headed back. When he topped the rise he saw Bryson sitting his saddle, he was looking down at Rowley and Fenton. "What happened?" Aldrich shouted as he neared.

"These two tried to kill me. When you made the other side they drew down on me, I had no choice."

Aldrich noticed Bryson was still holding his gun. He didn't trust the man, never had. He did trust the two men lying on the ground and knew they wouldn't have done what Bryson just said. Aldrich knew he was in a bind, his gun was holstered, at least the leather strap that held it in place wasn't attached. He worried more about the type of situation he found himself in now than having his gun fall out while he rode. He had no choice but to draw.

Bryson saw the look in Aldrich's eyes. The man didn't believe his story, no worry, he intended to kill him anyway. He brought his Colt up but to his amazement Aldrich was faster. He was looking at the business end of a .44 and knew at this range the man couldn't miss. The only thing he could think of was to toss his gun to the ground and try to talk his way out of this.

"I'm unarmed. Now put that gun down and listen to me. Those two turned on me. They figured once you were out of sight they would do me in and then when you came back they would do the same to you." Bryson stopped talking, he hoped his sincerity was convincing. Then he thought of something else to add.

"Oh no, you're in with those two. You're going to kill me same as they were going to do."

Now Aldrich didn't really believe Bryson's story, but it did sound convincing. He didn't know Rowley or Fenton all that well, maybe they had turned on the man and would do the same once he made it back. As these thoughts ran through his head Bryson eased his hand behind his back. While Aldrich considered the story he'd just heard, Bryson yanked a hideaway from under his coat and shot Aldrich. Bryson wasn't all that fast but with the confusion running through Aldrich's mind it was all it took.

Bryson stepped his horse over and looked down at the man, he was still alive, not by much, but still alive. "The difference between me and you is I don't need to slow down to figure if what I just heard was a lie or not."

Bryson aimed his gun at Aldrich's head. "It was a lie," he said as he pulled the trigger.

There wasn't going to be any graves dug or soft words spoken over the three. Bryson got down and retrieved a second set of saddlebags that held the other half of the money stolen from the bank. He left all three horses saddled but free to go as they pleased. After securing the extra saddlebags he mounted up and rode north, true north. If anything told the story of Heith Bryson's cold heart, it was that he never looked back at his handiwork.

The extra saddlebags were awkward and bulky. Once he got a chance he'd stuff all the money in a single pair. Better to have all the money in one pair of saddlebags than spread between two. If things got tight he could carry the single set easier than trying to handle two.

Bryson rode till past midnight, the going was slow, but his horse didn't have any trouble navigating the dark trail. At half past one in the morning the line cabin came into view. Most would have had trouble finding something so remote after dark, Bryson had worked this stretch of range for a month before the Dakota City job. He knew the terrain like the back of his hand.

Once at the cabin he quickly lit the stove and started coffee. He also tended to his horse and brought in his gear. He made the place look like he'd been there a full day. Not hard to do, just scatter his belongings around and dirty up a skillet. He already knew a spot about a hundred feet from the shack where he could hide the spare set of saddlebags.

After stuffing all the money in one set he quickly went to a deadfall. The tree was big and had been down for at least two years. The hollow he found was perfect. He stuffed the money inside and then scattered some branches and limbs to hide his activity. Rough going in the blackness of night but he was motivated. After finishing he hurried back to the shack for some coffee and jerky, not a bad day's work he thought.

Warrix headed away from the four but hoped to continue the hunt as soon as he found a horse. If there was one thing about the marshal that set him apart from other men it was his determination. He would find the four again and then he'd settle matters.

The marshal thought about Mae as he walked. When he found himself getting tired all he had to do was think of his sister, and the way she'd been killed, and he would find renewed energy. By late evening he knew he wasn't going to find help, at least not this day. He started looking for a spot to camp. It needed two things, water, and cover. Water wasn't a problem; it seemed every mile or so he came to a steady runoff. With plenty of streams his only concern now was cover.

The reason Warrix wanted good cover was that he would be forced to have a fire all night. He'd lost both his ground covers, the old one he owned and the new one the liveryman back in Dakota City had loaned him. The man had sent him away on a good horse and carrying a new ground cover, now both were gone.

When he saw the stand of spruce and pine he knew he'd found about as good a spot as there was going to be. It was about a half a mile away and slightly uphill. It seemed he'd been traveling uphill ever since the ambush. When he made it to the trees he turned and looked at his backtrail one last time before heading into the timber. Looking backward had occupied half his time that day it seemed. An ambush will do that to a man.

After entering the trees it didn't take long to find what he was looking for, rock. The mountain he was on wasn't big, but it was tall enough for some of the high rock to break loose over the millennia and tumble down into the trees. There seemed to be rock everywhere. He hadn't gone far enough to find a stream, but he knew one was close, he could hear it.

The spot where he entered the timber gave a good view of a wide valley broken by trees and rough terrain. He could size up a threat an hour before it got to him. Warrix doubted he'd need to be that concerned with the mountain behind him. It was rough and slide rock seemed to occupy every inch of the base. All in all, this was an easily defended position.

The first thing to do was select a spot back in the trees that would hide a fire but not be so far back that he couldn't keep watch toward the front. A campsite wasn't going to be a problem, there were several to choose from. There was one rock in particular that caught his attention. It was nearly ten feet tall and maybe twenty feet wide. Warrix could only imagine the racket the thing made as it tumbled down from the top, knocking over anything in its path, no doubt thousands of years earlier.

Behind the rock was a surprise, this spot had been used as a camp before. There was a fire pit against one side of the rock where the heat would be reflected outward. The spot was enhanced by several big spruce nearby that would hide the light from a fire and also scatter the smoke as it climbed toward the sky. Three rocks had been positioned near the fire for seating. As the marshal looked the camp over he realized it hadn't been used for years.

When Warrix scanned the side and top of the rock he noticed something else in the diminishing light, notches had been chiseled into the side about ten feet to the right of the fire pit. Inserting the toe of a boot into the lowest notch he lifted himself using the higher notches as handholds, it was a rock stairway of sorts. When he made it to the top he could stand on the rock and peer deep into the valley. This wasn't just a high perch; it was a fighting position. The outer most edge of the rock rose more than two feet from the standing position Warrix now occupied.

As he stood there looking at the scene before him he imagined an Indian war party holding off attacking braves from a competing tribe. As entertaining as these thoughts were he knew it was time to gather wood and build a fire. He'd also need to find that stream he could hear.

Wood for a fire was plentiful. Several of the big cedars had tumbled over in years past. Not only did they supply his fire with ample fuel, but it also helped to secure the camp. In all the years the marshal had been traveling and sleeping out of doors he had never had such a secure campsite.

As soon as he got a fire going he headed back out to the edge of the timber. As he peered into the darkening landscape he decided his view was better from the top of the rock. When he turned and looked into the timber he could see its upper edge. As he looked he figured out something else, the trees had been felled directly in front of the rock to give a better view of the valley. This answered another question, how long since this spot had been used by Indians. He guessed maybe ten years, not more than fifteen because the trees would have grown and hidden everything again. The men that used this place were most likely long dead. He might be the first person to use this camp since the last Indian slept here.

With no one in sight in the valley Warrix figured he could spare thirty minutes to fix himself something to eat. He dug into the canvas sack; it was the first time he'd actually looked in this particular sack to see what the mayor had sent him. There was a small sack of flour, useless without a skillet. There was tobacco, again useless because he didn't smoke or chew. Another small sack contained cornmeal for cornbread, again, no skillet no cornbread. There was a little salt and some baking powder in two small tins, good for making bread but without anything to bake it in he was again out of luck. A third sack contained coffee but without a pot he couldn't boil water. The skillet and small coffeepot were stored in the other canvas sack, along with the spare coffeecup the mayor had sent.

Warrix went and sat beside the fire, not on one of the special placed rocks but directly against the big rock. As he sat there he wondered if there might be something in his saddlebags. If there was it would be old and probably not palatable. He found a few strips of beef jerky that had been in there for at least a week, still good. He found a tin cup; his tin coffee cup he'd left inside since the last time he's been away from town.

With the tin cup Warrix managed to stir up a pone of cornbread, tin cup size. One big biscuit, again tin cup size. With that he sat back down and feasted. He even managed to heat himself a cup of coffee, but without a pot he was reduced to making one cup at a time which wouldn't be a problem. After he finished he decided he was stuffed. An hour earlier he had no way of catching a meal out here but with the help of his old coffeecup he had managed to make as good a meal as any camp had ever furnished.

Once finished he decided to make up the rest of his meal and flour into cup sized portions. He baked each and when they cooled he put them back into the canvas sack. He figured a campsite like this would be impossible to find anywhere else. He wanted his supplies converted into edible food while his cooking activities couldn't be seen by anyone. When finished he had seven cornpones and seven big biscuits. He also rationed the jerky to last seven meals.

The coffee could be made at each stop using his tin cup. That cup was going to burn out soon though, it wasn't meant to be put directly into the flame. No matter, new cups were being built every day. As he sat against the big rock he wondered if men in some factory built coffee cups, or made coffee cups, or was this done by some machine using heat and pressure. Afoot and without supplies and here he was thinking about coffee cups. A man will think of about anything to take his mind off more troubling matters.

With his meal finished Warrix hurried back to the edge of the tree line. He didn't want to risk climbing the rock with a fire built at its base. He would make a picture perfect target if he did. With no movement in sight he went back to his camp.

As he sat facing the fire he wondered how anyone could use the rock for defense if they couldn't be up there while a fire burned below. As he sat he studied that little problem and then it dawned on him. He put his hand against the side of the rock about five feet from the fire, it was warm, real warm. He knew that if the rock was warm here then directly behind the fire the rock would be hot.

Warrix stood and kicked dirt onto the fire, smothering all the flames. As he stood there he was still feeling the warmth of the fire. The rock would work similar to an oven. It should stay warm until daybreak. To think the opinion of most easterners was that Indians were nothing more than savages when in actuality they were intellectually equal. The real difference had nothing to do with brain power but lifestyle. It was simply a difference in how each group lived.

With the fire gone and the smoke nearly so, Warrix climbed to the top of the rock and examined his lookout position. As he scanned the valley he could feel the heat rising from the base of the rock. He would stay here a few hours and then retreat to the bottom. Not a bad situation considering how things could have been.

Without the benefit of a ground cover, or a bedroll, all Warrix could do was stay close to the heat of the rock. Before leaving Pulpit he had even tried to remove the saddle blanket but found it to be securely wedged under the saddle. He'd walked away leaving anything that could keep him warm.

Deputy Ray Beasley had spent the day keeping watch out the front window of the jail or sitting in a chair out on the boardwalk under the awning. After a while boredom began to set in. The marshal had ridden off that morning looking for the men that had killed his sister and robbed the bank. The deputy felt bad sitting there in the jail. He knew hunting for men as deadly as that bunch could only end one way, the marshal would get killed.

About three in the afternoon Doc Reynolds stopped by to check on the deputy's leg. "You know, Deputy, this ain't half as bad as I thought earlier. That bullet didn't do much damage, you can thank that awning post for that."

Beasley figured as much; his leg didn't hurt unless he poked it. "Now you tell me; the marshal done rode out of here this morning by himself. I should be out there with him."

"And you will be," Reynolds said.

Beasley looked at the man. "Now what do you mean by that?"

Reynolds looked around town, then at the sky. "It's too late to leave today, we'll ride out first thing in the morning."

"Did you just say we? Now don't go denying it, you said we. What did you mean by that?"

The doc again looked at the quiet street, again he looked up at the sky. "The marshal rode out of here because it's his job. And more than that, the men he's after killed his sister. I know how he feels."

Beasley had been leaning against the front wall under the boardwalk awning. He leaned forward resting all four legs of the chair on the floor. "What are you talking about, Doc?"

"The man they killed at the bank was my half-brother. After my dad died my mom soon remarried, the man's name was Bennett McCloud. They had a son, John. I was four years older than John. After I got my education and headed west John soon followed. I guess we weren't that close, I blame myself for that. He always looked up to me when we were young. Now he's dead. If I hadn't landed in Dakota City a few years back then he would have probably not been here either.

"At first light in the morning I plan on riding out. That leg of yours won't be a problem if you decide to go too. I would have rode out this morning with the marshal but figured I needed to tend to the needs of the town. This is personal, the town can tend to itself," Reynolds said.

Beasley stood; he never gave a thought to his leg. "John McCloud was your half-brother. I don't know as I've heard that story around town."

"And you wouldn't have. There was a woman back in St. Louis, a woman we both courted. I lost and he won, you might say. That's the reason I packed up and came to Dakota City. I found out later that she took sick and died. Soon after that my brother showed up here. I guess you could say each of us came west to forget."

Beasley stepped to the edge of the boardwalk and leaned against a post. It happened to be the same post that had slowed the bullet that hit his leg.

"No offense, Doc, but do you even know how to use a gun?"

Reynolds smiled. "I can use a gun, Deputy. I might have used one a time or two back in Boston. You might say it's another reason I hurried west."

Now this was mysterious. If the doc was willing to go out looking for the marshal then Beasley could care less what kind of trouble there might have been back in Boston.

"I hate to seem ungrateful for you volunteering to go but I doubt this is the kind of trip a buggy can make," Beasley said.

Reynolds started laughing. "I can ride a horse. And when have you ever seen me in a buggy, never! The only buggy I've ever seen in Dakota City is the one the two Slade sisters use each Sunday to go to church."

"I was only funning you, Doc. What's the plan?"

"As I said earlier, we leave at first light. Since we're trying to catch the marshal, and I hope we do, then I'd say a pack horse would be a welcome addition. Warrix said he might be gone for two or three weeks. We take enough supplies to do the three of us at least two weeks, maybe three. What do you say?"

Beasley knew a packhorse was a good idea. The marshal had some supplies, thanks to the mayor, but more would be needed. "We better be getting started. I'll see if Sanders has a horse we can use, maybe a pack saddle as well. How are we going to pay for all this anyway?"

"I have a tab I run at the general store. Just tell Quint and Maxwell what you need, they'll get it together and then charge it to me. How does that sound?"

"That sounds real good, Doc. I'll head on over to the livery and see what Sanders has in the way of horse flesh. We'll need a good pack animal and something for you to ride." Beasley thought a second, he really hated to ask but knew he had to. "Can you ride a horse, Doc?"

Again Reynolds laughed. "Stop asking, I can ride, I can shoot, and I can use my fists if the need arises. As I said, my time back east wasn't used just for studying."

"All right then, meet me at the livery an hour before first light. We'll take the packhorse to the general store and load the supplies. I'll make sure Sanders has a nice tame mount for you," Beasley said as he put weight on his injured leg. The thought of a trip, especially a trip to help the marshal, had invigorated the deputy. His leg even seemed to hurt a little less. As a matter of fact, it didn't hurt at all.

An hour before first light the doc showed up at the livery. Beasley and Sanders were already there. "Well would you look at that, I told you he'd show," Beasley said. He always liked to rib the doc and this trip was going to be no different.

"Did you have doubts? I've looked forward to this trip since I set my mind to it yesterday. I hope to settle a score with the men that attacked the town yesterday. What have we got in the way of horses?"

"Well, I've got my old plow puller, Jinx," Beasley said. Jinx wasn't a plow puller, far from it. He was a solid black horse that had energy and spunk, something this trip was going to need.

"Jinx, really? What else we got?" Reynolds asked.

The liveryman decided he better take over this conversation, the deputy was having too much fun. "I got a horse tied out back I took on trade a few months ago. He's a good horse, I paid boot to get him. His name's Yancy, don't know why but that's his name. He's a gray."

"Why don't you go bring him in Doc while me and Sanders put the packsaddle on Dusty," Beasley said.

"Dusty, that's the marshal's horse. I thought he was injured."

"I thought so too but he's fine. He had a slight puncture wound in the soft of his hoof. It was a tiny splinter of wood, but it must have been painful. I used a pair of tweezers last night and got it out. I treated it to keep infection away and this morning it had healed over. A horses foot heals fast," Sanders said. He almost laughed, here he was talking medicine to a doctor, go figure.

The three men led the three horses to the back of the general store. Beasley decided to load up away from any prying eyes out front, not that anyone was out at this hour. He also doubted there were any spies in town working for the outlaws. The secrecy was to not let anyone know the deputy was leaving.

With the help of Quint and Maxwell the job was done just as the eastern sky took on the look of a pinkish yellow. This morning saw the cloud cover thin and the snow flurries of yesterday gone. This late in October meant that wouldn't last long though. Heavy cloud cover was always just over the horizon.

The two mounted up with Beasley holding a fifteen foot lead for Dusty. The marshal's horse suspected they were heading to wherever the marshal had gone yesterday riding Pulpit. Dusty had no problem with Pulpit, he was a good sort.

"Let's get out of town before folks start to stir. I want to be a mile down the trail before that happens," Beasley said. To his surprise the doc mounted the saddle and then expertly turned Yancy up the street. He looked to be proficient as a rider. Time would tell.

Neither man spoke until they were well out of town. Beasley didn't know why but he felt being sneaky and quiet was the only acceptable way to start the trip. Maybe it was just the time of day, maybe it was nothing.

"Did you leave anyone at the jail?" the doc asked.

"I did, the mayor came over late last night and deputized James Hayes. He'll be staying at the jail until we get back," Beasley said.

"Isn't that the old prospector that came into town yesterday?"

"It is. I've known old Hayes for a couple of years. Ever since him and his two partners bought into that old claim over on Rimrock. I suspected the man that sold it to the three was a swindler. But Hayes says there's a rich vein in that mountain somewhere." After a moment Beasley added, "That's a big mountain though.

Warrix built a small fire a little before first light. He had coffee and one of the big biscuits for breakfast. He really wanted to just start walking but knew with the amount of energy he'd be expending he needed to eat. Once finished he again climbed the rock ladder to take a look out over the valley, it was just the way he'd left it the previous day. No one had changed a thing; the thought made him laugh.

After making sure the firepit was safe he slung the saddlebags over his shoulder and picked up the sack. Today he figured he could walk maybe twenty miles. He was a little tired from the previous day's walk and knew today would be worse. He scanned the valley before stepping from the timber. This was a quiet place.

The marshal headed east, that was the last direction the outlaws tracks headed. He'd gone maybe two miles when he came to a fast moving stream that he really didn't want to wade through. All he needed was to be drenched with the ice cold water coming off the mountains. As he scanned the stream he spotted a fallen tree about a hundred yards to his left.

Once he made it to where the tree was he was pleasantly surprised. It had fallen across the stream and was lodged against the other rocky bank. The water under the tree was fast moving on the side where Warrix stood but pooled on the opposite side.

Holding the canvas bag steady he put one foot on the tree and then the other. It would hold his weight. As he slowly moved across he couldn't believe how lucky he was to have found it. He could make it to the opposite bank without getting soaked. Then his foot slipped. He tried to grab a limb, but it was too late, he was falling. Then the jagged end of another limb caught his leg, it didn't just catch it, it stabbed it.

An hour later, after bandaging his leg and retrieving his saddlebags Warrix knew he was in a bad way. No horse, no food, and no supplies. The canvas sack was gone, swept away in the fast moving water. It was these thoughts that had him thinking of his own mortality. Today was a Monday, as good a day as any to die, he thought.

He sat there looking at the sky. It had snowed the previous day, not a lot but enough to cover the ground. Today was October 25th. This late in the year meant the weather would start to deteriorate and not in slow spurts either. If an early storm came now they would find his bleached-out bones lying here in the spring, not a pleasant thought.

As he looked at the sky he tried to analyze his options. He could stay here and die, not good. He could try and continue but to where, not only was he injured but he really didn't know where he was. His third option was to try and make it back to his previous campsite. It was safe and it offered some protection from the elements. Of the three the last one was preferable to the other two.

Warrix considered the distance, maybe two miles, maybe a little more. He would need to fashion some sort of crutch if he was going to make it that far. He would also need to navigate the fallen tree again, the one that had just tried to kill him. He'd do that first and if he survived he'd make the crutch.

Warrix looked at the fallen tree, it seemed to be looking at him. Before tackling the tree he tightened the bandanna around his leg again. The bleeding had stopped but the pain hadn't. This was no time to consider the pain though, he needed to make it back to the shelter of the big rock.

Warrix crawled to the tree and looked things over. He slung the saddlebags over a shoulder and then started. He'd decided the best way to tackle this was to stay on hands and knee. He would have thought knees, but he only had one good leg, thus one good knee.

Fifteen minutes later and he was on the other side. He'd done better as a cripple than when he had two good legs. After sitting a while to rest he looked for something to make a crutch out of. There were several branches and limbs lying around from where the big tree once stood. Most were fairly rotted but a few weren't. Fifteen minutes later and he had a crutch. It was rough, it was ugly, but it would work.

Once he got to his feet and tried his new crutch he was pleased. He could move, not fast but he could move. Again he grabbed the saddlebags and slung them over his shoulder. It was then that he thought of his rifle. He looked back into the stream but saw nothing. He stepped to the edge of the bank and looked hard, scanning every square inch of both banks and the water below. His Winchester wasn't to be seen. It must have hit more to the center of the water where it was deeper.

Warrix turned his back on the stream and the tree that had nearly killed him. Standing there looking at the trail that had led him here he figured again it was roughly two miles back to the rock. In his mind he had now firmly named the place where he'd camped the night before as, the rock.

As he walked he kept a close look out in all directions, especially behind. To be caught out in the open now meant death. With only his Colt and limited ammunition he felt naked.

If the four men came back then there was no way he could hold them off with just a handgun. He had once been told that a man with a pistol against a man with a rifle was a dead man. The man with the rifle only had to stay out of accurate range of the pistol and then pick off his target, this wasn't a pleasant thought. He wondered about his Winchester. Maybe he could come back this way and look again, after he got a horse.

After about two hours he figured he'd gone about half a mile. Staying to trees and off the rough trail was slowing him down about as much as his sore leg. He stopped occasionally to retighten the bandanna which kept trying slide down his thigh to his knee. The soreness seemed to be a little less after walking a while. He knew this was misleading, tomorrow he doubted he could walk at all.

After another two hours he figured he'd gone maybe a mile in total, no more than that. If his calculations were correct then he might be half way back. As he struggled along all he could think of was the safety of the rock. He would have a fire and a defensible position. He had no food and knew he needed to eat. He had a few ideas on that problem. Something that helped a man when he got hungry was that the more he wanted, and needed food, the more he could stand as far as taste was concerned. His father had once told of a Union soldier that got so starved and weak that he ate a raw possum. I guess that could be possible, once you got past the appearance.

Another two hours and Warrix began to think his calculations might have been off. He could be off a mile and if that were the case then he was in trouble. He needed the safety and shelter of the rock but was beginning to doubt he could make it before nightfall. As he continued he kept looking back, not just to keep check on any pursuers but to keep his bearings. As he walked away from the rock that morning he noticed things. Now he kept looking backward to make sure this was the way he'd gone before. He was looking backward in order to go forward, figure that one out.

When he figured the previous campsite, or the rock, was another mile he tried to pick up the pace. Another mile meant he was four hours away. It would be dark in an hour. Warrix knew he had to keep going but first he needed to rest. His leg had continued to hurt, the wound seeped blood the entire day. His pants leg was stained red with dried blood, all the way to his boot. He didn't know how much he'd lost but without food and rest he knew fatigue was going to come on hard and not leave.

As Warrix sat he continued to look the terrain over. He was thirsty, tired, and hungry. The next time he looked back he noticed something he'd missed a few minutes earlier, a fallen tree that had resprouted limbs along the upper side. The tree was crippled and bent but the good news was that he'd seen it this morning. He'd seen it not more than a few minutes after he left the rock. He was close, but close could still mean an hour or more.

The sight of the crippled tree gave Warrix renewed energy, but it wouldn't last. He stood and positioned his crutch. He noticed his arm was getting sore from the constant pressure of the limb that had been so crucial for him to make it as far as he had. He knew he could stand more, at least until he made it to the rock.

Now he seemed to move with a little more speed, a little more coordination with the third leg which was the crutch. As he continued he began to notice more of what he'd seen this morning. Then he saw the valley, the same valley he'd scanned so many times from the timber and the top of the rock. Twenty minutes later and he was where he sought to be.

He couldn't believe it at first, but a second check told him the rock was still slightly warm, or at least not as cold as the part farther from the firepit. There was still some firewood stacked nearby that he hadn't used during the previous night. As he scrapped the dirt from the firepit, the dirt he's used to cover the fire that morning, he nearly burned his hands on some of the embers. Using his crutch he finished cleaning the debris from the pit, everything but some of the charred remains of the previous fire.

Then he put some tinder in the base and some smaller twigs on top of that. As he dug for his matches the pit started to smolder, no flame but smoke just the same. The dirt he'd put on top of the fire that morning had preserved heat and embers. With a quick search of the nearby pine needles he found the driest and sprinkled them on top of the embers and waited. He knew there were matches in the saddlebags but wanted to save them, just in case.

Just when it got dark enough that he couldn't really see, just when he was ready to search for the matches, there was a flame. Slowly the flame grew and as it did Warrix sprinkled more pine needles on top. Finally the small flame took and soon he had a good fire going. The warmth was a welcome addition to his primitive situation. The heat of the fire felt good, he was tired and cold. Hunger pains had passed for the moment with the endeavor of restarting the fire.

Warrix leaned against the rock and soon fell asleep. When he awoke he didn't know how long he'd slept but judging by how low the fire burned it must have been an hour. He quickly piled more wood, hoping to heat the big rock enough to soon extinguish the flames, hiding his presence.

He might have put too much fuel on top because before long he had a good size fire burning. He let it burn, secure in the safety of his camp. This time when it burned down he would let it go out completely. He sat looking at his surroundings. Another thing he noticed about the rock was that it acted like a reflector, the woods and ground was illuminated with a pleasant soft glow. He could see far into the trees.

As Warrix sat he grew weary, even after his nap. For the next hour he thought of his situation. A new pain that made itself known was that of thirst. He'd drank at many streams along the way but the last water he had was an hour before dark. That was several hours ago. He figured his loss of blood, although not severe, was contributing to his thirst. He knew the stream was close but to go there in the dark, and trying to use a crutch was out of the question. He could stand the thirst until first light.

When the fire had ceased to matter he used the crutch to cover the pit. Soon the smoke was gone. Warrix hobbled to his feet and using the crutch he went to the stone ladder. With great difficulty he made it to the top without tumbling back down. He scanned the valley. After a few minutes his eyes adjusted and he saw exactly what he expected, no movement anywhere.

Warrix stretched out on his back and looked at the sky. It was cloudy, a moonless night. The heat rising from the heated rock felt good. Within minutes he fell asleep.

Beasley and Reynolds travelled the day without meeting a single person. The trail they used was one that had been used before. It was the same path the four outlaws had used as they left Dakota City. A fifth set of tracks were those of the marshal. Beasley was a good tracker, probably better than Warrix. He'd been a scout for the army years earlier. Not during the war, he was too young for that disaster, but the army still needed men and Beasley needed a job. He did his three years and then mustered out. Shortly after seeing the last tracks the ground grew hard and tracks were non-existent. Beasley had made a mistake, one that would cost the better part of the day, they were going the wrong way.

Dakota City had given Beasley a job shortly after he left the army, and for that he was grateful. The one comparison he always made was that the army paid better, and fed better. Small town deputy, full time starvation, he liked to say.

The two men travelled until past noon before stopping to allow the horses to rest and drink. No fire was needed, Beasley had made sure to include smoked ham in the supplies. He also had a chunk of cheese sawed from a big wheel of cheese the general store kept for the townsfolk. Most folks found cheese too difficult to make and only a store could afford to purchase the big wheels and then sell it to their customers by the pound. The Wilson brothers had put two pounds of the stuff in the supplies for the trip, sliced of course.

"This smoked ham and store bought cheese hits the spot. A slab of bread and some coffee would go a long ways in making this a veritable feast," the doc said.

Beasley just looked at the man. "It ain't 'veritable,' it's 'vittles.' Sometimes I think educated folk ain't that educated at all."

Reynolds just looked at the man. No need in arguing, or trying to set Beasley straight, that could take weeks. "No offense deputy, vittles it is."

"You're right about one thing Doc, a little coffee would make this food taste a mite better. I never did like drinking out of a canteen when I'm eating, crumbs make it into the water."

Reynolds just lost his appetite. "Now what's the matter, Doc? You look like a case of squeamish done set in on you," Beasley asked, then added, "If you ain't going to finish that ham and cheese then reach it here." Reynolds did as he was told.

"How far you think we'll make it today, Deputy?"

Beasley looked around and then at the sky. "I figure we got maybe four more hours before we need to find a spot to camp. We'll be using a cold camp, coffee, and fried ham at dusk and then the fire gets put out." The deputy wondered how the doc would like the idea of a cold camp.

"I thought as much. Actually I feel better under the protection of darkness. We got four murderers between here and a day's ride. My guess is the day's ride is the most accurate. I doubt they would have hung around just for giggles," Reynolds said.

This surprised the deputy. He imagined Reynolds the type that wanted a big fire to keep the critters away and to light the whole valley. "Now when did you figure out we was using a cold camp?"

"I knew it yesterday. We are after some terrible men. Men that would as soon shoot up a campsite as to say hello. We heat coffee and the skillet at dusk and then move on another mile, just in case."

Beasley was beginning to like the doc. He knew what he was doing, and it seemed he always had a plan. This would go a long way in seeing the job at hand to a resolution. "You act like you've done this before. I figure you been chasing someone, or maybe someone was chasing you at one time in your life. Which is it?"

"We better be moving. We need to make as many miles as we can before nightfall," Reynolds said. He wasn't about to share any of the adventures, or misadventures, he'd experienced earlier in life. Sometimes it was best to let old mistakes die off rather than keeping them fresh.

The men quickly mounted up and headed after the marshal and the four murderers. Both men were quiet as they rode, each wondering what would happen next. Reynolds patted his jacket, the gun inside his vest pocket felt reassuring. The first night's camp was uneventful, something both men were grateful for.

The two rose early and quickly had coffee and bacon. Would this be the day they caught up with the marshal? Time would tell. The deputy and doc would find out midday that they had travelled a half day in the wrong direction. By late midday it was decided they would turn and head back to the spot where they had camped the previous night. Both were mad that such a mistake had been made costing them a full day. As things would work out, it was the best thing for all concerned.

That night Beasley and Reynolds found a spot to stop and heat coffee and fix themselves supper. The three horses were allowed to drink from a cold running stream not fifty feet from where they built their fire. The two fried bacon and made skillet bread. After the coffeepot was hot they quickly extinguished the fire and hurriedly ate. They piled loose rock on top of the now extinguished fire and forty-five minutes after starting the fire they pulled out heading for a more remote, and safe, spot to camp for the night. This was the same area as the previous night's camp, not quite but still close. Neither man wanted to camp in the exact same spot, that would be admitting defeat they thought.

The horses were picketed within sight of the two men. It was decided that one should stay awake while the other slept. Both men were wary of the four men they were chasing. Caution would be the norm until the four were either caught or killed. The leader of the gang, Heith Bryson, had already taken care of seventy-five percent of that problem.

Little did Beasley and Reynolds know but they were camping within two miles of the rock. As an exhausted Warrix slept atop his rock fortress the deputy and Reynolds were nearby. Another mile closer and Warrix might have been able to smell smoke, maybe even the bacon they had fried.

The wrong turn earlier in the day and then the subsequent turnaround put them within minutes of the now injured marshal.

Ralph Bishop knew nothing of the bank holdup or the murders. He was confident in the fact that the money from the last cattle drive was sitting safely in Dakota City at City Trust Bank. Toler had taken three men with him early Saturday morning to bring back the cash his boss needed to pay the men and run the ranch.

City Trust Bank was open all day on Saturdays so there was no need to hurry. The four men went to the saloon upon reaching town. After that they would pay a visit to the diner. After taking care of their thirst and hunger then it would be time to go to the bank and sign the withdrawal papers. Little did they know but the withdrawal had been made earlier that morning, but without the paper work.

The four weren't doing anything against their boss's wishes, Bishop always allowed his men a drink and a meal when in Dakota City. It was another reason the wrangles that worked at the ranch stayed, they liked the work and felt they were compensated well. Bishop and Toler had done a fair job of hiring the crew that worked the Box W, that was until they hired Heith Bryson and the other three.

The four made it to the Rusty Spurs Saloon about an hour before noon that morning. They planned to be at the diner by noon and then the bank. Toler never suspected anything as the four rode into town. Some of the townsfolk were a bit nervous at the sight of four riders but the Box W men were easily recognizable, they had been to town several times in the last few months.

After tying the four horses out front the men entered the saloon. Each went to the bar and ordered beer, Bishop and Toler never let the men drink whiskey when transporting the money.

"Here you go," the bartender said as he sat four mugs on the bar.

"Say Burl, why is everyone so tense? When we rode in we were looked at like we came to rob the place," Toler asked.

The man named Burl; he was the bartender, looked at the four. "You didn't hear what happened this morning? Whole town got shot up. Even killed John McCloud and Mae Fuller over at the bank. Sad thing, real sad."

Toler sat down his glass. "The bank, did they rob it?" He assumed if someone at the bank got killed then the reason had to be robbery.

"They did, took a sizable amount. Don't know for sure how much but it was a lot. Story is they damn near cleaned it out."

"How much for the beer?" Toler asked. The other three quickly drained their glasses, they knew they were leaving.

"Dollar ought to cover it."

Toler placed the money on the bar and then headed for the door, they were met by James Hayes, he was carrying a shotgun and wearing a deputy's badge. "You hold it right there, mister," Hayes said as he pulled back both hammers on the old double barrel.

Toler held up both hands. He'd never seen this deputy before, the man was twenty years past wearing a badge.

"Hold on there, Deputy. We're with the Box W and here on business," Toler told the man. He hoped the man wasn't the type to shoot first and then get the particulars later.

"Wait just a minute, Hayes, that's Windell Toler from the Box W," Quint Wilson shouted from across the street.

Hayes didn't know Windell Toler and had never heard of the Box W. And for that matter he didn't know the two brothers that ran the general store either. He wasn't lowering the shotgun.

Finally Burl walked over to the batwings and looked out. "You don't know anybody do you, Hayes? Well you know me and I'm telling you to lower that shotgun. These men are here on business, don't go treating them like criminals."

This must have been good enough for Hayes, he lowered the shotgun. He might not have known that many in town, but he did know the bartender. On each trip into Dakota City to sell his silver he always left a little money at the Rusty Spur.

"Sorry, men, after what happened I'm a mite jumpy. Forget I was ever here," Hayes said as he headed back toward the jail. It was doubtful any of the four could forget nearly getting killed by an ancient deputy.

Word spread quickly that Ralph Bishop's men were in town. Mayor Farley was at home and once he heard he went looking for the four. He figured with the bank's president dead it would fall to him to give the news.

"Toler, I need to talk to you," Farley said as he approached.

The run in with the deputy and now this, what else was going to go wrong Toler wondered? He wasn't a fan of the mayor's and could do without the talk.

"What do you want, Mayor? Mr. Bishop sent us to town on business," Toler said.

"I figured as much. We might ought to get off the street where we can talk in private," Farley said.

"Tell it while you're walking. Me and the boys are headed to the bank," Toler harshly told the man.

Farley could tell by the tone that Toler was in a hurry. He didn't know if the man had heard about the robbery, he decided to just walk along with the four and tell them at the bank.

As Toler approached the bank he saw one shot out window and a couple of bullet holes in the façade. Well, guns were used he thought. He walked into the bank and looked around. The place had been cleaned up a little. The furniture didn't look out of place, but he did notice a couple of holes in the ceiling and a couple more in the wall. They must have fired a couple of rounds upon entering the bank to let everyone know they meant business.

"The bank was robbed early this morning, as soon as they opened. Two people were killed," the mayor said. He felt he needed to explain although he really didn't know why. Was this part of the job of being mayor?

"Two you say, who were they?" Toler asked. He knew most of the people at the bank. He'd also been told who was killed by the bartender. He just wanted to hear it from the mayor. The bartender might have been wrong, he really hoped he was.

"Mae Fuller and John McCloud," was all Farley said.

"Where's the marshal?" Toler asked.

"He went after the four. He's riding alone," the mayor said.

"What about the deputy, is he around?"

"He's around somewhere, he got wounded by them four. The doc patched him up, he might be at doc's place. I think the marshal, or the deputy gave a badge to that old prospector to help out at the jail," Farley said.

"You say four men did this? Anybody get a description," Toler asked.

"Not really, no one got a good look at the men's faces. I think everyone was staring at the guns they were pointing. They took damn near every dollar the bank had. I reckon your boss had his money here, if he did then it's gone now." Everything the mayor had said so far was bad. Then again, there really wasn't any good news to share.

Toler had stopped listening to Farley. He was thinking about the four men that did this, he was also thinking about the four men he'd sent to the southern line shack. He had no proof, but he did have his suspicions.

"We're heading back. I got to get to the Box W and let Mr. Bishop know what happened here," Toler told the mayor. He also intended to ride over to that southern line shack and find out what he could. Later that day Toler and his three men made it to the line shack where Bryson and the other men were supposed to be stationed.

The line shack looked to have been used but it was hard to tell how recently. Could have been a week could have been a day. He knew the four had been told to ride north to scout that boundary, if they did then they were innocent. Heith Bryson had never instilled much trust in Toler and for good reason, Toler just didn't like the man. He'd check further but now he had to get back to the Box W.

Bishop took the news hard. He knew both Mae and John, he dealt with them for the last few years on nearly every visit to Dakota City. As bad as the deaths were he also had the matter of the money that was stolen. Most of what Bishop had was in that bank. He had some cash for emergencies, this was an emergency.

"Ride up to the northern boundary. Find Bryson and the other three and bring them back here," Bishop said.

"We'll leave now. The three I chose to escort the money will be going to. They know how to use a gun," Toler said as he headed for the door.

"One more thing. When you find them make sure you take their guns. I don't trust those men and you don't either," Bishop told his ranch foreman.

Toler smiled at his boss. "Don't worry about that. I plan on riding in there with guns drawn." The way he said it looked like the man wanted nothing more than to mix it up with Bryson, time would tell.

Bishop walked to the porch and watched the men ride away. He hoped Bryson and the other three men were innocent, but something told him it wasn't going to be that simple. He went to the rocker he kept on the porch and sat down. He had a lot to consider, the rocker always helped.

As he sat and looked over his ranch, at least the very small portion he could see from the ranch house. He began to wonder how he was going to meet his financial needs for the near future. The small amount of cash he kept in the office safe would see him though for a couple weeks and then things would start to get tight. His wranglers wouldn't work if they didn't get paid.

As he thought of his problems another one came to mind. It wasn't really a problem, just a suspicion. The man in Chicago knew how much money he'd sold the last four-hundred head of cattle for. He knew when the money would make it to the bank in Dakota City. The date always varied and was never public knowledge. The coincidence was probably just that, a coincidence. But Bishop hadn't gotten as far in life as he had by tossing aside his suspicions. He'd spend more time thinking about the possibility that Bernard Rumford had sold him out. For that matter he might even be involved. More thought was needed.

Heith Bryson spent his first night at the northern line shack trying to figure out his next move. He assumed he wouldn't be a suspect in the robbery and killings in Dakota City. He was a good twenty-five miles from that town, maybe he would be considered innocent due to the distance. The only other men that could identify him were now dead, all shot out of the saddle by Bryson himself. He had all the money safely hidden in the fallen carcass of a tree. The only person left that could implicate him was Bernard Rumford.

As for anyone identifying him from Dakota City he felt that couldn't happen. He was the only one of the four that wore his neckerchief up over his mouth and nose. He'd told the other three not to worry about being recognized. Most folks only look at the guns. And most folks are afraid to give a description, who would want to be on a witness stand testifying against men that have no qualms about killing? Nope, don't worry, he'd told the three.

The information Bryson shared with the three had a small shred of truth to it, but he was really protecting his own hide. If those three were identified then that wouldn't be a problem. He couldn't be implicated because of the neckerchief. There were only four men that could point a finger at Bryson, three were now dead. He kept telling himself that Bernard Rumford was the only man he had to worry about and that wouldn't be a worry because they were working together.

Bryson kept telling himself these things but was having very little success in believing it. He ran through his conversations with Rumford. He was told there would be three or four thousand dollars in the bank on the day of the robbery. Bryson was promised a thousand dollars for his part. The other three were promised three hundred each and this would be paid by Rumford. If Bryson had it figured right then he was getting a thousand and Rumford twenty-one hundred.

The amount was acceptable because Rumford had put the plan together. Plus, if there was less in the bank then Rumford got less, Bryson would still get his thousand. They had also agreed that if any of the men got killed then Bryson could have their three-hundred dollars. It now looked like his thousand had grown to nineteen hundred. Not a bad day's pay.

As he sipped his coffee he began to wonder how much he should trust Rumford. He'd met the man a month earlier, that was the meeting where the plan was hatched, and fees agreed upon. Now though, he began to wonder. What if Rumford had designs on doing a little killing himself, he could keep it all, four-thousand dollars. Bryson suddenly became worried; he decided to go ahead and take out his nineteen-hundred and hide it some place safe.

The tree was close so it wouldn't take that long to count out his share and put it someplace other than near the line shack. He quickly went to the tree and grabbed the bulging saddlebags. As he carried them to the shack he was trying to guess how much the bags contained. They must be filled with small bills, he thought. He'd know soon enough.

Bryson scanned the surroundings, no one was anywhere in sight. He quickly went inside and dumped the saddlebags on the small table and began counting. When he made it to four thousand he realized the pile hadn't gone down all that much. At eight thousand the table was still covered with money. When finished the count was north of twenty-thousand dollars.

Bryson whistled; the amount was astounding. Either Rumford underestimated the amount, or he'd lied. Bryson suspected he lied. He quickly put the money back into the saddlebags and hurried back to the tree. He had a decision to make, take out his nineteen hundred and deal with Rumford on the remainder or something else. He decided then and there that he wanted to renegotiate the deal. He'd do the new negotiations with the help of a gun.

Bernard Rumford knew the bank job had been planned for Saturday the twenty-third. He wanted to arrive in the territory at least a week after the robbery. He planned on meeting Bryson and acquiring his share of the money. He was also going to acquire Bryson's share, he planned to kill the man, and his three accomplices if necessary. With the money from the robbery added to what he had already stolen, it still left him shy of the amount he needed to buy the Box W Ranch.

A loan for the remainder had already been arranged using the ranch as collateral. The bank that now held the loan was a Chicago bank. Ralph Bishop had borrowed heavily in order to purchase all the land he wanted. He had bought fifteen thousand acres outright and used that as collateral to purchase the other thirty thousand acres. This was now leverage that could sink the Box W.

Rumford had arranged the financing to cover his shortfall with the bank that now held the lien on the ranch. His argument had been that the bank was in for two thirds of the ranch's value, an amount that was beginning to make the bank, primarily its loan committee, nervous. Rumford would own a full two-thirds reducing the bank's exposure to one third. If the bank took the deal they would cut their exposure by fifty percent, from two thirds to one third. The loan committee liked the argument Rumford made and decided to back the man the first time the ranch's current owner missed a payment. That day was getting close with the theft of Bishop's funds from City Trust Bank in Dakota City.

Rumford purchased tickets for the four-o'clock train heading west. He was traveling on a Pullman. This would be the first time he had used such a car. It was also the most he had ever paid to travel to Butte City, the closest town to Dakota City that had a depot. He figured to ride in style because he wanted to be well rested when he took possession of the Box W.

The next installment on the note for the ranch was due in two weeks. Bishop was planning to use the proceeds from his most recent cattle drive to make the payment on the loan. This had been the way he'd operated for years. He made three payments a year, one every four months since putting the ranch together. Another reason to make three cattle drives a year, each coincided with a loan payment.

Rumford had the bank's foreclosure documents in hand. The day the note was due he would have the papers served, that was assuming Bishop didn't make the payment. This was something Rumford knew couldn't happen; he had managed to steal the money Bishop was going to use.

As he settled into his seat on the train he could only imagine how life would be when he became the full owner of the Box W Ranch. He might even change the name, or maybe he would leave it the same. Then again he might use the original name, the Double R. After all, there were two of the letter R in Rumford. He almost laughed at the thought.

Tuesday morning Warrix awoke to a heavy frost. It was heavy enough that he first thought it had snowed during the night but one look at the sky told him a clear sky rarely snowed. He shook the frost from his jacket and sat up, nearly falling from the top of the rock as he did. After catching his balance he looked out over the valley. There was no movement, and this was what he expected.

After making sure he was fully awake he slowly climbed down. The rock ladder wasn't slippery, probably due to the warmth of the fire that kept the surface temperature above freezing. Once on the ground he grabbed his crutch and tried out his leg. It was sore but not as bad as he expected. One thing that was worse than the day before was his shoulder. He suspected using the crutch was something that took getting used to. He hoped to not need it very long but that was just a hope.

He was more thirsty than hungry but not by much. Warrix decided to go to the nearby steam before starting a fire. He grabbed his tin cup and hobbled the fifty feet or so to the water. Once there he drank his fill, eight full cups as best as he could tell. He wasn't really counting. The cup was small, but he figured if it was a canteen he'd drank it dry twice. After finishing he refilled the cup and then made his way back to the rock.

After he got there he quickly built a fire, this time using a match, not the slower method of using the previous night's embers. Once he got the fire going he gathered some pine needles making sure to get ones that had recently fallen. Using his folding knife he cut the needles into tiny pieces and then put them in the cup. His mixture needed to be half water and half needles, so he gladly drank half the water.

After the fire caught he stirred the ashes and then sat the cup as close as he dared. The problem with having only one cup was that he had to get it away from the fire at some point and to do that he had to touch the handle. He let the water and needles simmer for a while and then using a stick he slowly slid the cup away from the flames so it could cool. Ten minutes later he took a slow sip.

Warrix had never sampled pine needle tea but knew it was drinkable. It was also medicinal, these things he'd heard early in life but hoped to never actually experience. The taste was surprisingly good, well maybe not good but tolerable. It seemed to have a citrusy taste, maybe even minty.

After drinking half the tea he took off the bandage and looked at his leg. The injury was easy to see because the rip in his pants leg was enormous. The wound didn't look all that bad this morning, but it did need stiches or so he thought, something he had neither the means nor the stomach for. He slowly poured a little of the hot tea on the wound, he was ready to grimace as he did, but the pain wasn't that bad. Actually it didn't really hurt at all. The more he cleaned the wound the more he realized it wasn't that bad after all. It had looked worse yesterday but now it wasn't nearly as disturbing.

After slowly using the tea until it was gone he decided to get more water and make another batch. He would also wash out the bandanna. It was covered in dried blood and who knew what else?

Thirty minutes later and he was ready to give the wound another washing. After using the full cup he put the freshly washed bandanna back around the leg and tied a knot.

As he sat there he wondered how long he'd be using this camp. Maybe two, might even be three days. He had fuel for the fire. He had plenty of fresh water nearby. The real concern was food. He knew he could continue to drink the pine needle tea. There were ample pine cones lying around and of these he could harvest the pine nuts, something that was edible. There was even a freshly fallen tree, maybe two or three weeks down. He knew he could strip the bark and boil it. He'd never eaten pine bark but knew it was edible if the tree was a fresh fall. Hell, he'd eat the whole damn tree if it got him out of this mess.

Warrix sat by the fire and considered his options. He figured in three or four days he might be able to start walking back to Dakota City. If his leg didn't get worse that is. Infection could set in and then he would die. As he thought things over he decided walking was impossible and there were several reasons.

Yesterday he had traveled about one mile every four hours. A ten hour day meant two and a half miles. It would take him a month, not an option. He would also lose the protection of his rock fortress. It might not have been much, but it was way better than trying to camp out in the open. He had no blankets, and his clothes were lacking for a multi-day trek back to civilization. If he tried to walk he would die of exposure.

The only option was to stay here and keep doctoring his leg with the pine needle tea. He wouldn't freeze to death if he stayed here. He wouldn't die of thirst if he stayed here. Food could be obtained from the freshly fallen pine tree. He might also kill something from the cover of the rock. A deer, a rabbit, a squirrel or even a coyote would be acceptable. The more he thought of his situation the more he knew he was stuck here for the foreseeable future.

 

The deputy and the doc had spent a fitful night even though both had been tired. The thoughts of badmen sneaking up in the darkness had both on edge. What began as one trying to stay awake during the night ended up being both. When the first light of a new day found the two they were bleary eyed and exhausted. Reynolds knew they were in no shape to hunt down outlaws. The stress of wasting a full day yesterday while heading in the wrong direction was also adding to their stress.

"Tell you what, Deputy, you stretch out and grab fifteen minutes sleep. It's good and light and I can see anything within a mile of here. You nap and then you keep watch while I sleep. Fifteen minutes each might not sound like much, but it should double our senses. As tired as I am right now someone could walk right up and hit me over the head before I knew it," Reynolds said. Before he even finished talking the deputy was snoring. Funny how daylight makes a man less afraid. After fifteen minutes he woke Beasley and told him to return the favor.

The doc was right, the little nap helped refresh the deputy. "You go right ahead, Doc. I'm going to start a fire, fix some coffee, and fry a little bacon. By the time you wake up I'll have breakfast ready, but don't you go thinking you're getting breakfast in bed."

"Wouldn't dream of it, Deputy." Reynolds fell asleep almost immediately. What seemed like seconds, but was actually the allotted fifteen minutes, were soon up and he was jostled awake by what had to be a rock.

"Did you just throw a rock at me, Beasley?"

"I did no such thing. It was the third rock and I planned on tossing one of these burning firebrands next if you didn't wake your doctoring self-up. Get over here and sample this coffee before it's all gone."

Reynolds did as he was told, he really could use some coffee. As he tasted the brew he noticed the deputies canteen lying nearby. "Say, Beasley, did you fill the coffeepot over at the stream?"

"Naw, I just used the water from my canteen. I'll refill it before we leave."

Reynolds spit out the coffee as he remembered the story of crumbs falling from the deputies mustache back into the canteen. He felt as though he was going to be sick.

"Something wrong with the coffee, Doc?"

"Nothing, Deputy. It was just a little too hot for me. You finish it."

"Be glad to. You'll regret it an hour or two from now."

"I really don't think so." It was then that Reynolds decided to make all the coffee and cook all the meals on this little trip. The deputy might have been a good lawman but his abilities with a bar of soap were lacking.

Warrix decided to go to the stream and have another drink. He'd also bring back a cup of water for more pine needle tea. As he made his way to the water he noticed a slight breeze. He hoped it didn't mean a storm but decided storm or not he was going to gather more firewood. He was also going to make some sort of lean-to using pine and cedar boughs. It would go a long way in keeping him dry, and maybe even warm.

As he made his way back he definitely noticed a breeze coming from the west. This could only be the makings of a storm. There was something else he noticed, the breeze had the distinct smell of coffee, and at times, smoke. Once he even thought he smelled bacon. His injury and solitude were playing tricks on him. But then he decided it wasn't his imagination, he actually got a whiff of bacon.

After making what was now his fourth cup of tea he decided to climb back up and keep watch. That would be much easier than hobbling out to the edge of the tree line every hour to scan the valley. Again he put out the fire knowing the heat would keep the top of the rock tolerable. Back on top he stretched out and looked at the sky. He figured the clouds would be back soon, along with the promise of a storm, he could just feel it. Before long he'd dozed off.

Beasley quickly packed up the few items they had used in camp. The two were actually running late this morning. Rather than getting started at first light it was now a good hour and a half past. The extra time had allowed the two weary travelers to have breakfast and look the terrain over. Having arrived here at dusk the previous evening didn't allow for much scouting around.

Another reason for the late start was it took a good thirty minutes to saddle Jinx and Yancy. The pack saddle came last, Dusty didn't seem to mind. He figured they were going to find the marshal. The reason he thought this was because he had never traveled without the marshal. Surely there was a reason these two strangers were heading off into the wilderness, it had to be for the marshal.

"This valley leads away from the Box W. I guess the men that we're after know this range pretty well and want nothing to do with that crew of wranglers that work for Bishop," Beasley said as he took up the reins of Jinx. He climbed into the saddle holding the lead for Dusty.

The doc took one last look around before climbing aboard Yancy. The big horse tried to protest; it was the first time Yancy had given anything that looked like trouble to the doc. "Whoa now. It's a little too early in the morning to be giving me attitude, horse." Again Yancy protested. He did a sideways step and then backed up a few feet, all the while tossing his head up and down. After he got the horse under control he looked back at the deputy. "Now what do you reckon that's all about?"

Beasley was looking the valley over. "I don't reckon I got an answer for you, Doc, but I got a guess. There might be something in this valley that Yancy don't like. He senses something, could be a bad something, or it could just be a different something. Might be another horse he smells. I guess we'll find out," Beasley said as he tied the lead to his saddle horn and then pulled his Winchester. "I'll just keep this handy," he said as he patted the gun.

The two men soon picked up the trail of the four previous horses that had been through here, the same trail they had managed to lose the previous day. They moved slow, Beasley keeping a close eye on the trail ahead. As they moved he noticed Dusty had moved up beside Jinx. After a mile the big tan had moved in front. He also knew he was on the trail of four horses. What happened to the marshal and Pulpit? There was no sign of the marshal's horse.

"Now would you look at that. Dusty wants to lead," Reynolds said.

Beasley had noticed it too. "He senses something up ahead. That might explain why Yancy was acting so peculiar a little while ago."

The men continued but Dusty was doing more of the leading as the other two horses followed. The trail had split off going left and right. One going the way Dusty wanted to go while the other, with the tracks of the four horses, veered right. Beasley stopped Jinx and looked around. That's when he noticed something.

"Those are boot tracks. I thought I noticed a boot print a time or two late yesterday evening. I figured it was one of the riders that had dismounted and was walking his horse," Beasley said.

After looking the tracks over he came to a conclusion, a guess really. "I think the four we want to follow are headed more to the east. But I got a hunch this single set of tracks belongs to the marshal. He's headed more to the north. I believe we better head that way. I'll be able to pick up his horse's tracks soon."

The two men headed north with both now holding Winchesters. The tracks were faint in spots and nonexistent in others. Beasley was having trouble tracking the man who was on foot. He had yet to find a single horse track.

"Something just ain't adding up. Why would anyone be out here on foot?" Beasley asked.

"I don't see any tracks that would indicate a horse had gone through here. I can't see any tracks made by a man on foot either. Are you sure you're not imagining things, Deputy?"

Beasley stepped to the ground and bent at the knee; he wanted a closer look at the tracks. "Horse leaves good sign, a man, not so much. Something weighing over a thousand pounds and wearing steel shoes leaves heavy prints. A two hundred pound man wearing boots can walk a mile and not leave a single print in hard packed ground. If we follow the man on foot we might lose the trail. He ain't leaving much."

Beasley had released the lead he held as he looked for sign. Dusty noticed this and decided to head on up the valley. As soon as he started walking Beasley stood and tried to catch the lead, but he was too late. He quickly mounted up and went after the horse.

"Did you let Dusty escape?"

"I did no such thing. He won't go far, we'll just see where he leads us," Beasley said. The deputy was a mite embarrassed that he'd dropped the lead. It wasn't intentional, he was so focused on the tracks he just dropped it.

Dusty continued up the trail. As he went he would stop from time to time and lift his head, something either had him spooked or he was following a familiar scent. Each time he would start again heading in the same direction as before. Something had the big horse acting like a bloodhound on the hunt.

"Would you look at that. Dusty is acting strange," Reynolds said.

"He senses something. A horse is nearly as good as a bloodhound when it comes to tracking. The reason they don't track is that most horses just don't give a damn. We'll let him have his way and see where it leads us," Beasley said as he followed along letting Dusty do as he pleased.

Dusty kept going, he had no intention of stopping now. He sensed something and he was going to investigate. As they made their way up the valley they came closer and closer to the tree line. Finally Dusty stopped. He looked toward the trees but made no attempt to go further. He was trying to figure out what he sensed and whether he wanted to get any closer.

"We better hold up here, Doc. Until Dusty decides whether he wants to go any further we stay here, and stay alert." Both men still had their Winchesters lying across their saddles. Beasley did ride up and grab the lead where it attached to the bridle. Dusty thought about giving the deputy a nibble just to say, 'leave me alone,' but didn't. He was too focused on the tree line.

Warrix had fallen asleep again. The top of the rock made a good bed. It was safe and not all that uncomfortable, mainly due to how flat the top was. A rock for a bed, who would have thought?

Warrix was dreaming that he heard voices, a dream that had gone on for quite some time. When he realized it wasn't a dream he eased up and peered over the front of the rock. He saw two men and three horses. He pulled the Colt from its holster and checked the cylinder. The one empty chamber he always carried wasn't empty for long.

After loading the gun he looked back at the riders. The range meant he couldn't make out much in the way of details, but he did see that both men had rifles at the ready. Could he hold off two men with Winchesters? Probably not.

Then he noticed the pack horse was leading the two men, what the hell? He continued to watch, something about the pack horse looked familiar, maybe it was the color, or maybe the way it walked.

Beasley kept a tight grip on the fifteen foot lead attached to Dusty. Until the big horse started acting normal he wasn't going to give him much space.

"Let's ease on up a bit, Doc. Keep that Winchester at the ready," Beasley said and then thought of something else. "You said you could shoot, and I assumed you were talking about a six-shooter. Can you shoot a rifle?"

"Stop worrying, Deputy, I might have been in a gunfight or two in my younger days." He looked at Beasley and added, "And I might have not."

"You are a strange one, Doc. I don't know what kind of trouble you had back in Boston, and don't care. What I am worried about is now."

Again Dusty started toward the trees. This time he was moving with purpose, he wasn't skittish at all. He wanted the tree line, and he wanted it now.

"We'll let him go a ways more and then we stop. Damn horse might be leading us into an ambush, but I don't think so," Beasley said. Whatever was in the trees didn't seem to spook the big horse. As a matter of thought, he wanted to get there now and not later the way he was moving.

Warrix kept looking at the men and horses as they continued to approach. Finally he thought he recognized the packhorse, it was Dusty. Naw, that can't be right. Dusty was laid up at the livery with a sore leg. And who in their right mind would put a packsaddle on his horse?

Five minutes later he was sure of it, Dusty was being used as a packhorse and he was leading the other two men and horses to him. A minute later he recognized Beasley and

Reynolds. They had come looking for the killers and found him on the way.

Warrix stood on top of the rock and watched as the group got closer. He didn't want to shout or wave his hands, that would be a good way to get shot.

"Stop right here a second, Doc. We got a man standing on top of that big rock. You see him there just inside the trees?"

Reynolds held his hand to his forehead to decrease the glare. He saw the man. "Now why would anybody stand out in the open like that?"

"It's probably the man we've been following that was afoot. He must have lost his horse." Beasley looked harder, "I believe that's the marshal. Let's get a little closer and make sure. Stay alert though, it might be a trap."

Warrix continued to look at the two men from the safety of the rock. He wasn't going to come down until he was absolutely sure they were who he thought they were. Injured and without the benefit of a rifle made him overly cautious. Another minute and there was no doubt who they were.

Dusty was intent on making it to the rock, so intent that he pulled the rope out of Beasley's hand. Once free of the lead he trotted to the big rock and stood there looking up at the marshal. He probably thought the man had lost his mind or something standing up there. People could be downright crazy acting sometimes.

Beasley and the doc hurried to the rock, both looking at the camp the marshal had.

"Howdy, Marshal, we figured to not let you have all the fun, so we decided to follow. By the looks of that leg we might have got here at a pretty good time," Beasley said.

"You did at that. Come on around back while I climb down."

As the two men rode around behind the big rock they looked the place over. Dusty was already there checking everything out. The first thing he wondered was where Pulpit was, maybe the marshal had him staked out near water and grass, yeah that was it.

Beasley and Reynolds tied their two horses and looked at the back of the rock. They also watched as Warrix nimbly climbed down. He was cautious until he got to his homemade crutch.

"Boy am I glad to see the two of you. I was just about to make tea, would either of you like a cup." Both men looked at the extinguished fire and the nearly burned up coffeecup.

Beasley paid close attention to the rock and the chiseled steps leading to the top. Without a word he walked over and climbed to the top. He looked at the way the front of the rock rose higher than the part he now stood on. It made a protected firing position.

"Marshal, do you know what this is? This is Medicine Rock. I've heard of this place all my life but thought it was just a story, but it really exists." The deputy looked, and sounded, like he had discovered the New World.

"Medicine Rock," Warrix said as he scanned the area, the same area he'd scanned at least a hundred times, as well as slept there.

"Haven't you heard of it, Marshal? You must have. This place is sacred to the Lakota Tribe. I doubt there's a Lakota warrior within a hundred miles of here. This place is powerful medicine," Beasley said with the excitement of a child.

"Lakota you say. I don't recall ever hearing stories of a Medicine Rock. Maybe I did and just forgot. I do know one thing, this place hasn't been used in years, many years," Warrix said.

"Looks like you had an accident, Marshal. Better let me take a look at that," Reynolds said as he got his saddlebags from Yancy.

Dusty figured he wasn't getting his due attention, so he stepped over to the marshal and nudged him with his nose. Warrix patted the big horse. "Looks like they made a pack horse out of you, Dusty."

"We did at that. His foot is fine. Randal Sanders said he had a splinter was all. He said the big bastard was as good as new, so we decided to use him to haul our grub. Say, where is Pulpit? You got him staked out somewhere?" the deputy asked.

As Reynolds doctored the wound Warrix was wearing, the marshal told the story of how the four killers had ambushed him and killed his horse. He told of the mishap at the river and how he barely managed to make it back to the rock. He told of pine needle tea and how the big rock kept him warm at night. The other two men listened as if it was the best story they'd heard in ages, and it probably was.

"Well I'd say luck, and this rock, were on your side. How about we fix you some coffee and bacon, that is unless you'd rather have tea?" Beasley said with a grin. He and Reynolds were glad they'd decided to chase after the marshal, it probably saved the man's life.

Heith Bryson sat at the line shack the entire day. He was supposed to be checking boundaries for strays to make it look like he'd been there longer than just one day, but he couldn't. After counting the money he figured his working days were over. All he had to do was confront Rumford and settle things, man to man.

Then another thought dawned on him, why confront Rumford at all. Grab the money, mount up and ride off. That was the thing to do. Head south to Mexico or maybe west to California. He had the money to do whatever he pleased. He was having these thoughts when he heard riders coming hard up the trail toward the shack.

One quick glance and he knew this was some of Bishop's men. Now he had a decision to make, stay and try to sound convincing that he'd been here longer than one day? Mount up and ride out? Against four men he figured he couldn't get far enough away before one of them caught him.

The last option was to stay and fight, not a good option but it was looking like the only one available to him. He grabbed his Winchester and made sure it was fully loaded. He checked his Colt and as a last thought he put the hideaway behind his back. It was the same gun he'd killed Aldrich with.

Rather than going out the front he slipped out the back and headed for the nearby timber. His horse was tied up deep in the trees near a small seep that offered good water and grass. It was completely out of sight. Bryson found a good spot among some deadfalls and knelt. He was going to stay quiet and out of sight until he figured how the four Box W men were going to handle this.

"There's the line shack. Let's spread out, no need to make an easy target for a shotgun," Toler said. All four men had their rifles out and at the ready. If Bryson and the other three men were innocent then they could prove it. Until that time Toler wasn't taking any chances.

They rode within fifty feet of the shack and then Toler shouted. No response. The four dismounted and eased toward the shack, each expecting to be shot. Once at the front door Toler used the barrel of his gun to shove the door open. The shack was empty and the stove cold. It looked like the place had been used recently but looks could be deceiving. The smell of coffee and sweat was thick but that could linger for a month in a closed up cabin.

"I got tracks around back. Looks like a horse was here in the last twenty-four hours. Sign is fresh," one of the three wranglers said.

The four men scouted around the shack but didn't find anything other than the horse tracks. It had gotten cold during the night and the ground was frozen solid. A man walking couldn't leave a mark of any kind now. Even the horse tracks were frozen. The more they looked the more they decided the tracks could be a week old, even longer.

"I didn't think them four would be here. If four men had stayed here and had four horses tied out then we'd know it. Them bastards must have stayed at the southern boundary," Toler said.

They mounted up and headed off the mountain. They needed to get back to the Box W and report what they'd found. Toler didn't want to be away from the ranch longer than needed with four killers on the loose. He figured his boss could take care of himself but against four, well he just didn't want to risk it. There was another hand or two around the big house but still, anything could happen.

Bryson watched as the four men scouted around the line shack. He kept his Winchester trained on Toler the entire time. He was going to make sure the ranch foreman got it first. Then he'd deal with the other three. He was in good cover and well-armed. He also had the advantage of surprise. This was Bryson's favorite way of fighting, surprise, and brutality.

Just when he figured they were coming his way they turned and headed back to their horses. When they mounted up and rode away he couldn't believe his luck. He doubted, if things came to a shootout, if he'd survive unscathed. He would have taken some lead, but he was confident he could have killed two, maybe even three, before he went down.

As he walked back to the shack he stayed out of sight. He could still see the riders and until they were completely off the mountain he was going to stay hidden.

Reynolds patched Warrix up, at least as good as one would expect this far from town and with limited supplies. The marshal was in good spirits. He had just gotten his leg looked at and he'd eaten, and not just eaten but eaten ravenously. And now there would be three men hunting the outlaws. He regretted heading out on his own, probably not one of his smartest moves. He might have two men traveling with him now but he damn sure wasn't going to double up on a horse.

"How we going to handle this anyway, you two done made a packhorse out of Dusty?" Warrix asked as he watched the doc finish up with his leg.

Beasley stood and went to the fire. He'd used one of the rock seats as he listened to the marshal and looked Medicine Rock over. He felt as if he were in some sort of majestic place, not meant to be disturbed or sullied by the likes of the three.

"We got no choice but to offload the supplies and push ahead. We can come back in a few days and replenish. I figure we can store what we can't carry up on the rock. Should keep the bigger critters away from it," Beasley said.

"What about a saddle?" Reynolds asked.

Now this was a problem. "I can ride without a saddle if one of you has an extra saddle blanket. After walking, or should I say hobbling, back to this camp, I can definitely manage to ride without a saddle."

"Alright then, we better get a move on. As we sit here the men we're after are getting farther away. The trail is going to grow cold real fast," Beasley said.

It took nearly an hour to get the supplies secured on top of the rock. Warrix stood on one of the rock seats and easily mounted up. It was odd using only a saddle blanket, the lack of stirrups was something different too. At slightly before noon the three men pulled away from Medicine Rock.

Let's head back to where the trail split. We should find the tracks the four left day before yesterday. Unless it rains the trail shouldn't be that hard to follow," Beasley said.

The three men headed out and within an hour they had met back up with the old trail. Another hour and they spotted something lying to the side of the trail.

"That looks like a body lying there," Beasley said as the three approached.

"Looks like three bodies," Reynolds added. The men grabbed their Winchesters, at least Beasley and Reynolds did, the rifle Warrix owned was at the bottom of a creek.

"Doc, why don't you and the marshal keep watch while I investigate," the deputy said as he reached the reins to Warrix.

There were three bodies, all had been scavenged by predators that would just as soon take advantage of dead food as hunt for live food.

"Marshal, whoever did this didn't take their guns, all three look to have been shot and just left by the side of the trail. What do you figure went on here?" the deputy asked.

"My guess is this is part of the gang that attacked the bank. Check their pockets for any papers that might shed some light on who they are," Warrix said. "Maybe there was an argument and gunplay erupted? I doubt a stranger rode up and just shot the three."

"Looks like a horse coming this way, Marshal," Reynolds said.

The other two men looked in the same direction as the doc was pointing. Sure enough, a saddled horse was heading their way. It walked all the way to where the men were and just stopped. The horse not only wore a saddle and bridle but there was also a scabbard and inside was a rifle.

Beasley took off his hat and held it in his hand as if he were offering something to the horse. He'd done this, everybody had done this at one time or another to try and catch a horse. The animal stepped forward to investigate. The deputy grabbed the bridle and patted the horse's nose.

This must be one of these men's horses. I'd say two more are roaming around here somewhere. What do you want to do, Marshal?"

"First, reach me that Winchester," Warrix said.

The gun was a seventy-three, one of the latest versions. It was fully loaded and looked to be in good condition. "I'll be keeping this," Warrix said as he eased down.

"Let's switch that saddle to Dusty. Then we'll head back and get the packsaddle and our supplies. This horse not only brought me a saddle but will now become our packhorse. The trip back is going to waste a couple more hours but at least we'll be well-supplied and ready to continue the hunt," Warrix said.

By three that evening the men left Medicine Rock for the second time that day. The marshal was riding Dusty and he had a saddle. His leg had been patched up and he was fed. All in all, the day was ending way better than it had begun.

The three bodies they'd abandoned earlier didn't have anything that would help identify who the men were. Still though, both lawmen figured they were three of the four that had robbed the bank. They had left the three as they'd found them, a burial wasn't even considered. They did take their guns and ammunition though. Warrix and his small posse now travelled with three additional Colts, all in good condition and all fully loaded. The three dead men had furnished a horse, saddle, and guns. It was probably the only instance of generosity any of the three had ever offered, and of all things, it was after they were dead.

"What's the plan, Marshal?" Reynolds asked as they rode away from Medicine Rock.

"This late in the day I say we head to the Box W. I want to talk to Ralph Bishop. He needs to know about the bank robbery. I'll still see if he can send a couple of men to Dakota City to help out until we get back."

"Dakota City will be fine, Marshal. The mayor done deputized James Hayes. He'll be staying at the jail if needed. They've also organized a twenty-four hour watch. Several of the townsfolk are helping until we get this all sorted out," Beasley told the marshal. Warrix seemed surprised at first but soon came around to the plan.

Toler and the three men that had gone to the line shack the previous day were at the ranch. It had been decided that until a few more wranglers could be brought in they would stay and keep check on things. It was doubtful anyone would attack the ranch house operation, but it'd also been doubtful anyone would attack a bank in the center of Dakota City.

Toler had brought the news that the northern line shack didn't look to have been used. If it had then whoever had used it wasn't there when they investigated. He was sure that four men hadn't used the shack. Bishop figured the men led by Heith Bryson were suspects in the robbery and killings. He had no proof, just a hunch.

"Got three riders coming up the road boss. One's pulling a packhorse," Toler said.

Bishop went to the front porch. The three looked well-armed, not your normal travelers. "Get a few more hands, have them grab a couple of shotguns until we know these men's intentions," Bishop said.

The three riders rode up to the ranch house, a well-guarded ranch house. Warrix recognized one of the men on the front porch as the owner.

"Hello the house. I'm Marshal Joshua Warrix."

"Come on up, Marshal, I thought I recognized you. Sorry about the welcome, you might say we're a bit on edge after what happened in Dakota City last Saturday," Bishop said

The three dismounted, Warrix taking a little longer than the other two.

"You get shot, Marshal?" Toler asked as he and a couple of hands grabbed the reins.

"Fell off a tree. It's a long story."

"I'll bet it is. We'll take care of your horses," Toler said as they led the four animals toward the barn.

It took Warrix longer than the other two to climb the steps to the porch. Once there he collapsed into a chair. His injury, and subsequent loss of blood, was taking a toll on the man. Sleeping on a rock probably wasn't helping that much either.

"We came to tell you of a robbery at the bank in Dakota City, but it sounds like you've already heard the news," Warrix said after he caught his breath.

"I know what happened, Marshal. I sent Toler and three men there Saturday afternoon. I'm afraid the men that robbed the bank took nearly everything I had. Their timing I find suspicious, to say the least. They hit the bank as soon as a large payment for my last cattle drive arrived. It was almost like they knew. I'm still trying to figure out what could have happened."

"We came across three bodies about three hours back. They weren't on the trail that leads from Dakota City to the ranch here. It was actually more to the east. You got any ideas about that?" Warrix asked.

Bishop thought a second. "I might. I sent Toler and three men to one of the northern line shacks to see if four wranglers that work for me were there. The shack looked to have been used but not by four men. One man maybe, but not four. As soon as Toler gets back from taking care of your horses we'll ask him. What are you going to do next?"

"We'd like to stay here for the night and start tracking again first thing in the morning. This late in the day, and this close to dark, we couldn't get far before having to make camp."

"That was what I was going to suggest. I'll let the cook know. I've had a cook now for about a year, ever since my wife died. One thing I never learned to do was prepare a meal. I can fry bacon, and drink water from a canteen, but that's about it," Bishop said as he got up and went inside. He was back in only a minute.

We've got a bunkhouse, but I'd prefer the three of you stay at the house. There's plenty of room and the company will be a welcome change. We're having meatloaf and potatoes; I hope that's acceptable?" Bishop asked.

"Sounds fine to me," Warrix said. He would have been happy with baked groundhog as hungry as he'd been the last few days.

"About those men you found back on the trail. My guess is that four men that work for me robbed the bank. They were on the southern boundary, but I had them sent north. Apparently I waited too long. They must have had a falling out and one managed to quadruple his one quarter share. You remember that old saying, 'No honor among thieves,' probably came into play," Bishop said.

Toler had come back to the ranch house after seeing to the four horses. He listened and was curious about something. "You say there were three bodies. Can you describe any of them?"

The three members of the impromptu posse thought a minute. Finally it was Beasley who spoke up. "The critters got there before we did. The bodies were in pretty bad shape."

"Well that horse you're using as a pack horse belonged to one of the four. Sam Aldrich owned that horse I'm pretty sure. If the killer done away with all three and then rode off then there's two more horses out there. And if my guess is right they both are wearing saddles same as the horse you found. With your permission boss I'd like to take three men to where the bodies are and see if we can bait the other two horses in. They're probably wondering why they're out there anyway," Toler said.

"You can't get there before nightfall. You'll be looking in the dark," Warrix said.

"That's true but if my hunch is correct those two horses will gladly come to other horses. We got wolves in the territory and even the occasional bear. Catching the two horses after dark might be easier than daylight."

"I like it, take three men, and see what you can find out. Take shotguns, better to shoot wide in the dark if it comes to it," Bishop said.

Toler turned and headed for the steps, but stopped short and turned back around. "Once there we'll look for an hour or so. That will put us back here around midnight at the latest. You want to know what we find out tonight or in the morning?"

Without hesitation Bishop said to come to the ranch house as soon as they got back.

"I believe the survivor of the four was at that line shack on the northern boundary. I believe he'd been there a few hours, maybe half a day, and then hid like a coward when he saw Toler and the three wranglers ride up. Toler said he could have seen if four men had been there, he said four hadn't. He also said the place looked like someone had been there, but it was hard to tell. One man don't make much of a disturbance in a line shack. The damn things are in a perpetual state of disturbance," Bishop said as he watched Toler and three of his wranglers ride out in the direction of where the bodies lay.

"Sounds about right. My guess is the man was trying to act innocent by being there. He figured he wouldn't be suspected of the killings and robbery down in Dakota City if he was found at that line shack. He must have lost his nerve when he saw

Toler and his men ride up. Like you said, he hid," Warrix told the three.

"If the man was there when Toler rode off then I'd say he ain't there now. He's headed for the far and wide if you ask me. A man that knows he's being chased by four men won't have much stay-put about him," Beasley said.

Doc Reynolds just looked at the man. "Where in hell did you learn to talk like that?"

"I learned to talk good a long time ago. You hang around me long enough and I'll teach that Boston accent right out of you," the deputy said. Reynolds could only shake his head in defeat.

"And another thing. He knows he's being chased. My guess is he'll hole up somewhere safe. He'll stay put until he thinks folks quit looking. That's when he'll foul-up and he'll get caught. Mark my words, it's like I say," Beasley said. He was half serious and half just aggravating the doc. He knew how to irritate the man.

Just then a woman came to the porch. She was probably in her forties but that could be misleading. Her appearance was neat, and she had the air of an educated woman. When she spoke her voice was pleasant but not weak or standoffish. Her wording and diction were perfect, maybe an eastern accent.

"Dinner is ready. Stella and I have placed everything on the table in the dining room. I hope that's alright with you, Mr. Bishop?"

"That's fine Maggie. We'll be in shortly," Bishop said.

The woman named Maggie smiled as she went back inside. Each of the men were trying to evaluate whether she was forty five or twenty nine. She was of the type that carried herself well and whose looks could deceive. Bishop didn't think twice about the woman's appearance. She was his sister.

"Well gentlemen, let's not keep Maggie waiting. If supper gets cold then she feeds it to my birddogs. Usually that happens at least twice a week. She doesn't really mind though, two of the dogs belong to her."

Beasley wondered if he was also invited, after all he was a lowly deputy traveling with a marshal and a doctor. Bishop noticed his reluctance. "Deputy, why don't you join us. I promise my sister hasn't poisoned anyone since, well let me think," he said as he started laughing.

Maggie met the men at the door. "The washroom is around back. I'll also see if a pair of my brothers pants might be better than the ones you're wearing, Marshal. I'll have Stella bring them to the back porch."

After the woman was out of earshot Bishop said in a whisper, "One of my line shacks is starting to sound pretty good to me. That woman runs this place with an iron hand. You three hurry to the washroom and then meet me inside. Remember, she runs the inside of the house so if any of you find yourself in trouble don't look at me, you're on your own. And I apologize in advance, I know how to stay out of her way, you don't." Again the man started laughing, this time though it was at a whisper, if that were possible.

The washroom was elaborate to say the least. It was even heated by a flattop wood burning stove. There was a hand pump and if you had the time you could heat a tub of water. The doc decided he would make use of the tub if it were offered to him. All three hurried and cleaned up. Warrix hobbled out when he heard the woman say she was hanging the pants on the outside of the door. He was anxious to have a sit down meal. He wondered if they had any pine needle tea.

Once cleaned and wearing new trousers Warrix decided he couldn't wait any longer. He was tired and sore, but hunger trumped both of those problems. All three men stepped to the back door and knocked. The woman named Stella answered and then led the three to the dining room. She immediately took a seat to the right of Bishop.

If the outside of the house looked big then the inside looked bigger. They were led through the kitchen, an elaborate kitchen, and into the dining room. The table had eight chairs, three on each side and another one at each end.

When the men entered Bishop was already seated, along with the two women, Stella, and Maggie. Each took a seat as they looked at the food spread before them.

"Gentlemen, we run things in the dining room as informally as possible. Each of you can serve yourself," Bishop said.

As the men ate they heard footsteps and then the front door open. A lean rangy man entered the dining room carrying a Winchester. Warrix and Beasley were ready to go for their guns when the man spoke.

"I got a man in front and another out back. Got another two at the barn. I'll be walking the property on all four sides until Toler gets back," the man said.

"I think that should do it. Until we catch that last man I want guards posted day and night. When Toler and the three men with him get back some of you can rotate out. Each of you try to get a little sleep but daylight would be best," Bishop said. The man nodded and then turned and left.

"I run a big crew, but most are away from the main ranch house. A few more than sixty men work the ranch but at any given time only five or six are here. As men check in I'll be adding to the crew here until this business is over," Bishop said.

"You suspect the ranch might be attacked? I doubt there's more than one of the killers left," Warrix asked.

"I'm not that worried about that bunch, like you said I think three are already dead. Maybe we can talk after dinner in my study. I got a bottle of Kentucky Bourbon that's been asking to be opened for a few weeks now. It's a pretty dangerous brand, maybe the three of you can help me tame it?"

"Be glad to, I've tamed a few in my day," Beasley said with a grin. He'd already decided he liked Bishop.

Warrix ate two full plates as he listened to the others talk. He added nothing to the conversation. Bishop had heard the story and knew the man needed to eat. He also knew about Medicine Rock.

"You say you've heard of the rock, Deputy. Most folks haven't," Bishop said.

"I've heard of it nearly all my life, thought it was just an old story that's been handed down for years."

"Well now you see the story is true. I've owned this property for years; Medicine Rock came with it. I believe the marshal here is the first one to use it as a camp since I've owned the property."

The men finished the meal and then were led by Bishop to his study, it was also his office. The room was big and had ample seating in the form of overstuffed leather chairs. All four took a seat.

"You say Maggie is your sister. Does she always refer to you as Mr. Bishop?" the doc asked. He was curious.

"Only when we have guests. She came west shortly after my wife died. Her husband was afflicted with a wandering eye and shortly before my wife died he ran off with another woman. I don't know the particulars and don't care to.

"The other woman is Stella; she is my sister in law. My wife only had one sibling and when she became sick she arranged for Stella and Maggie to come west to see after me. I really think it was my wife's way of tormenting me from the grave." After some thought Bishop added, "I was only kidding about that. The two see to the needs of the ranch house and leave me to the running of the ranch itself."

"You mentioned some other happenings, something other than the robbing of the bank," Warrix asked.

Bishop stood and went to a cabinet. He grabbed a bottle of whiskey and four glasses. After everyone had a glass he sat back down and began his story.

"About six months ago the ranch started having trouble with rustling. This is a big ranch, a little shy of fifty-thousand acres. A spread like this is hard to patrol. The rustling might have been going on for a year or longer before we began to notice. I've got a lot of cattle; it's how I pay my bills.

"We run four-hundred head at a time to the railhead. We do that three times a year, on a good year maybe four. The last three drives took us longer to put together, had to range farther on my spread to gather the four hundred. At first I figured the bad winter from three years ago might have thinned the count.

"A bad flood last year took the numbers down too. This is a rough environment, lots of cattle never make it to market due to the extremes in weather. But on a good year the grass grows thick and so do my cattle. I've always counted on some bad luck but that just didn't add up to the shortages in my numbers.

"Of the sixty or so men that work the ranch I've got eight men keeping tally books on the herds. After careful consideration it could only add up to one thing, rustlers," Bishop said as he took a sip of his bourbon.

"How many head are we talking about here?" the marshal asked.

"I figure year before last it was around four hundred. That would amount to one full cattle drive to the railhead. Last year maybe seven hundred. This year it's looking like a thousand and the year ain't done yet." Bishop was telling the story but not looking at the three men in his study. To talk about it was painful, that you could tell just by the look on the man's face.

"With that kind of operation going on there would be evidence. No one can steal that many cattle and not leave any sign," Beasley said. The deputy was a natural born tracker, everything to him boiled down to what was left in the way of evidence.

"Toler thinks we got fifteen men running fifty head at a time to the railroad. They touch the brand and then move." By the look on the doc's face Bishop felt he had to explain. "To touch the brand means to change it. The Box W brand is a tough one, but it can be done. We figure they stop short of the railhead each time and rebrand the fifty head. If they can head that many cattle east then they're getting top dollar."

"Wouldn't that take an agent, someone like the man you got handling the transfer of your own cattle?" Warrix asked.

"It would, someone like Bernard Rumford. That's the agent I use, for the moment. An agent is necessary to keep tabs on when the market is high. When I get a telegram telling me that prices are up I quickly put together four-hundred head and start the drive. If I hear the market is down then I might put off a drive for a month or two. The market is volatile and playing it right can make a difference of several thousand dollars," Bishop said. The way he said the agent's name and the fact that he said, 'for the moment,' seemed ominous.

"The way you spoke of your agent sounded like you have suspicions about the man. Either that or he's doing a bad job," Warrix said as more of a question than a statement.

Ralph Bishop sipped his bourbon. He seemed lost in thought. Finally he said, "I'm starting to consider that Rumford might have something to do with the missing cattle. I really can't say why, just a lot of little things that are starting to add up. Whoever is rustling Box W beef is doing damage to my bottom line. If it keeps up at this rate I'll be out of business by next summer." Bishop didn't tell about the fact that he couldn't even make his next payment on the ranch's substantial loan.

Bishop decided to turn the conversation away from his missing cattle. "What do you think of the bourbon?"

"I like it but instead of bourbon why don't they just call it whiskey?" Beasley asked.

"Well, Deputy, all I can say is that all bourbon is whiskey but not all whiskey is bourbon." He knew he probably confused the deputy even more.

At a little after ten that night Toler, along with the three wranglers that had traveled with him to check out the dead men, rode back into the confines of the ranch house and the barn and corrals. It had been an interesting trip. Toler reached the reins of his horse to one of the other hands and then walked toward the house. It was well lit which indicated his boss was still awake.

"I didn't expect you back this quick. Any luck?" Bishop asked his foreman.

"Got to where the three bodies were. Wolves were there first. They didn't want to give up their find but a couple of shots from my Winchester sent them away, but not far. I figure they are back cleaning up the scraps now.

"There wasn't much left, anyway, not enough to try and identify the bodies. If it was the same three that hired on with Heith Bryson the remains didn't show it. After we got rid of the wolves though the other two horses came trotting up. The way they acted they weren't liking being out in the wilderness like that, especially with wolves around.

"I checked both, they belong to two of Bryson's men. Just like the horse the marshal found and used as a packhorse; they were still saddled and carried all the dead men's gear. Got two of the hands stripping the gear off and putting both in a stall as we speak. Neither horse needed any coaxing to come on in with us."

After giving his report Toler left the men in the study. He needed to see about the men stationed around the ranch house and barn. In the last couple of days Toler and Bishop had transformed the main house and adjoining buildings into a veritable fortress.

"Looks like the only man left is, Heith Bryson. How certain are you that Bryson and his men actually did the killings and robbed the bank?" Bishop asked.

"Can't be certain but everything points in that direction. If you don't mind I'd like to take the three horses back with me to Dakota City. Some of the folks there might be able to identify them as the ones the killers rode. Plus, we'll need to use one as a packhorse," Warrix said.

"Take all three, I got no need for them here. As a matter of fact take all the gear, it might help in the identification. When do you plan to head out?" Bishop asked. With the three dead men being tentatively identified as the men that rode with Heith Bryson there was less need to continue the chase.

"First light, we need to get back to Dakota City and at least put folk's minds at ease. Once they find out that three of the killers are dead it will go a long way in calming their nerves. First light will put us in town by late afternoon," Warrix said.

"I'll make sure breakfast is ready an hour before. The three of you can enjoy some more of my sister's cooking. One other thing, Marshal. The money that was stolen, do you think there's any chance of getting it back?"

"Maybe, if we can find that last man, Heith Bryson. Everything now depends on finding him and bringing the man to justice. I'll send word to the other towns in the area. That's the best we can hope for at the moment. To continue the hunt might pan out but most likely it won't. We'll wait for him to make a move."

"As far as the Box W goes, I plan on having every available hand riding the boundaries looking for the man. If we find him I can't guarantee what kind of shape he'll be in when we turn him over," Bishop said.

"You or any of your men find him try to take him alive. I want to see him stand trial. One other thing, if your men kill him before he tells you where the money is hidden then you may never find it," Warrix said.

The thought of losing the money had consumed Bishop ever since he'd heard of the robbery the previous Saturday. "Believe me, Marshal, retrieving the money is foremost in my mind. If Bryson is caught I can assure you he'll stay alive, at least until I find the money."

The wording left nothing for chance. If Bishop and his men found Bryson before the marshal did then they would find out where he'd hidden the money. Warrix doubted if Bishop would allow the man to live after he found his money but there wasn't anything he could do about that scenario.

Early the next morning Warrix was awakened not by gunfire, or a thunderstorm, or anything life-threatening, it was his nose. The smell coming from the kitchen was thick in the house. No sooner had the marshal made his way to the big dining room than he was met by Beasley and the doc.

"Well Marshal, looks like you might be chasing some breakfast," Beasley said.

"As are you, Deputy. Have any of you seen Bishop this morning?"

None of the men had seen the ranch owner. Rather than sit down Warrix went to the kitchen, both Maggie and Stella were there. When asked he was told that neither of the women had seen Bishop.

"Is it usual for him to not have breakfast?" Warrix asked. He knew very few men started the day on an empty stomach.

"Actually, he never sleeps this late. An hour before sunrise is the latest he sleeps, the man is an earlier riser," Maggie said.

"Why don't you go tell him breakfast is ready. I'll finish up with the biscuits," Stella said.

Maggie took off her apron and then headed for the stairs. The big corner bedroom's door was wide open, she thought her brother must be awake and ready to come downstairs. She gently knocked on the door frame. He wasn't in his room, it looked like he hadn't even slept in his bed last night.

Maggie went inside the room, while standing there trying to figure out what was going on she noticed a slight breeze. The room was also cold. Upon closer inspection she found one of the widows slightly open. She stepped to the window and pushed it shut. Maybe the marshal could come up and have a look around she thought. She really didn't think anything was wrong but was beginning to worry anyway.

Warrix was standing at the base of the stairs. His right hand on the right hand baluster, his left boot on the first step. He suspected something was wrong when the ranch owner didn't greet them as they entered the big dining room. He had Bishop pegged as a man that ran things on a tight schedule. It was the only way to describe a man that had come so far in life and acquired so much.

"He's not up here, Marshal. It doesn't appear he's even slept in his room. Another thing, one of the windows was unlocked and open," Maggie said as she stood at the top of the stairs.

Without a word Warrix climbed the stairs, once at the top Maggie pointed him toward the room. The air inside the bedroom was noticeably cooler, it was actually downright cold. The room had two large double-hung windows on one wall, a second wall had another window.

"Which window?" Warrix asked. He had to ask because all three windows were closed, undoubtedly by Maggie after finding one open.

Maggie indicated which window had been found open. Warrix went to the window and checked the lock, it looked alright on the inside. Just outside the window was a narrow balcony that led to the left and around the corner. A balcony adorned most two story houses to allow escape in case of fire. Warrix opened the sash and stepped through the tall window and stood on the balcony. He looked toward the yard and the road, nothing out of the ordinary could be seen.

As he prepared to climb back through the window he noticed splinters of painted wood on the windowsill. Upon closer inspection he could see that someone had used a thin bar, or maybe a pocketknife, to separate the two sashes and then slide the lock to an open position. Someone that didn't want to use the main staircase had crept up the back stairs to the balcony and then broken into Bishop's bedroom.

Warrix descended the stairs in a hurry. He needed to find Windell Toler. The ranch foreman might be able to shed some light on where his boss was. Maybe there was an explanation for the happenings upstairs, and then again, maybe not.

The marshal found Beasley and Reynolds sitting at the big table, neither man had taken a bite although the table had several plates of food sitting there. While Maggie and the marshal were looking upstairs for Bishop, Stella had gone ahead and prepared the table. By the look of things, the two women had risen early and prepared a big breakfast. Before Warrix could speak the ranch foreman walked in, he didn't look happy.

"Marshal, we've got a problem. One of my men is dead, knifed in the back while on guard duty. Four of the others are gone, I'd expect they had something to do with the killing," Toler said. The fact that the ranch foreman hadn't mentioned the disappearance of his boss indicated he was unaware.

Warrix looked at the man. He seemed disturbed about the knifing, as any man would. The marshal wasn't a trusting man by any means. He was searching Toler's expression and demeanor for any sign that might give away the man's loyalties. For all Warrix knew, Toler might have killed the guard and kidnapped Bishop. Time would tell but until then he'd keep a careful eye on the man.

"How many more men have you got? Men that you can trust."

"Four more. I've got them guarding the house. Until we get some answers I don't know who to trust," Toler said as he looked at the others in the room. The murder of one of his men was clouding the man's thoughts and possibly his judgement. It might take a while for him to snap out of it.

Warrix was about to tell the foreman about Bishop when Maggie spoke up. "Have you seen Ralph? We've checked the house, but my brother is nowhere to be found. I'm hoping he just went out and maybe let you know something."

The expression on Toler's face indicated he was unaware, but that could be an act. "I haven't seen him since last night when we got back. Are you sure he's not somewhere outside? You know how he likes his pipe. He may just be outside for an early morning smoke."

"I don't think so, but we really haven't checked other than the house," Maggie said.

"I've checked his room; it doesn't appear he stayed there last night. It also looks like someone fouled the lock and entered through the window. My guess is whoever came in waited in the room until Bishop retired for the night. When he entered they forced him out the same window and down the stairs that lead from the balcony. I'd say the men that did this waited until the time was right, probably knifed the man you mentioned as well," Warrix said.

Toler stood in the dining room as the others gathered. He didn't really know his next move. His boss was gone, four of his men were gone and another one was dead. He was a ranch foreman, not a detective. All this was a bit overwhelming.

"You said four men are now guarding the house? How many men have you got left besides those four?" Warrix asked.

"The four outside are all I've got. There were ten of us but now with one dead and four others unaccounted for that leaves me and the four I got posted."

Warrix didn't like the sound of that one bit. "Can you trust the four you've got stationed outside?"

"I can. They hired on about the same time as I did. The ranch has men stationed at the line shacks but that doesn't help, those men won't be back to the main house for weeks. And if they did show up I don't know how many we could trust. If someone got to the men that I work with everyday then we can assume they also got to some of the men at the line shacks."

Warrix wasn't sure what to make of the disappearance. With Bishop gone he really didn't know who that would leave in charge. He decided to answer that question right now.

"As of now you and your men will be taking orders from me. When we find your boss then I'll relinquish authority but until then I'm in charge. The way I see it whoever took Bishop must want him for leverage," Warrix said.

Beasley came in. He'd heard only part of the conversation but knew by the sound of what he did hear that things weren't good.

"Maybe until we figure out what's going on we might ought to carry rifles. That's big country out there and a Colt won't do much against a man a couple hundred yards away with a Winchester," the deputy said.

"Do the men you've got stationed outside have rifles? Like the deputy said, a man with a Colt against a man with a Winchester doesn't stand much of a chance from a distance," the marshal added.

"They don't. I figured night time was close up work, best to do it with a Colt. It'll be light soon, I'll see they each have a rifle," Toler told the marshal.

"Does the ranch have any extra guns, maybe some extra ammunition and such?" Beasley asked. He knew if things got bad then having a little extra was way better than having barely enough.

Toler smiled. "The boss saw to it that the ranch has plenty of guns and ammunition. He had a room built to the side of the barn, built out of masonry and stone. The man spent some money on that room then he spent some more stocking it. I'd once thought he overdid it a bit, but the way things are happening around here maybe he had a premonition. You want to have a look?"

Beasley's eyes lit up. "I'd say me and the marshal both would."

The three men headed for the barn. First light was getting close. The four guards should be armed properly for day work. Day work meaning work with long guns.

Just outside the gun room was a lantern. Toler picked it up and sparked a match to the wick. With the help of the lantern the two lawmen could make out the door in better detail. It was solidly built and secured by not one, but two heavy locks, one at the top and the other near the bottom. Toler pulled a ring of keys from his pocket and unlocked both. The big door swung open to reveal a room about twelve feet square. There was a workbench on one side where repairs could be made, or cleaning could be done.

Beasley let out a whistle. The room was now well lit and the contents in full view. There were ten or twelve Winchesters of various calibers. Six shotguns, three Greeners and three Parkers, all of the twelve-gauge variety. Beasley and Warrix were familiar with the Greener brand but neither had ever held a Parker. If it came right down to it, the two would stick with what they knew. Besides the long guns there were at least a dozen Colts and Remington's, even a couple of Smith's.

"What about ammunition? Me and the deputy are thin on cartridges," Warrix said. He was ashamed to admit the reason. The town of Dakota City was too cheap to furnish proper supplies for the operation of the jail. The two lawmen were expected to use very little in the way of ammunition. If they used more than what was considered *'sufficient'* then they were expected to pay for it themselves.

Toler pulled another key from his pocket and unlocked a cabinet that adjoined the workbench. It was well stocked with a variety of ammunition. Again Beasley let out a whistle.

"Take what you need. I'll send the four guards over, one at a time. If you don't mind staying while that happens I'd feel better. Make sure each man takes a Winchester and a box of cartridges. After the last of the four is armed I'll come back and lock up." With that Toler turned and headed back toward the house.

"Deputy, this sounds like a job for one man. You stay and see to the needs of the four guards Toler is sending. I'm going outside to have a look around before it gets full light." With that Warrix left the gun room and headed for the main door to the barn.

The air was crisp. The marshal hadn't noticed it when he first left the house, he'd been too wrapped up in his thoughts. Now though, he felt the chill as he looked at the sky. It was difficult to tell if it was storm cloudy or just plain cloudy. There was little wind to mention but the air smelled of snow. As he stood there he did notice a few fine flakes twirling around in the light breeze.

Warrix found Toler at the corner of the big house talking to one of his men. In the darkness the marshal silently stepped in their direction hoping to hear the conversation. He still didn't know who to trust and anything he might hear would help make a determination. What he heard was unexpected.

"Still alive you say. Where is he now?" Toler asked.

"He's inside. It was Sid that found him earlier. He thought he was dead and came straight and told me. That's when I came to you. I never thought Sid had much of a brain and this morning he's proved it," the guard said.

"How bad is he?" Toler asked. A minute earlier the foreman thought the man was dead from a knife wound and now he finds out the man is still alive. If he'd been looked after earlier it would have helped his chances, now it was anybody's guess.

"He's bad. Three of us took him to the house. I heard last night that one of the men that rode in was a doctor. He's looking at Tazwell now," the man said.

Warrix had heard enough to convince him that these two might be trustworthy. As he approached both men turned and drew their weapons.

"Hang on there, it's me," Warrix said as he stepped into the dim light cast from one of the windows. What he just did was a fool thing to do, walk up unannounced. He'd try to do better, at least until one of the spooked ranch hands shot him.

"Damn, Marshal, I almost shot you," Toler said.

"Sorry, I wasn't thinking," Warrix said. He thought his description of what he'd just done was pretty accurate.

"I was about to come find you, Marshal. The man I told you that had been killed earlier appears to still be alive. He's inside with the doctor. If he makes it that'll be some good news in a day that ain't had any. His name is Tazwell."

Toler looked past the marshal toward the barn. "I left the door unlocked to the gunroom. Is your deputy still inside?"

"He is, I told him to stay put until your men each grab a rifle. I was going to have a look around before it got good and light. I'll be in to have a look at this Tazwell you mentioned when I get back. I hope he makes it. Maybe he can give us a description of who did this and how it happened."

Toler looked toward the house. He couldn't go in until the last of his men were better armed.

"Sounds like a good idea, but it could also be a bad idea. The other three men I got outside don't know you and might just shoot you to be on the safe side."

"I figured as much. I plan on scouting out about a quarter mile, do a circle. By the time I get back it'll be good and light. I'd appreciate it if you told the other three."

"I'll do it now. Make sure that badge is out in the open. My men are spooked and that makes for a real delicate trigger finger," Toler said as he scanned the darkness.

"I'll be back in one hour. Tell Beasley to stay inside until I make it back," Warrix told Toler. With that he turned and walked away from the house, and hopefully any of the other three guards.

The marshal was cautious as he left sight of the ranch. The route he decided on was low, through trees and gullies. He wanted to be out of any direct line of sight before he exposed himself to anyone at the house. As he went he checked for any sign of where the men from the previous night might have went. At what he guessed was at least a quarter mile he found a small clearing, in the center of that clearing was what appeared to be a used up campfire.

Warrix scanned the surrounding area. He was in a crouching position in a stand of timber. He felt uneasy, as any man might if he were looking for men that had tried to kill a ranch hand the previous night.

When the marshal finally felt it was safe to investigate he stood but before stepping from cover he took another look. He saw nothing other than the long dead fire. Before stepping from the trees he checked his Winchester, this was the second time since leaving the ranch that he'd looked over his gun. Making sure it was fully loaded and operational just made him feel better, but not by much.

The fire might have been long dead but the stones that surrounded it were still slightly warm. Again the marshal peered into his surroundings. Whoever had stayed here had left not that many hours ago, they could still be around.

Warrix figured the best place to be right now was back in the timber. Standing next to this firepit and out in the open like it was might be a bad place for a man wearing a badge. As he headed away from the fire he decided to investigate a little more. Once in the trees he made a wide circle looking for a spot where horses might have been picketed during the night.

The marshal slipped deeper into the timber all the while looking for any sign. To station a horse anywhere for longer than five seconds would leave ample sign of it being there. It didn't take more than ten minutes to find the spot, it was near water. The little stream came down from the west where the mountains began. The elevation here was not that much higher than the ranch, maybe even a little down grade. The spot looked like a horse had been tied up for the better part of the night going by what winter sage had been either knocked down or eaten. One thing that felt a bit reassuring was that it was only one horse.

Warrix followed the trail the rider took when he left, it was the same trail the man had come in on. This was leading the marshal farther from the ranch, maybe farther than he felt comfortable with. Still though, he felt he had to continue. He wanted to know which way this man went.

The sky had been cloudy at first light but now seemed to be darkening, a storm might be brewing. Any precipitation today would be in the way of snow, way too cold for rain. Storms in October could turn into a blizzard this far north. A blizzard could spell the end of a man caught out and unable to return to shelter. Warrix wasn't concerned about being trapped by a severe snowstorm, those would come a month or so later, but then again, anyone that had been proven wrong was dead.

The path the rider took seemed to be well-worn, maybe from cattle or even elk. The horse and rider were traveling on the trail of least resistance. For this reason Warrix stayed about ten yards to the north of the trail. His path was easy enough for a man on foot but would be hard for a horse and rider.

After thirty minutes the trail led out into a more open stretch of grass and scrub, cattle had foraged in the area before moving to lusher pasture. The trees became more sparse but not by much, just enough to allow a little sunshine during the warmer months, thus the grazing.

It didn't take much searching to find where the solitary rider had met up with others. Warrix counted, at least six horses had waited here in the clearing. The marshal went low as he scanned his surroundings. He'd been searching for one man riding a solitary horse, no pack animal. Now it looked like there were seven men somewhere in front of him.

The situation wasn't bad, at least not yet. The marshal was here alone and the man, or men, he tracked didn't know they were being followed, that was before the sound of a rifle and a geyser of dirt being kicked up near the marshal's feet. Warrix had only gone low a moment before, it probably saved his life. Whoever fired that shot was aiming where he thought the marshal was. If he'd been standing the bullet would have probably been aimed at his chest.

Warrix moved left as fast as he could doing something similar to a duck walk. He hoped his bobbing hat didn't give him away. After ten yards he went prone between three or four cottonwoods. He removed his hat and again checked his Winchester, if he kept it up he was going to wear the damn thing out.

As he eyed his surroundings he thought he could hear the faint sound of men talking, they were talking low. It seemed they were on the other side of the clearing; it was a clearing in name only. It was really just a spot where the trees were spread out a bit more than usual.

Warrix used the time to check his Colt, something he had failed to do so far, being more concerned with the Winchester. The gun held five rounds with an empty cylinder under the hammer. He quickly pulled a cartridge from his belt and added the last round. The talking continued but now that the men had gotten closer he could make out more of what they were saying.

"You sure you got him? That was a pretty long shot and you ain't known for your shooting ability," a man by the name of Oz Taylor said. If anyone thought Oz was a strange name they better keep it to themselves. The rumor was that Oz had once shot his pa for allowing such a name to be pinned on his son.

The elder Taylor had survived, the gunshot was only a graze. Some speculated that either Oz was a terrible shot for only grazing his father. Others said he was an excellent shot for not killing the man, but only slightly wounding him. At any rate Oz was designated as a ruthless killer for what he'd done. It was told that the man's pa now kept a sawed off shotgun over the front door, just in case.

"I got him, Oz; don't you worry none about that. I saw where he went down and sent a bullet at that exact spot. How about we ease on over there and take his rifle. From what I saw he was carrying a nice looking Winchester," Ty Arnold said. Ty might not have been the best shot in the outfit, but he did have the best vision. He could see things only a hawk or eagle might see. Oz hadn't even seen the man Arnold shot at.

Warrix could hear nearly everything being said, and that was bad, these two were getting close. He didn't mind exchanging lead with the two, after all they had shot at him first. What he did mind was the chance that more men might be close and would soon be here to investigate what the shooting was all about. Before the two got any closer he backed away and into a depression.

The marshal now found himself in a dry wash. It ran left and right of the direction the two were coming from. He decided to head left, it would put him in the general direction of the ranch house. He figured he was too far away for the shot that had already been fired to have been heard. Even if some of the men at the ranch had heard the shot they wouldn't head this way, at least not yet.

Warrix knew he was on his own and needed to get back to the others. Before he could make good his escape he heard the men again. They had made it to the spot where Warrix had been when he was shot at by Ty Arnold.

"You missed him, Ty, I told you so. Looks like he headed toward that wash. We better ease over there, it'll give you another chance to do what you already said you done," Taylor said.

"Let's spread out a little. No need giving the man a chance at getting even. He probably knows where we are, and I doubt he'll miss if we aren't careful. You head over where the wash narrows. I'll head left, maybe you can flush him toward me," Arnold said. He still thought of the Winchester he'd seen earlier; he wanted that gun.

Warrix eased up and out of the wash into a spot that offered good cover. He was careful to leave as little sign as possible, no need making his adversaries' job any easier. He knew he needed to be getting back to the ranch, but something told him there was more information to be gathered here. The two men were careless in what they said and how loud they spoke.

Warrix eased into some brush and rock, it was his good fortune to find the spot. The brambles and brush would make it nearly impossible for a man on horseback but perfect for anyone trying to find cover and concealment. Once in the rocks he found it to be a readymade blind. He could stay here and fend off ten men if he had to. Now all he had to do was wait, he wouldn't need to wait long.

"You spot him, Oz?"

"Not a sign of him. If he came in here then he's long gone by now," Oz Taylor said.

The two men looked in both directions of the wash. Warrix had been fortunate that the bottom of the wash was dry and mostly made of gravel and stone. That type of footing held secrets really well. If it'd been wet and muddy then they could have followed him without any problem. Oz Taylor was beginning to doubt Arnold had seen anyone at all.

"You say you shot at a man standing at the edge of the clearing. Are you sure you didn't imagine it? We've looked each way of the wash for a good hundred yards, there's not a trace," Taylor said.

Arnold was indignant that he was being questioned about what he saw.

"I saw him alright. Just as I turned I saw a man duck for cover. I put a shot right where he was, you can count on that."

"If you saw a man, and you put a bullet where he was standing, then where's the body? Where's the blood? Maybe that famous eyesight of yours is starting to fail you. Either that or your starting to see things in your old days."

141

"Old days you say. I'm telling you he was there, right where I said he was. You see the way the sage was flattened in spots."

"Could have been a deer last night making its nest. You know how they curl up and make a flat in the grass," Taylor said.

"Be quiet a minute, I think I hear Bradley and the rest of the men," Arnold said. He really hadn't heard the men but knew they should be close. He was just glad to change the subject of him seeing ghosts.

Bradley Allen was the man in charge of this rabble. He'd been one of the ranch hands, that was until the night before when he knifed Tazwell and made good his departure from one job as an underpaid cowpuncher to another as a gun for hire. He'd been on the payroll of Bernard Rumford for more than a month. The timing all depended on when the bank in Dakota City got hit. The plan Rumford put together was working out, it now meant a sizable increase in pay for Allen.

Allen and three other men from the ranch had taken care of Tazwell before kidnapping Bishop. It wasn't part of the plan to kill Tazwell, it was just a bonus; Allen didn't like the man. He knifed him for the sheer enjoyment of it.

What Warrix and Toler didn't know was that they were facing more than just the four men that had slipped off during the night. The number was more than thirty, a good size portion of the men that worked the ranch. Sure, Bishop had more than sixty men on his substantial spread but that was before Rumford became involved.

Rumford had given instructions that anyone that stayed at the ranch had two choices, join him, or be killed along with anyone else that tried to stand in his way. He'd sent this message by way of Bradley Allen. The men that hadn't defected to Rumford and Allen were now long gone. They knew to fall in with the two meant they would be criminals. Best to head for a warmer climate than take the chance of getting their faces on a wanted poster.

As Warrix stayed hidden he kept a close eye on Oz Taylor and Ty Arnold. The two men were still looking around trying to find any evidence that someone had been there. No more than ten minutes had gone by when the sound of horses could be heard, it sounded like several.

"Sounds like Allen is on his way. Maybe we shouldn't mention anything about me seeing someone. Like you said, it might have been my imagination," Arnold said. He was starting to doubt what he saw. Maybe it was a crow or a buck that flushed his thoughts into thinking it was a man. At any rate, he didn't want to look foolish. There was the sight of that fine rifle though, maybe he'd imagined that too.

The two men stepped back to the clearing and waited. A minute later five horses came into view. Each carried a rider holding a Winchester across the saddle. These men meant business.

"Was that a gunshot we heard a few minutes ago, Taylor?" Allen asked as soon as he saw the two.

"It was, boss, we came upon a bobcat. Arnold took a shot at the varmint but missed. That was one fast critter," Taylor said hoping to satisfy Allen. He didn't want to get into trying to explain what really happened.

"Next time just say shoo. Bobcat means no harm unless it grabs you by the ass. You two seen anybody from the ranch?"

"Naw, not a soul. We've scouted since daybreak. We got that ranch house bottled up real good. The way I see it, they only got four men besides Toler," Oz Taylor told the man.

"Alright then, you and the others stay put. Make sure no one leaves the ranch. I got to meet Rumford in a few hours. He'll be wanting to see Bishop and inform the man of how things are going to be handled. There'll be a new owner of this spread by tomorrow. As soon as he finishes with Bishop we'll hit the ranch. I really wish there was a way other than burning the house, but that's what the man wants, no witnesses and no evidence," Allen said.

"Is Bishop to be brought to the ranch house before we start the fire?" Taylor asked.

"No, he won't be joining the others for that little fire. Rumford needs to keep him alive a few more days to make sure everything goes to plan. After the deed is authenticated and registered at the courthouse Bishop won't be needed any longer," Allen said as he turned his horse and headed away.

Warrix had heard every word. He now knew the plan was to attack the house and kill all the witnesses. Bishop would be spared, at least in the beginning but would eventually be killed, most likely after he signed over his property and this Rumford got his deed posted in the land office. The marshal needed to get back to the ranch as fast as possible. He needed to warn the others and try to establish a defense, something he doubted if more of Toler's men didn't show up. That was assuming anyone that came was trustworthy.

Bernard Rumford had departed Chicago on a late departing train ten days prior. His lodgings on the Pullman were better than he'd expected. Once he acquired the ranch he'd make sure to travel more and always on Pullmans. The trip had been uneventful, actually it was downright boring. He wanted to get to the ranch and orchestrate his plans using the men Bradley Allen had hired.

The spread Bishop owned amounted to roughly forty-five thousand acres. Rumford would be one of the largest land owners in the territory. He might never go back to Chicago but if he did he'd travel in style. Money worries were about to become a thing of the past.

The days of scraping by as he made fortunes for others were over. He would now use his skills to expand the fortune Bishop had. Within a couple of years he would expand eastward. The ranch that adjoined Bishop's spread had been poorly managed for years. This particular piece of property was ripe for acquisition. Rumford intended to start there and then continue to move east. It was a domino effect and Bishop would be the first domino to fall.

Warrix eased from his hideout and started making his way back to the ranch. He needed to get there before his path was blocked. He didn't know how many men stood between him and the house and there was no time to scout around for the answer to that question. What he'd already found out was reason for worry, men were going to die.

Five minutes after leaving Oz Taylor and Ty Arnold, Warrix was well enough away to chance moving at a trot. He paced himself not wanting to be too badly winded in case he needed to move fast. A man that was all spent would be an easy target in a stand up fight. Warrix didn't want to be that target.

When he figured he was halfway he stopped to look over his surroundings. As he waited he noticed a man on the next ridge over. The man was looking in his direction, but Warrix wasn't sure he'd been spotted yet. It was then and there he decided to even the score a little, if he could. He was going to capture this man if possible and take him to the ranch.

The marshal went left where the timber was a bit heavier. As he moved through the trees and undergrowth he kept an eye on the lookout. Warrix was in his element now. He moved with stealth; he moved as if he were part of the forest. It took ten minutes to work his way around behind the man. He looked his situation over. He could simply ease up a little closer and at the right moment he would step from the trees and get the drop on the man. Everything went fine, right up until a second man got the drop on Warrix.

"You there, drop that rifle before I shoot you. Don't try anything, I've got a Winchester pointed at your head," the second man said.

The marshal froze. He hadn't seen the second man; he must have been hiding somewhere covering the first man he'd spotted. To move meant almost certain death, to give up definitely meant death. Definite death or almost certain death, Warrix took the almost certain death route.

The marshal dove to the ground and then rolled to his right. Two gunshots, both in quick succession, hit the spot he had just rolled away from. Warrix rose up using a big cottonwood as cover. When he stepped from the protection of the tree he had his Winchester at the ready. He raised and sighted the gun in one smooth motion. He fired two quick rounds, both hitting the man. It looked like one was dead center of the chest, the second jerked the man's head back. He was dead before he hit the ground, probably dead even before the head shot.

The marshal quickly went to ground hoping the second man didn't have him in his sights. Two quick shots told another story. One bullet grazed Warrix but did little damage. The second hit a tree and scattered bark and splinters in every direction. Warrix caught a few splinters but that was way better than lead.

The marshal knew he had to dispatch this last shooter before more men showed up. If he was going to make it back to warn the others he would need to try something bold, and that's exactly what he did.

Warrix brought the Winchester to his shoulder and stepped from the cover of the tree. The man who had just shot at him had made the mistake of lowering his rifle. When he saw the marshal he brought his gun back up, but he was too late. Warrix took the shot first, he hit the man just below the chin. The man's arms flew up as the bullet severed his spinal cord, a reaction not uncommon to such a wound.

Warrix knew he needed to move and move fast. He headed directly between the two dead men but as he passed he had an idea. He saw both men as he shot them and knew which was clothed in the same dark checkered pattern shirt as he wore. He went by that man and as he did he grabbed his hat and quickly put it on. He had to leave his hat and that was just too bad, he really liked that hat.

The marshal sprinted along hoping to find either of the two men's horses. He found the two just over the rise, he didn't know which man rode which and he damn sure wasn't going to go back and ask. The thought almost made him laugh. He grabbed the reins of the horse he liked best and climbed in the saddle. Again he wondered what he was thinking, just grab a damn horse and get out of here. This wasn't the time to be picky.

He headed toward the ranch at nearly a full gallop. The trail was wide and had seen its fair share of cattle and game over the years. Just when he thought he was going to make it he came face to face with two riders heading his way, no doubt heading in the direction of the shooting.

As the two men reigned up Warrix decided to do the same. It was a risky bet, but he'd rather face a threat head on than get shot in the back.

"What was all the shooting about back there, Ace. We heard three or four shots," one of the two asked as Warrix rode up, his head down and the brim of the borrowed hat hiding most of his face.

As Warrix raised his head he also drew his gun. In the split second before anything happened he figured which of the two was the most dangerous and which looked most able to draw in a hurry, both turned out to be the same man.

As the two realized their mistake they each went for their guns. Warrix hurried his first shot toward the man that looked the most dangerous. He blew that man clean out of the saddle. In the time it took to move his gun an eighth of an inch to the right a scheme entered the marshal's head. Funny how time seems to slow when death is staring you in the face.

Warrix knew he only had a split second before the second man fired. That was the split second he needed to hit the man in the right shoulder. It wasn't a fatal shot, probably didn't even hit bone, but it was enough to make the man's gun fall to the ground.

"Now you listen to me. You head toward the ranch house as fast as that horse will carry you. It's not far and we got a doctor there that can tend to your injury. Any deviation and I promise to finish the job I started here. You understand me, mister?" Warrix asked as he scanned his backtrail to make sure he wasn't about to catch a bullet himself.

Being disarmed and with a bullet hole in his shoulder the man was glad to cooperate. "Alright, you'll have no more trouble out of me," the man said as he raised the reins of his horse with his good hand.

"Alright then, turn that horse and touch spurs," Warrix said.

Both men headed over the rise at a full gallop. It might have been a little too fast, there was a drop or two of blood from the man's shoulder that hit Warrix in the face as they rode. He had to admit, these outlaws rode fast horses.

As they rode they passed three more men on the next hill. It was maybe four-hundred yards. Not an impossible shot if any of the three had any notion to shoot, they didn't.

With the ranch house in sight Warrix took off the hat he'd borrowed from the man he'd shot and threw it to the ground. He hoped the men guarding the house could recognize him before they started shooting. Then he realized only one of the four guards had seen him that morning. Well, if he got shot now then it was what it was.

"Got two riders coming hard, Toler. You better get out here and tell us what to do," one of the two guards said. Neither of the men guarding that side of the house had ever shot at a man before, much less killed one.

Toler had been just inside the door waiting for a cup of coffee he'd been promised. What he really wanted was a beer, maybe two. He hurried out and immediately recognized the marshal. He knew the man had left alone earlier and he also knew he'd been on foot. The man on the second horse seemed to be injured.

"You two stay alert. I recognize the marshal and that other rider looks like Albert. I'll be damned, looks like the marshal has brought one of our wayward hands back to the ranch to face a little poetic justice," Toler said. He always wanted to be a poet. The more time you spent around the man the more you began to wonder about some of his word choices.

Warrix smiled as he rode up to the house. The wounded man's disposition changed from one of injured outlaw to fearful prisoner. He was now back where he'd started from, and it hadn't even been twenty-four hours.

"Well, Marshal, looks like you've had a busy morning. Howdy, Albert. I suppose you've come home to roost," Toler said.

"I was forced to do what I did. You've got to believe me," Albert said.

Albert Treadway was one of the least favorite of Bishop's cowpunchers. The man was lazy. Some of the other hands said there was two things Albert disliked about a day of hard work. First was the hard part and second was the work part. The man gave lazy a bad name.

"I hear you, Albert. Them men knifed poor Tazwell and then woke you up from the bunkhouse and asked if you would like to go for a little ride. I guess the part about Bishop being tied and gagged and mounted on a horse against his will didn't occur to you as a mite strange?" Toler asked the man.

"Now how did you know all that? That's exactly what they done; I was forced at gunpoint to cooperate. It was that or be shot. Now which would you have done?" Albert asked.

This was more than Toler could stand. He grabbed Albert by his good arm and yanked him from the saddle. He let the man hit the ground before kicking him in the stomach with his boot. The other guards and the marshal just let him have his way. Toler was taking out some of his anger, Albert was receiving it.

"Get off your sorry ass and tell me what they've done with, Mr. Bishop. If he's harmed I can promise I'll hang you right here in this yard," Toler said through gritted teeth.

Albert got the message real quick. He got to his feet fully expecting to get more of what he'd already been served.

"Alright, you get me to the doc, and I'll tell you what I know. You got to promise me though that I'll be let go as soon as you've heard me out."

Toler grabbed a handful of shirt and nearly lifted the man off the ground. "You're in no position to negotiate, Albert. You'll tell us what you know and then if we feel it's the truth we'll decide whether or not to do the hanging. Until then start talking."

"Alright, alright. Take me to the doc and I'll tell you what I know while he patches me up," the man said through gritted teeth. The gunshot wound had started to hurt more, probably due in part to the rough handling of the ranch foreman. It was apparent that Toler wasn't a man to be trifled with. The marshal figured the ranch foreman had a story to tell.

Once inside Reynolds cut the sleeve of the shirt to expose the wound. He didn't know if the man had a second shirt and really didn't care. If he froze to death it wouldn't happen before he shared what he knew.

The bullet had gone clean through without hitting bone. Albert was lucky if you could call it that. Less than thirty minutes later and the doc had both the entrance and exit wounds cleaned and stitched up. He'd done all this without offering the man a drink of whiskey to help dull the senses. Fair enough.

"There you go. It'll be sore for a few days, after that we should be able to hang you," Doc Reynolds said. He didn't know what type of punishment the man might get but he felt a little fun would go a long way in relieving some of the tension. It might have helped the doc and the others but it terrified Albert.

While Albert was being patched up he never really gave any information. He was in too much pain; about all he could do was grit his teeth and squint his eyes. It seemed Doc Reynolds didn't have much in the way of bedside manner when it came to outlaws. Toler and the marshal sat sipping coffee while they enjoyed the show. At one moment during the treatment it looked like Albert was going to pass out.

Once the doc was finished Toler grabbed the man and stood him on his feet. "You got two seconds to start talking. You're wasting time and I think I know why. You're hoping your friends will attack and release you. Well I can help you with the outcome of that little plan. The last bullet I fire before I die will be between your eyes. Now, if you want to live then you better hope we live."

After a second of thought Albert felt his only chance was to tell them everything he knew.

"Alright, I'll tell you. They took Mr. Bishop last night around eleven. Two men went up the stairs that lead to the balcony and broke into his room. They waited until the old man came up and then tied and gagged him. He was taken out the window and down the stairs."

Toler wanted his information a little faster than Albert was talking. He pulled his gun and rested the end of the barrel against Albert's forehead.

"Where did they take Bishop? Say it fast or you'll say nothing ever again."

"They took him about a five hour ride from here. I believe it's called the Brewer Ranch."

"I know that ranch. Old man Brewer lives there alone. He's all done in. He just sits his porch all day waiting for the end.

He's been that way since his wife passed a year or so ago," Toler said.

"Well he don't have to wait for the end no more. Bradley Allen shot the old man yesterday as soon as we got there. He didn't even bury him, just had the men take him to the barn and put him in a stall. I swear I didn't know what I was getting into when I agreed to this. If I'd thought for a minute that an old man would be killed like that then I wouldn't have signed on," Albert said. The man seemed ready to cry. Probably not for the loss of Brewer but for his own hide.

"Well now, if you ain't an accomplice to a murder, Albert. You better keep talking if you want to try and save your ass," Toler said. The marshal just let the ranch foreman do the questioning, he was doing a pretty good job of it.

"Allen says there's a man by the name of Bernard Rumford calling the shots. He's some sort of cattle agent from Chicago. He's going to force Bishop to sign over his ranch. I think Rumford is either on his way to the Brewer place now or soon will be. He's coming in on a train, seems like they said it was yesterday. I believe he's already in the area by the way Allen spoke earlier."

Warrix looked at Toler and Beasley. "Sounds like this has been coming together for some time, maybe months. If this Rumford was an agent for Bishop then he would have known nearly every move the man made."

Something just hit Warrix, this agent would have known when the money for the last cattle drive would have arrived at the bank. This was the man that arranged the murder of the two miners and then the bank robbery that ended in the murder of his sister.

The marshal felt the blood rise in his face as he grew flush. An anger was building. He'd been so busy hunting the outlaws and then with this business of the ranch that he'd given little thought to Mae. He almost felt guilty for his lapse. To avenge her death would be his sole purpose from this moment on. He wondered if justice and vengeance were the same thing. It didn't matter, he wanted both.

"You got some strong rope in the barn, Toler?" Warrix asked.

"Got some real good rope, Marshal. Got thick rope and thin rope. Good for tying a man up, good for hanging too. Which kind do you want me to bring?"

Warrix looked at the man. If Albert looked a bit scared earlier, the look he presented now was one of sheer terror. "Bring the tying up rope for now. But keep a length of the hanging rope close by, just in case."

As Toler trotted to the barn Beasley stepped out on the big wraparound front porch. He wanted to have a look around. He also wanted to make sure the four men guarding the house were where they were supposed to be, they were.

"Marshal, we got some tired men out there," Beasley said as he stepped back inside.

"I'd say that's about right, Deputy. They've been on guard duty since last night. That leg of yours feel like letting you stand guard duty?"

"It feels way better, it really does. Maybe I'll set the corner of the porch and do my stint of guarding. You got an injury too, Marshal. How you holding up?" the deputy asked.

Warrix had nearly forgotten about his injury from a few days prior. He reached down and poked his leg. He still wore a thick bandage under his trousers, but he could feel a little soreness. Not bad considering the shape he was in a few days prior.

"It don't feel that bad. The doc really did a good job cleaning it up. I think it felt a lot worse than it really was when it happened. Even with all the walking this morning I never really gave it any thought."

"That's good, Marshal. Before this is over we're going to need every man here," Beasley said.

"Don't forget about the women. Me and Stella will do our part in this," Maggie said as she came through the door.

Beasley and Warrix turned to see Bishop's sister. She was carrying a Winchester.

"Maybe it would be safer if you and Stella stayed indoors," Warrix said.

Maggie gave the marshal a quizzical look. "Do you really think my sister in law and me will be safe if the ranch is overrun. The men that took my brother won't give safe passage to me or Stella if you men are overrun and killed. The two of us have talked it over and decided we'll fight alongside the men. We both know how to shoot; my brother saw to that."

Beasley looked at Warrix before saying, "She makes a fine point, Marshal. The part about them being in danger, same as us, I believe is an accurate statement."

Warrix knew they were right. After thinking about it he realized that two more guns might come in handy when the attack came. If one or both of the women were injured or killed he would feel responsible. But if he did nothing and they still suffered the same fate he would feel worse, that was assuming he was alive to feel anything,

"Alright then. I would ask that the two of you use the weapons you feel most comfortable with. Make sure Toler gets them for you, along with extra ammunition. Stay in the house when the shooting starts. If it comes to close quarters then be my guest to send as many to the other side as possible," Warrix said. Everyone knew what the other side meant.

"I'm glad you see things our way, Marshal," Maggie said as she turned and went back inside.

155

The two lawmen didn't say as much but both were pleased to be associated with strong willed women. It was refreshing, but then again, if things went wrong it could be disheartening to see any harm come to the two. At least it was reassuring to know they could help in their own protection rather than depending on the men. Some women were strong that way.

"Say, Deputy, did you ever get to enjoy that big breakfast that was prepared this morning before I left," Warrix asked.

"I did. Just after you went on your one hour scouting trip I went inside. Ate more than my fill. I might have even eaten your share too. Those two women can really cook."

Warrix figured as much. His starving deputy was a match for anyone when it came to free food.

"Is anything left? I just realized I haven't had a bite since last night."

"You bet there is. Those two cooked enough for ten men, and with Bishop and you gone, there was plenty left over."

Warrix turned and went inside. He didn't know exactly how to ask, so he decided to just ask. The first person he found was Stella. She was in the kitchen cutting up vegetables. A big pot was on the stove, and it looked and smelled like some sort of stew was being prepared.

"Pardon me, I was wondering if there might be something I might have to eat? You see, I left without breakfast this morning. I hate to be a bother," Warrix said.

Stella put down her knife and turned to the marshal. "Maggie and I know you left before getting to eat. We saved a plate. It's cold but it's the kind of food that eats well cold."

Stella opened a cabinet and took out a big plate. It was covered with a cloth. She carried it to the big dining room and sat it on the table. "I hope you don't mind, maybe this will do until supper."

Warrix looked at the plate. There were two big biscuits, four sausage patties, a big portion of scrambled eggs and a small cup of gravy. The biscuits looked more like pones of bread they were so big.

"Why this will do fine and your right, I like this kind of food anyway I can get it."

"Would you like a cup of tea or maybe some coffee? The tea will take a few minutes, but the coffee is ready now."

"Coffee will do fine. If you have a pepper shaker I might like that too."

"We do, I find it odd that men like to put pepper on everything they eat." Stella didn't say that in a demeaning way, it sounded more out of curiosity.

Warrix ate his fill, as a matter of fact he ate past his fill but did manage to clean his plate. If supper was getting close he doubted he could hold a bite.

By now it was nearly three in the afternoon. It was time to see what could be done about securing the ranch against attack. The marshal had made a few mental notes during the day. He'd been around the house and barn and knew he needed more men, men he knew weren't coming. He found Toler and Beasley on the front porch. Both men were armed with Winchesters.

"Howdy, Marshal. You find anything left over from breakfast?" Beasley asked.

"I did, seems they hid a big plate from you. I'm glad they did because it was delicious, I hadn't realized how hungry I was."

"Them two can cook. I can't remember when I've had such as meal as that. From the smell coming from the kitchen I'd say supper will be just as good," the deputy said. The look on his face said it all, he was looking forward to supper.

"Where are the four men that guarded the house last night?" Warrix asked.

"I sent them to the bunkhouse just after you got here. They needed rest. I figured to stand watch with the deputy until just before dark. They should have had enough sleep by then. It's going to be a long night. When do you figure they'll hit us?" Toler asked.

"Actually, I don't think it'll be tonight. From what I gathered I believe they aren't quite ready. One of the men I heard talking said he was going to meet with that Rumford feller this evening. I believe Rumford will want to call the shots," Warrix told the two.

"Sounds about right. They probably want to see what they can get out of Mr. Bishop before they attack. Attacking this place will cause a lot of damage. I'd say Rumford wants the ranch intact," Toler said.

This surprised Warrix. "But I heard them talk about burning the house and barn to hide the evidence. I believe if we all died in the fire he would just blame it on a lightning strike or a fireplace fire." Warrix said this low not wanting the two women to hear.

"I know that's what you heard, and I have no reason to doubt that. It just seems to be a waste for a man that wants this place to go and burn down such a house as this. That might be the plan but I'm sure they have a backup plan in case things change. Maybe Bishop signs over the ranch to protect his family," Toler said.

Warrix considered this. The old man would do just that if he thought he could save the lives of the two women. What good were possessions if you lost the ones you loved. Losing Mae had proven that to the marshal. He'd give anything to bring her back. He knew that was impossible, all he could offer her memory now was to avenge her death.

158

As the two men talked Stella came out. "Supper will be ready in about an hour. I hope you like elk stew?"

The notion of a stew seemed to put a smile on the deputy's face. It seemed any food, especially food Beasley didn't have to pay for, put a smile on his face.

"Well now, I believe that will be right nice ma'am," Beasley said.

"We better get the other four up. We got to get some things done before nightfall," Warrix said.

Once the four men that had spent the previous night guarding the house were awake the marshal shared his plan. It wasn't much of a plan, but it was a plan just the same.

"Alright, listen up. The windows of the house all have storm shutters, I want all those closed and locked tight from the inside. If shooting starts they will at least offer some protection. Does the ranch have any barbed wire?"

Toler wondered what the marshal wanted with barbed wire. "Got a few rolls of twelve and a half gauge in the barn. You got a plan that requires fencing wire?"

"I do. Those outside stairs leading up to the bedroom balcony are a liability. We need to fix it so no one can climb up that way like they did last night when they kidnapped Bishop. Take the wire and make an obstacle course. Make it so no one can climb up there and come in a window. It'll be one less worry."

"But what if they manage to set the house on fire? Wouldn't that prevent anyone from escaping?" Toler asked.

"It would but no one will be up there. I want everyone down here that can shoot a rifle. Anyone that tries to go out an upstairs window would be a target anyway. We stay downstairs until the danger's past."

"Sounds about right, Marshal. Let Stella and Maggie know to cook up some rough grub. Stuff that can keep and be eaten

159

cold. If this becomes a siege then we can't spare anyone to cook, everyone will be watching through the gun opening in the shutters. We also need to arm Doc Reynolds. I doubt he'd mind."

"That sounds pretty good, Marshal. What about the barn? If we are all guarding the house then they can occupy the barn and raise hell from there," Beasley asked.

"I want two men in the barn. One on each end with a Winchester. Take some heavy boards and barricade the two hay doors about half way up. It'll make a good gun rest and also offer some protection. We also need to barricade the door opposite the house. Make it so no one can enter the barn from the side."

"Alright, Marshal, we better get at it. One thing I might suggest, we bring all the guns and ammunition inside the house. If we need any of that stuff we won't be able to get to it if there's a gun battle going on," Beasley said.

"Good idea, now let's get to it. Our lives might depend on it," Toler said.

By the time the women came out to let the men know the food was ready they had nearly completed the preparations the marshal had suggested. Toler and Beasley stepped to the porch and looked the place over. The only noticeable difference was the closed storm shutters. Everything else appeared as it had earlier.

"No one would be the wiser if they suspected anything had changed," Toler said.

"It don't look that different, but it offers a little protection if the shooting starts. That little idea about the two upstairs hayloft doors will be a big surprise for any attackers," Beasley said.

"We got the back of the barn locked up tight, both doors are barricaded from the inside. Anyone attempting to get through that way will need to make it past the man in the loft first," Toler added.

"I want your two best shooters in that loft. You got anybody that is dependable out to two-hundred yards?" Warrix asked.

"Any of the four can shoot about as good as the next man. I'd say we spell the two men in the loft in four hour shifts. That way the four can switch out and the two coming off watch can come in for a little coffee," the ranch foreman said.

"Good idea, go ahead and put two up there now. The rest of us can eat and then we'll relieve the two. From that elevated position they should see anyone from either direction. We got about another hour of daylight left, we better get to it," the marshal said.

By the time everyone had eaten it was completely dark. Warrix and Toler walked the perimeter of the house and the barn. Hardly any light escaped the wooden storm shutters of the house and there was no light at all in the barn. Both went upstairs to the loft of the barn and peered out. Once their eyes adjusted it was still nearly impossible to see farther than a few feet. If shooting started the two men stationed up there were instructed to shoot at the muzzle flashes. At least they could hold anyone at bay, maybe.

"Toler, I need to speak to you and Beasley inside where we can talk without being heard by anyone out here, friend or foe," Warrix said.

A few minutes later the three men were in Bishop's study. Each looked longingly at the liquor cabinet in the corner. Before anyone could say a word there was a slight tap on the door and Stella stepped in.

"I thought you men might want a drink to finish the day. You can help yourself. I think my brother in law would agree that you've each earned it. If you need anything me and Maggie will be in the sitting room." With that she left, closing the door behind her.

Beasley, being the lowly deputy, looked at the marshal for guidance. "I think a drink will do the three of us some good. That includes you, Deputy."

The three quickly poured three glasses and then sat down.

"What did you want to say, Marshal?" Toler asked.

Warrix sampled his whiskey, not bad he thought. "I'm leaving tonight. Now before you two get the wrong idea, let me explain myself. I'll stay until about two in the morning. If anyone is going to hit the ranch tonight it will most likely happen by then. If it does I'll be staying. If we haven't had any trouble by then it's safe to assume the coast will be clear until tomorrow night."

Beasley wasn't sure of what he was hearing. "Where are you going, Marshal. I doubt you got enough time to ride anywhere for help if that's what you're thinking."

"I'm not riding for help, like you say, I can't accomplish that in any reasonable amount of time. I'm going to the Brewer place. I plan on raising a little hell there. With any luck I might be able to help Bishop before they kill him. I know it's a longshot but it's the only chance Bishop has."

Toler took another sip; he was deep in thought. Finally he spoke. "I like it but there's going to be a twist, I'm going with you."

Now the deputy spoke up. "Well with all due respect, you two are crazy as hell. And since you two are about the craziest men I know at the moment then I'm going along too."

"No Deputy, you're not. You got a busted leg and I'm depending on you to run things here while I'm gone. If Toler is serious about coming along then that will leave eight of you here to defend the house. That's counting the two women. Like I said, I don't think tonight is the night. Me and Toler will head out around two, if we meet up with anyone then we'll turn around and head back here as fast as we can," Warrix said.

"I didn't think you'd agree to let me come along," Toler said.

"Normally I wouldn't, but I don't know the way," the marshal said. All three men got a laugh out of that.

"Another reason to attempt this is if we can free Bishop then they'll be busy hunting us. I doubt they will attack the ranch here if all Rumford's men are tracking us in order to recapture Bishop," Warrix said.

When the men considered the plan they agreed it was worth a try. Warrix then let the other two in on the rest of his plan. "We're going to ride the two horses me and Albert rode in on earlier. It won't help in the dark, but it might once it gets daylight. I went back out and grabbed the hat I threw down when we rode in, you take the hat Albert was wearing. Maybe riding the outlaws horses and using their saddles and gear, not to mention their hats, we might get close enough to do some damage before we're found out."

The three men sat in silence for a while, each enjoying their drinks and wondering what tomorrow might bring. They were wondering what the night might also bring.

Finally Beasley broke the silence. "I believe you said I'm in charge now, Marshal. As for being the new ramrod my first act of authority is to order the two of you to get some sleep. I'll make sure both the horses are saddled and ready to leave at two o'clock. I'll also see if the women wouldn't mind having some breakfast waiting. Maybe even a little traveling food. Now git," Beasley said.

Warrix and Toler just looked at each other. Both knew Beasley was right, they needed rest. Warrix was wondering though if he'd created a monster.

At one forty-five in the morning Beasley walked into the bunkroom and told the two men it was time. Warrix was sleeping soundly when the deputy walked in. He'd been dreaming about fly fishing in a shallow stream. He wasn't standing in water; he was sitting a horse. The horse in his dream was none too happy about standing in icy water. Then the deputy came in and put an end to that little fishing trip. Toler hadn't been dreaming anything, at least that's what he always thought. He was just the sort to never remember a dream.

"You two hurry over to the house. There's some food and coffee waiting in the dining room. The horses will be ready in fifteen minutes. Now hurry yourselves up before I start deducting the time you two are wasting from your pay." Beasley laughed as he headed back toward the house.

"Is there a law against shooting your deputy?" Toler asked.

"Probably, but we might overlook it just this one time."

The two quickly headed to the wash bin. The bunkroom had been thought out nicely. There was a handpump that fed into a sink with a drain. During the conversations of the previous night it had been agreed that both men would be clean shaven for this little trip. The reason was that the man Warrix killed the previous day and Albert Treadway were both clean shaven. If they were going to try and pass themselves off as two of the men that worked for Bradley Allen then they would need to shave. It was a long shot but anything that might give them an extra second would be used.

When the two walked into the dining room they found both Stella and Maggie there. The two women had heard about the plan to rescue Bishop and felt the least they could do was offer a hot breakfast.

"If I knew a breakfast like this would be waiting I'd wake every morning at this hour," Toler said.

Warrix didn't comment, he wanted to get a head start on the food, having missed breakfast the previous day made him that much more determined to not miss out this morning. As the two men ate the women made food for the trip. Not a lot because a saddlebag wouldn't hold a lot. Beasley had told the women that the men were going to be traveling fast and light. No coffee pot or skillet, two items that were handy but also held the disadvantage of making noise. Noise would be an enemy on this trip.

Once finished the two thanked the women and then headed for the barn. Beasley was there gathering ammunition for the Winchesters and Colts Warrix and Toler were taking.

"Any idea how many cartridges you want to take, Marshal?" Beasley asked.

A box of Colt and another of Winchester for the both of us. If we need more than that we're probably dead already," Warrix said.

"Tell you what, Deputy, put an extra box of Winchester in for me. Two boxes will only fill a rifle three times. I can always haul it back if I don't use it," Toler said.

Beasley looked at the marshal. He decided to add an extra box for Warrix too. If the two ran into trouble then the last thing they needed was to run low on ammunition. He knew the extra box of Colt apiece was probably enough, both men had full belt loops.

"You're about ready to head out. Best of luck to the both of you," Beasley said.

"Thanks, Deputy. Push that door open, I believe I'll walk the first half mile. I'd rather be on foot if we run into trouble.

This close to the ranch we can scoot back pretty fast," Toler said.

The two men led their mounts for the first half-hour. They met no one on the trail.

"You say you know the trail to Brewer's spread?"

"I do, it's a good five hours in daylight. I'm guessing seven or eight with us traveling at night and using as much caution as we are."

"Why two hours more than normal? Darkness won't slow us down that much."

"You're right, Marshal. But it ain't the darkness that's going to slow us down. If we use the regular trail we stand a higher chance of running into trouble. I elk hunt this trail every fall, been doing it for the last five years or so. I know some trails that a man would be a fool to travel."

"If that's the case then why would we want to use it?"

"Because the way I see it, we are fools, Marshal. We're attempting a two man rescue against what could be an army. Now don't get me wrong, I'm all for this attempt but the fact remains, we're fools for trying."

The two had been talking in little more than whispers. Both felt exposed riding horses in the middle of the night with men around that would shoot first and investigate later. Warrix felt particularly vulnerable, he was riding blind and not just from the darkness, he didn't know the terrain this far north and surely didn't know the trail they were taking. The farther they traveled, and the later it got, he knew his trepidations would only increase.

After two hours on the trail Toler called a halt. He wanted to rest the horses and also have a look around. He wasn't a suspicious man, but something told him they better stop. Warrix too had a funny feeling, something just didn't feel right. The two men found a spot and tied out the horses. A small stream trickled nearby; it pooled in several places. The horses went to the water first, the two men went upstream a ways to fill both canteens.

"Do you sense something out of the ordinary, because I sure do? And I'm not talking about the fact that we're going on a rescue mission where we're probably going to be outnumbered ten to one," Warrix asked.

Toler looked over his surroundings. It was dark but a man's eyes can adjust to darkness. The sky was cloudy but not to the point of blocking out everything. Every now and then the moon even shown through.

"I would have to agree, Marshal. It seems the farther we get from the ranch the more uneasy I feel. I'm not a superstitious man but I'm starting to think we're being followed. Can't say for sure, just a feeling."

As the two men scanned their surroundings one of the horses stirred a bit. With head raised high and ears perked it sniffed the air and looked nervously around. Soon the other horse did the same.

"Seems the horses are uneasy too. Think it might be a bear or maybe a coyote?" Toler asked.

"Doubt it's a bear. Both horses would be trying to tear free if that were the case. I guess we better be moving," Warrix said.

The two men mounted up and headed for the Brewer place. The horses seemed glad to be moving, especially away from where they'd just been. Both men knew a horse had good instincts. If a horse seemed nervous then the man that rode that horse better take notice. More than one man had been saved by his mount.

The two traveled in silence for the next hour. Both carried their Winchesters across their saddles, just in case. Toler would have been happier with a Greener but knew the Winchester would be his weapon of choice once it got daylight.

"How much farther?" Warrix asked. It had been a long night, morning actually. The two men had been in the saddle for nearly five hours when the first hint of daylight began to make an appearance. The eastern sky had grown dim rather than dark. The glow of morning would soon take over from night.

"Maybe an hour. We need to start considering a plan. I don't think we can just walk up and knock on the door."

Warrix considered the remark, was Toler becoming a smartass? "Never said we'd do any such thing. I can't formulate a plan until I see the layout of the Brewer place. I can say though that if it comes right down to it, I'll just stand off and blast hell out of the place with the outlaws inside." The marshal was talking the harsh talk of a man who had just lost a sister to the outlaws. He was in judge and jury mode, kill those responsible as quickly as he could.

"The Brewer spread is rather large. The main house and barn occupy about an acre that backs up between two low hills. Both hills are rocky, so is the land the buildings sit on. That's probably why old man Brewer built there. He used the least productive of his land for his home. It was smart on his part if you ask me, why take any acreage away that would be better suited for grazing?"

The fact that the house was joined by rocky hills might work to the marshal's advantage. "Can we come in by way of those hills? We might be able to get close without being spotted."

"The trail comes in directly in front of the main house. We can divert our path a little and make our way around back. I know a spot where we can tie the horses and then make the last half mile on foot. We should be able to get close without being spotted."

This suited the marshal just fine. He'd know more once they got there. As they rode both men kept a close watch on their surroundings, especially their backtrail. No rider ever wanted to pay so much attention to where he was going that he allowed someone ride right up behind him.

An hour later both men headed farther away from the trail and up the left hand valley adjoining the ranch house property. Again the route taken was through a dry wash. Neither man wanted to get spotted. It took nearly another hour to get to a spot where the two horses could be tied. Another fifteen minutes of sneaking and dodging put the two in a position to observe both the house and barn.

From their concealed location they counted four men at various positions guarding the house. It was unknown how many more were inside.

"Alright, Marshal, how do you want to play this?" Toler asked.

Before the marshal could answer the door to the house opened and a man stepped out. He was carrying a bowl and a cup. He stepped from the porch and went to the barn. Not more than a minute later he came out of the barn and went back inside the house.

"Are you thinking what I'm thinking, Marshal?"

"I believe so. That man just took breakfast to someone in the barn. Now what's the chance they got Bishop locked inside the barn and just carry him food?"

"Well if he is in the barn then he's not tied up. If they leave food and coffee then he would have to use his hands, how else could he feed himself?" Toler asked.

After thirty minutes the same man came from the house and went back to the barn. He retrieved the bowl and the cup and headed back inside but not before relocking the barn door.

"I believe that answers our question, someone is locked inside. Unless this bunch has more than one man held prisoner then it's Bishop," Toler said.

"How good a shot are you with that Winchester?" Warrix asked.

"I don't know but I will say this, I win the turkey shoot every year at the ranch. What have you got in mind?"

Warrix scanned the surrounding terrain before answering. "If I can get down around back of the barn can you cover me? I'm going to scout around and see what we're up against."

"Won't be a problem. I see anyone while you're out in the open I'll put a bullet at his feet."

"Sounds about right but I ask one thing. If that someone is about to shoot me then you aim a little higher than at his feet."

Warrix left Toler and headed around through the timber. The going was slow because he didn't want to come across anyone who might be scouting around. It took a good ten minutes to make it to the back of the barn. The marshal could see inside through some of the gaps in the wood siding. It didn't take long to find Bishop sitting in a stall on an old ladderback chair.

"Bishop, can you hear me?" the marshal asked as quietly as possible. He hoped the man wasn't hard of hearing because he sure didn't risk talking any louder.

"I can hear you. Who's there?"

"Marshal Warrix from Dakota City. Are you roped to that chair?"

"No, Marshal," Bishop said as he stood. "Boy am I glad to see you. How many men you got with you?"

"It's me and Windell Toler. Is there a way out of this barn other than that front door?" Warrix asked.

"Just you and Toler? There's at least ten men holding me prisoner here, Marshal. You and Toler can't go up against that many men, it's suicide."

"Talk a little lower. I plan on getting you out of here now answer me, is there another way out of this barn?"

There was silence for a second as Bishop considered his situation. "I believe there's a back door, but the latch is in here with a big padlock attached. It's either the front door or nothing, Marshal."

Warrix went around back to have a look. There was the door, just as Bishop said. It seemed solid, more solid than a man using only his bare hands could deal with. As he stood there looking he noticed a pile of scrap wood lying nearby. Upon closer inspection he found a hammer and a handsaw, along with a crowbar. It looked as if the elder Brewer had been doing some repairs on his barn, repairs that would forever go unfinished.

Warrix picked up the bar and went back around to the spot where he'd been talking to Bishop. The barn looked to be fairly old, some of the wood was warped and trying to pull away from the purlin. It might be possible to pry a couple of the wider boards loose, at least enough for Bishop to squeeze through.

"I'm going to try to remove a couple of these boards. You listen for anyone coming through that front door," Warrix said.

"Will do, Marshal, but you better be hurrying."

The job was easier than Warrix first thought. It didn't take but a couple of minutes to pry off two boards, hopefully enough for the skinny Bishop to squeeze through.

"Alright, see if you can make it through," Warrix said.

Bishop was outside in no time. As the two men headed around the barn they came to a corral that contained six

171

horses. The best piece of news was another horse was tied outside the corral, it was saddled and ready to go.

The marshal looked at Bishop. "I'm going to open the gate so the rest of the horses can escape. You grab the reins to that buckskin and head for the timber, I'll be right behind you."

Bishop quickly untied the horse and headed in the direction he was told to go. Warrix unfastened the gate and swung it wide. He stepped in the corral and used his hat to shoo the horses out. They headed for the timber apparently trying to get away from this crazy man using his hat like a windmill.

So far everything was going better than either man expected but that was about to change. Five of the corralled horses headed for the timber but the last one out decided to head in the opposite direction. It ran past the ranch house at a full gallop.

The men inside heard the horse and came outside to investigate. They saw the horse that made the racket, but they saw something else too, two men leading another horse into the timber.

"That's Bishop leading that horse into the trees. Why he's stealing my horse," one of the men said. The fact that a man that participated in a kidnapping would think to accuse another man of stealing his horse was almost laughable.

The only one of the bunch that carried a rifle quickly raised it to his shoulder and sighted in the second man. Before he could fire there was another gunshot farther up the ridge. The man holding the rifle fell face first off the porch, he was dead before he hit the ground.

"Sounds like Toler is giving us some covering fire," Warrix said. He didn't know a man had him in his sights and was only a split-second away from pulling the trigger. Warrix also noticed the older man starting to slow, that just wouldn't do.

"Let's stop here a minute, we've put enough space between us and the house. We can't wait long though. It might be a good idea if you mount up, try out that horse me and you just stole. It'll be easier on you, and we can make better time. Toler is at the top of the ridge and our two horses are tied about a quarter mile back." Thirty seconds later Bishop was safely mounted on the buckskin. Now it was Warrix that found himself getting tired.

"Marshal, you mentioned, *'the horse me and you stole.'* I know for a fact that this is a stolen horse, but it was them hombres back at the house that stole it first. How in hell can either me or you steal something that's already been stolen?" Bishop asked.

"You make a good point and as soon as we get somewhere safe maybe we can debate the matter but right now we better keep a close watch. I doubt anyone that is associated with your kidnapping will hesitate to shoot either of us."

"You also make a good point, Marshal. I'm just so glad to be shed of that bunch that I had to say something, even if it was something stupid," Bishop said with a slight chuckle. Warrix had to agree.

It only took a few minutes to make it to where Toler was. The man was laying prone and had his Winchester resting across a small log. It looked like a log that had been placed there on purpose.

"What's happening at the house," Warrix asked as soon as he got there.

"They backed inside once I put a few shots between their feet. I also dug up some ground near their horses, they took off for the high country. I doubt anyone can give us any trouble until they find their mounts. That'll take some time."

Bishop looked at his ranch foreman. "I ain't seen a man in a shooting position like that since back in the war. We had a few sharpshooters in our outfit, they could do some damage with a gun not half as good as the one you're holding, Toler."

"You done real good when you built that gun room and stocked it the way you did. I wish you'd listened to me though about the scopes. Even one would make a difference in the situation we're in," Toler said without looking away from the house.

"I didn't see anyone in my old outfit with a scoped rifle and they was plenty good with a gun. But I will admit, a scope might make a world of difference. As soon as we get this business settled I'll let you make a list. We'll order off for anything you see fit to put on that list, that's assuming we live past our present troubles," Bishop said.

"You got yourself a deal. How long are we staying here, I'm starting to draw dampness from the ground," Toler said.

"Put a couple more shots into that front door and then let's head toward our horses. We stay here much longer those other men might show up," Warrix said.

"It'd be my pleasure," Toler said as he sighted his rifle and slowly squeezed the trigger. The shot hit the knob of the door, shattering wood and steel. He moved the rifle ever so slightly and put another round through the metal flue that ran from the kitchen stove out the roof. A cloud of black smoke puffed from the damaged pipe. It didn't take a second for more smoke to seep from the windows and the damaged front door.

"I believe you knocked the vent pipe off the kitchen stove with that last shot. Wouldn't want to be inside breathing that right now," Warrix said.

"We better be moving. I know for a fact that there's a back door and I'd say everyone in the house is heading that way right now. This would be as good a time as any to make our escape," Bishop said. It was good advice.

Warrix, Toler and Bishop headed toward the other two horses. Ten minutes later and all three men were mounted and ready to head out.

"You got any ideas on which way we're heading?" Warrix asked. This was his first time in this part of the country, and he was about as lost as he'd ever been.

"I say we head north. It's the opposite direction of my spread. It might buy us some time, then again it might not," Bishop said.

Toler looked back toward the rise they'd just left; he expected men to top the hill at any minute and start shooting. "I agree, we head in the direction they'd least expect. There's a small town about fifteen miles from here. We can rest the horses there and figure out our next move. Heading straight back to the ranch from here wouldn't be a good idea."

"You're right, there's men between here and my place, I know it for a fact. We'll head to Elkton, it's far enough away and like you said, we can rest the horses," Bishop said.

"If it's fifteen miles wouldn't that be putting us close to the railroad?" Warrix asked.

"It would at that. The nearest railroad depot from here is in Fenton but that's another twenty miles or so. We head for Elkton and see what happens. I doubt anyone will be the wiser," Bishop said.

"What about the ranch? Shouldn't we be getting there to lend a hand?" Warrix asked.

"The ranch will be okay. Every member of that gang will be searching for the three of us. I doubt they'll give the ranch much thought since the two of you have managed to make good my escape. I heard a few things when they brought me here. Not much, just a word or two now and then. But what I did hear was enough for me to understand what's going on and who's behind it, Bernard Rumford," Bishop said.

175

"I always suspected that man as being dishonest. Something about the way he eyed the place and some of the things he said. I was never around him that much but the time I was around I noticed things," Toler said. The tone the man used didn't mask his resentment at the trouble Rumford had caused.

As the men talked they were also moving away from the Brewer Ranch. The three doubted the men they'd put afoot could have rounded up their skittish mounts in so short of time, but you could never tell.

"We make it to Elkton without any trouble won't that still put us there too late for a trip back to your place," Warrix asked as he scanned their backtrail.

"I'd say you're right, Marshal. By the time we make it there and then rest the horses it'll most likely be getting dark, probably an hour or two past dark. I for one don't want to ride that trail back to my place knowing how many men are hunting us," Bishop told the two.

The men rode in silence for the next few miles. The trail wasn't that bad, apparently it was used by old man Brewer and a few of the other ranchers in the area. The only problem with living in this part of the territory was that a close neighbor could be as far away as five miles. This suited most but could be inconvenient when trouble came calling.

The three rode into Elkton at five in the evening. If this place was trying to be a town it was failing miserably. There was one main street with a saloon on either side. A livery and a general store made up the rest of the business establishments. A few houses lined either side of the street and that was about it. Every chimney produced smoke; every door was shut tight. There was a post office and a few other building, mostly abandoned.

During the day the weather had managed to stay about the same, cold, and windy. As if that wasn't enough the wind also came with snowflakes. Not the kind that would accumulate but it was the type that stung a bit when the wind hit you in the face. The flakes were more like sleet than fluff. It didn't hit and stick, it bounced off either clothing or skin.

"You mentioned staying here for the night. Exactly where would a man stay, surely not at the livery?" Warrix asked. Still though, a livery was way better than camping out. None of the three had the gear to survive a night out of doors.

"I never really gave that much thought, Marshal. I guess we'll find out from someone in one of the saloons," Bishop said. He too was dreading the option of staying in a livery.

"One of the saloons, you mean either of the saloons, there's only two."

"That's right, one of the saloons. I know how to count to two, Marshal."

It had been a long day and Bishop was starting to show some wear and tear. In the last forty-eight hours he'd been kidnapped, held prisoner, busted loose, and ridden an unfamiliar horse for fifteen miles. He was in no mood to humor the marshal, or anybody else for that matter.

The three rode to the front of the least busy of the two saloons. It was a place that looked to have been there for ages but that could be deceiving. In this environment a newly built building started to age the minute the last nail was driven in place. A building a year old might actually look ten. A ten year old building might look a hundred. The place had a shingle nailed over the door. On that shingle were the words, Last Stop Saloon.

"The Last Stop Saloon. Now that is one ominous name if I ever heard one," Toler said.

"Last Stop for what?" Warrix asked.

"You two want to stay out here and debate the name or do you want to go inside?" Bishop asked. His tone revealed the fact that he was tired and didn't want to be out of doors any longer.

The three tied their mounts to a ramshackle hitch rail and headed for the door. There were two batwings, but both were sprung wide and latched in a full open position. Those two doors were for warmer temps and milder days. There was another door that looked to be older than the building itself. There was also two bullet holes near the top.

"Looks like your kind of place, Toler," Bishop said as he turned the knob.

The three quickly stepped in and were immediately met with stove warmed air. The room was about typical for a saloon of the area. Rough tables and chairs, rough built bar and stools, rough looking crowd. As rough as everything was the exception was the bar top. It was dark and shined to perfection.

As the three pushed in they were met with stares from the patrons. Toler and Warrix both carried their Winchesters; Bishop carried a sneer. The sneer looked more deadly. All three headed for the bar but before getting there Bishop brushed against a man that was playing cards, he looked to be losing.

"Watch it you old bastard," the card player said without getting up. He was holding five cards and apparently didn't want either of the two men he was playing against to have a sideways glance.

"Well pardon me all to hell. But let me ask you something, you plan on bluffing your way to a win while holding a pair of nothing?" Bishop asked.

The man at the table knew his hand hadn't been seen. He kept his mouth shut as the other two players quickly raised their bets. The man stayed in the game and even re-raised, he was holding a full house, three sevens and a pair of queens.

Needless to say he won that hand and took the pot. As he counted his money he realized the man he'd insulted had set him up for the win by leading the other two men at the table to believe he didn't have a hand.

As the pot was being taken the other two men at the table looked at the three strangers. They'd just lost a hand they would have probably lost anyway but they both wouldn't have raised. That old man had cost them some money.

The barkeep was a surly looking man that seemed to have better things to do than be here. But in a town like Elkton what else could any man find to do, other than drink.

"You got any money, Boss?" Toler asked as he eyed the bottles behind the bar. Toler might have been a drinker in his earlier days but not so much lately, he was a mean drunk and knew it. Best if he stayed sober, especially around his boss.

"Actually, I do. The kidnappers checked me for weapons but nothing else. They let me keep what money I had on me." Bishop reached in a pocket and pulled out a wallet. He looked to be set for a while.

"You three here to drink or just sit and get warm?" the barkeep asked.

"We need a drink, and we need information," Warrix said.

"Drinks will cost but the information is free. What'll it be?" Both Warrix and Toler ordered beer, Bishop wanted a shot of something stronger.

After pouring the drinks the barkeep leaned on the counter and quietly said, "You might want to have them drinks and then get out of here. I believe one of you might have made an enemy on your way in. Two of the men you spoke to a little while ago have been eyeing you."

Bishop wasn't in the mood for trouble, he also wasn't in the mood to run from it. He picked up his whiskey and drank half before turning and looking back at the table the barkeep had spoken of. Sure enough, two of the three cardplayers were eyeing him.

He knew he'd set the third man up for a win and really didn't care. He was just defusing a situation; he might have started a worse one in the process.

Warrix wasn't wearing his badge. He'd taken it off shortly after leaving Dakota City. He was a small town marshal and knew his jurisdiction stopped at the edge of town. At a time like this a badge might go a long way in preventing a bad situation from getting worse. As the marshal thought of things like badges and the such the two men from the card game stood.

"I believe I lost four dollars on that last hand, mister. You must be working with this cheat because you led us to believe he had a losing hand and instead he lays down a full house. Now I might be able to forgive and forget, but it's gonna cost you four dollars," the man said.

The second man now spoke. "Yea and I lost three more. You pay me the three and we might just let you drink your beer in peace."

The man they had called a cheat now stood. "Why you son of a..." Before he could finish one of the card players stepped over and hit him square in the face. It must have been a good swing, blood gushed from the man's nose as he fell to the floor. He was knocked out cold. With the third card player now on the floor the two could return their full attention to Bishop and his two friends.

"Now as we were saying, you owe us some money," one of the two said. Warrix wondered how they had gotten in this situation, but he had also about heard enough.

"I believe you are mistaken. We owe you nothing," the marshal said as he turned to face the two.

"We'll now, looks like you want to help the old man pay. Between the three of you there should be enough money to cover our losses. And while you're at it throw in an extra five dollars for our trouble."

Now the two were wanting what they lost along with an additional five. This was more than Bishop could stand. "You two can go straight to hell. It should be easy to find because I figure you both got family there."

One of the card players started toward Bishop but was stopped in his tracks by the sight of a Colt. Warrix had drawn and was now pointing his gun at the loud mouth's face.

"You like the looks of this gun? You must the way you're looking at it right now. Let me take this opportunity to introduce you, this is Colt. He don't like you. As a matter of fact I don't like you. Now you and your mom there have a choice to make, continue acting the way you are and get shot. Or you could pick up your friend there and go back to your game of cards, your decision," Warrix told the two. He was working off a little steam and these two were on the receiving end of it.

The two men grudgingly picked up the man that had his nose busted. He was groggy but not mad. The three headed back to the table where they'd been playing cards.

"And you can give up those guns your wearing. The bartender will be glad to hold them until we leave." Warrix looked at the bartender, he was shaking his head in agreement.

Once the three cardplayers had their teeth pulled Warrix walked to the end of the bar to finish his drink. He wasn't about to turn his back on them, one or all of the three might be carrying a hideaway. He would drink where he could keep a close eye on the game. He would also keep an eye on the barkeep, a man that acted like he had something to hide and didn't like having Warrix and the other two in his bar.

"Now that everyone is friends again maybe I'll have a second beer," Bishop said as he looked at the man behind the bar. Just when he was wondering if he was going to have to get the beer himself the barkeep grabbed his glass and refilled it.

"There's something familiar about you, mister, have we met before?" Bishop asked as he grabbed his glass.

"Naw, I've never seen any of you three before. And as soon as you're gone I hope to never see you again."

This was the first time the barkeep had spoken, at least that many words in a sentence. If Bishop had thought he recognized the whiskey peddler before then combining the face with the voice brought the memory back, front and center. Toler now knew who the man was.

"It's been a while but tell me I know you. Your name is Samson Bradley. Am I right?" Toler asked.

The barkeep was hesitant to answer. His hesitation told the answer even if his mouth refused to cooperate. Bishop, upon hearing the name, realized that he did know the man.

"I believe you worked for me a few years back. Am I right?" Toler asked

Suddenly the barkeep found the need to wipe the top of the bar. His silence seemed to be contagious, the three card players had grown quiet as well. Warrix, from his position at the end of the bar, noticed everything. He was keeping a close eye on the card game and also on the barkeep. From an angle he could see the butt of a double-barreled shotgun sticking out from underneath the bar. He couldn't actually see the gun directly, but the mirror behind the bar gave a good view of what was underneath.

"I asked you a question, mister. When I ask a man something I expect an answer," Toler said. The menace in the ranch foreman's voice was evident to anyone that heard it.

"I used to work at your ranch. Been a few years," the barkeep said. The words seemed to pain him.

"And if I remember correctly you were run off for stealing, am I correct about that?" Toler asked as he eyed the man.

"I was accused of stealing but there was no evidence. You and that bastard made it up just to get rid of me," the barkeep said. For some reason he had developed a little backbone.

"Naw, you got that all wrong. You stole some saddles and sold them to a couple of no goods. As a matter of fact I believe I recognize two of those cardplayers. They were the ones buying the tack you were stealing. We ran you off because to have sent for a marshal or the sheriff would have taken manpower away from our roundup. We just couldn't spare anyone plus we figured the stuff you stole was long gone. Now what do you have to say, barkeep?" Toler was about to get worked up. He'd only had one glass of beer and that was a good thing. Even with only one beer he was having a hard time keeping his drinking attitude from taking over.

"That was years ago, mister. Why are you coming in here now and trying to cause trouble?"

"Cause trouble, did you really just say that you stealing sack of horseshit?"

"That's right, Toler. I remember you. You're just the errand boy for Bishop. If you want to come in here and start accusing me of something then do it by yourself. You talk real big when you got two men backing you up."

Toler had heard enough. He reached across the bar and pulled Bradley off his feet. After a second he muscled the man clean over the bar and dropped him to the floor.

"Now, Bradley, maybe you can repeat yourself. I like to be face to face when a sniveling little bastard like you starts talking tough. Now before I beat the living hell out of you I'll give you one chance to try and talk me out of it."

"I took the saddles, two of 'em. I took a couple of bridles and one set of saddlebags. And before you ask they were empty saddlebags. I know I done wrong, and I was never raised to do such a thing. I've got no beef with you Toler and I'm sorry for what I said. Now if you don't mind I'd like to get back to the other side of the bar. The next round is on me."

Warrix was surprised at the change in tone from the barkeep, then he remembered the shotgun. Toler released his grip on the man and then reached for his empty glass. As the barkeep circled back behind the bar Warrix kept a close eye on the man. What happened next was totally unexpected.

"Before we do anything I'd like to hand over this shotgun from under the bar. I don't want anyone to get the wrong idea about it and shoot me just for kicks," the barkeep said. He grabbed the shotgun by the end of the barrel and eased it out where everyone could see it. "Who wants to hang on to this?"

Warrix had his hand on his Colt as all this was happening. "I'll take it, Bradley. After we leave I'll see that you get it back."

The barkeep reached the Greener to the marshal. "Here you go."

Warrix took the gun and immediately unloaded it. He stood the two shotgun shells on the bar and leaned the gun beside his stool. Now that the three cardplayers and the barkeep had been disarmed he felt better. Still though, for three men that only wanted to come in out of the cold and have a drink, things had deteriorated really fast.

The barkeep was good to his word, he poured a shot of whiskey and two glasses of beer. He gingerly slid all three to the three men that had made his evening a living hell. All in all though, it had a cleansing effect on the barkeep. He had never stolen anything in his life and wouldn't have stolen the tack from the ranch if he didn't need the money so bad. But then again, don't all thieves steal because they need the money.

"You men staying in town tonight?" the barkeep asked. He felt he could speak since there were no more secrets to hide.

"Might be. If we were of the mind to stay in Elkton where would we find lodgings?" Bishop asked. The ranch owner was suddenly a forgiving man. Old man Bishop was a man that treated folks the way he was being treated. If someone was rude or rowdy then that was what they got in return. The barkeep, although an admitted thief, was now acting sociable and Bishop always felt the need to reciprocate such behavior.

Bradley felt comfortable enough now to go back to wiping the bar top and some of the beer mugs. The fact that the barkeep liked to serve his wares in clean glasses satisfied Bishop that maybe he wasn't such a bad man after all. If what Bradley said was true then he'd only stole the one time. As he sipped his beer Bishop was glad no one was still around that knew of his younger days. He'd stolen, and more than once. He'd shot a man, didn't kill him but shot him just the same. Those days were long gone, no one would ever know.

As the temperature cooled, and the temperament, things took on a slower pace. Three men sipping drinks at the bar. Three card players behaving themselves. And one barkeep that was glad his past sins had been brought before him for all to see and he'd survived. Everything was as it should be on a cold fall evening, or at least that's the way it was at the moment. Things were about to change, and not for the better.

There was a commotion outside, horses could be heard. Horses that sounded to have been rode hard. The heavy breathing and snorting gave that little fact away. Toler and Warrix thought nothing of the sounds. It was a cold evening and men liked to end the day with something stronger than coffee to warm them up. The barkeep heard something that gave him an idea of who was outside. His nervousness came back.

The door to the saloon was roughly opened by a mountain of a man wearing a chest length beard. He was big, he was dirty, and he was ugly as a raw skunk.

"Bradley, line em up. We done made us some money today and aim to spend a little of it right here in your saloon," the man said as he eyed the others in the room.

Again Warrix was glad for his position at the end of the bar. All he had to do was stare into the mirror and see pretty much everything that went on. It also put him farther away from the smelly polecat that just walked in.

If the sight of the first man through the door was startling then what came next was worse. Four more men came in behind the bearded man. They all ranged in at about the same size, enormous. They all had the same grungy look and grungy smell. The room was filling up fast with men that ate too much and bathed to little.

Bishop and Toler had the disadvantage of being closest as they came to the bar. Bishop actually choked on his beer when he got a whiff of the mountain man. Both he and Toler moved toward the marshal, not from fear but in the hopes the air was a little more pleasant, it wasn't. The five men had managed to fill the entire saloon with their unpleasant smell.

The five to a man went to the bar and slapped a hand, each telling Bradley what they wanted to drink. It was easy to remember, all five ordered beer.

"Bradley, I reckon the drinks are on the house, same as usual," the bearded man said with an evil grin.

The barkeep didn't answer, he drew five glasses of beer and placed each on the bar. "That'll be a dollar," he said.

All five men grabbed a glass and in unison each turned their faces toward the ceiling. The five beers were gone in seconds. Once finished five glasses slammed down on the counter. "Five more," the man said to Bradley.

The barkeep refilled the glasses and then said, "That'll be two dollars."

The five men didn't say a word, they were too busy looking at the ceiling while they poured beer down their throats. Once finished the five looked longingly at the row of whiskey bottles lining the shelf behind the bar. Directly behind the bottles was the ubiquitous mirror that nearly every saloon had. A saloon mirror was originally used to make the inventory of whiskey seem to be more than it really was. More than one hardscrabble saloon owner invested in a mirror rather than stock more whiskey.

"What's the best whiskey you got back there? That beer seemed to cure my thirst, now I need something to rid the chill from my bones," the bearded man said.

Samson Bradley didn't answer the question. He was waiting to see if he was getting paid the two dollars for the beer the men had drank. This didn't go unnoticed by the bearded man. Warrix and Toler wondered who this stinking loudmouth was. If his attitude wasn't overbearing enough then his smell surely was. Bradley wasn't going to pour any whiskey until he saw some cash.

"You want another drink Chaney then pay up for the beer," Bradley said.

The bearded man, the man known by the barkeep as Chaney, stepped from the bar and straightened to his full height. The man had to be well past six feet tall. In all his winter robes he looked nearly that wide as well.

"I asked you what kind of whiskey you got. I expect an answer."

Bradley swallowed hard. He looked to be hunting courage and wasn't having a good go at it.

"I don't own this place, Chaney. You know that. If you drink again and don't pay then I have to pay," the barkeep said.

Chaney's face took on what seemed to be a smile. It was hard to tell with the beard. "You hear that, boys, Bradley just said if we don't pay then he will. Just reach me a bottle and five glasses. Since you're buying the least I can do is pour."

The other four men thought this was the funniest thing they'd ever heard by the way they laughed. Warrix wondered what Bradley would do if he still had the shotgun under the bar. The three cardplayers had stopped paying attention to their cards, they were now wondering how the drama at the bar was going to turn out. They were also wondering if it would soon involve them.

The barkeep stepped back from the bar. The memory of Toler dragging him across the bar top was still fresh in his mind. With a little space between himself and Chaney his courage seemed to stiffen, but not by much.

Chaney saw this and also saw the lack of cooperation. "This is the last time I gonna ask, now reach me a bottle."

Chaney stepped toward the end of the bar; he was followed by the other four men. Warrix decided he wasn't going to let the five have their way. He didn't like the way they talked, or smelled for that matter.

"I think you should pay the man his two dollars. Then he'll see to the whiskey," Warrix said.

Chaney stopped and glared at Warrix. "Who asked you? If you know what's good for you you'll keep quiet."

"I don't think you have earned the right to tell me a damn thing, Mister. Now as I said, pay the man and he'll see to the whiskey."

Chaney started toward Warrix but stopped when Toler and Bishop stood next to the man. "Well you three must be together. Suits me just fine. There's five of us and we'd just as soon kick the living hell out of three as one."

"Make that six," one of the card players said as he stood. The other two also stood up. Warrix figured he might have been wrong about the three, especially if they were going to lend a hand.

While all attention was on the situation at hand Bradley walked to the end of the bar and grabbed the shotgun that Warrix had taken from him. He quickly inserted the two shells and then turned to face Chaney.

"I said pay me the two dollars for the beer you've already had. That way I get my two dollars and save the expense of buying two new shotgun shells," the barkeep said. With the shotgun in hand his whole demeanor had changed.

Chaney held up both hands, palms out. "Now don't go getting feisty with that shotgun. I got your two dollars. I'm going to reach into my coat pocket, that's where my money is."

"You just do that but if it's a gun then I promise to send you to the Hereafter," Bradley said.

No one took a breath as Chaney reached into a pocket and pulled out two dollars, it was all the man had. "Here you go, Bradley. Now would you please point that cannon somewhere else."

"This all you got," the barkeep asked.

"It is. Me and the boys haven't done so well since we lost our jobs a few days back. I guess we should have spent the two dollars on grub instead of beer."

Bishop wondered where the five worked and why they lost their jobs. "You say the five of you are out of work? Was it of your own doing to lose a job in these parts?"

"Weren't our fault. Some men rode in and gave us a choice, join them, or ride out. The foreman told them to go to hell; they shot him. We decided then and there to put some space between us and them. The old man that owns the place stayed.

189

Last we seen he was sitting on the front porch," Chaney told him.

Bishop didn't know where the five worked but he had a hunch. "This old man that owned the ranch, what was his name?"

"Brewer, Stanley Brewer. Me and the boys, along with the foreman, been working that spread for the last few years. Brewer was a good man to work for. When that bunch rode in all we could do was watch. Brewer didn't like men carrying guns. We all had guns but were made to leave them in the ranch house. Them murdering bastards let us leave with our horses and saddles, nothing else," Chaney said.

Bishop had known Stanley Brewer, how could he not have known him, their spreads had an adjoining property line. Chaney could tell by the look on the old man's face that he knew Brewer.

"I don't believe I know you, mister, but I'd say you know my boss," Chaney said.

"I did know your boss. Stanley Brewer and me have shared a fence line for years. Why I remember years ago when we were both young and just getting started, we shared a campfire a time or two. I never had a reason to think poorly of the man," Bishop said.

Chaney picked up on the way the old man spoke. "You speak as if Mr. Brewer is dead. Well he's not dead. When we rode out he was rocking on his front porch. The men that ran us off promised that no harm would come to Brewer if we left in peace, so that's what we done."

"Brewer's dead. Those men you spoke of killed him and are at the ranch as we speak. We rode away from there earlier today," Bishop said. He still wondered why anyone would kill Stanley Brewer. The man hated violence, that was one of the reasons he didn't allow his ranch hands to carry guns. Maybe if these men had been armed things would have turned out differently.

Chaney walked over to a table in the corner and sat down. He'd worked for Brewer for the last four years. He didn't earn much money but while at the ranch he was well taken care of. A bed in the bunkhouse or one of the line shacks and three squares a day. He even got a day off once a month, not that he wanted it, but it was offered just the same. As he sat there his four friends joined him.

"Give me a bottle and five glasses," Bishop told the barkeep.

After getting the bottle he walked over and sat it on the table. Bradley followed with the glasses, which he sat beside the bottle. Chaney looked up at Bishop, even with the beard and grime anyone could tell the man was shocked that someone could kill Stanley Brewer.

"This one is on me. You men enjoy," Bishop said as he walked back to the bar.

Things had gone from tense to sad all in the span of a minute. Even the three card players began to shuffle the cards for another hand.

"Say, Bradley, where would a man stay if he was in Elkton? I didn't see a hotel in town, only a livery," Toler asked. It was nearly dark and the thought of spending the night camped outside of town was starting to trouble him.

"Got no hotel but the livery will rent you a spot with your horses. Not in the same stall though, you can bed down in the hallway. The general store has a bunkroom they rent by the bed. Dollar a night per man if my memory serves. It ain't bad, I stayed there a night or two when I first came here," Bradley said as he again wiped the top of the bar. The man spent so much time wiping the bar that it was no wonder it was so shiny. The gloss was enough for a man to nearly see his own reflection although that might be a bad thing, no man wanted to see himself getting slobbery drunk.

Toler looked at Warrix and Bishop, "Looks like the bunkhouse at the general store will have to do."

Now that sleeping arrangements had been taken care of it was time to consider food. None of the three had eaten since earlier that day.

"I don't suppose that other saloon serves food. It's about past supper time for me," Bishop said.

"Naw, they don't. We don't serve anything here either, other than the type of supper a man can drink. The general store has a few tables in the back. The old couple that runs it keeps something on the stove nearly all the time. In cold weather it's usually a stew, maybe a roast of beef or hog, something like that I reckon. That old woman can surely cook," Bradley said. He smiled at the memory of some of the meals he'd enjoyed there.

"Well, it looks like the general store is our next stop. But that's after we stable our horses," Bishop said.

The three stood but not before Bishop asked the barkeep how much he owed the man. With the drinks and the bottle he'd bought for Chaney his tab was four dollars and seventy-five cents. He paid with a five and told Bradley to keep the quarter change.

The three men left but not before telling Chaney they were sorry to share the news about Brewer. Chaney seemed to be a different man. He was a bully when he first came in and now he seemed withdrawn and somber. Maybe the man wasn't as bad as they'd first thought.

Once outside they saw the additional five horses at another hitchrail in front of the saloon. These five must belong to Chaney and his men. The horses looked solid, and the tack seemed well kept. The story of these men working for Brewer

192

seemed appropriate. They must have been hard workers and to have worked that long for one man meant they must have done their jobs to satisfaction.

Rather than mounting up the three just untied their horses and walked them down to the livery. It was now completely dark. The only light was from the occasional window where a house had a fire and a kerosene lamp lit.

The livery was about the same as the rest of Elkton, run down and in bad need of repair. One of the double barn doors was off a hinge and had been nailed shut to keep it from falling off. Rather that open the second door Bishop knocked with his fist. After the second knock a man shoved the second door open.

"I reckon you know that a man that works for a living should already be in bed. Well if you didn't know then I'll tell you, I work and was already sound asleep. Now what do you want?"

"We got three horses that need stabling. Are you awake enough to handle something like that?" Bishop asked. He was unhappy with the reception he'd gotten for trying to give the hostler some business.

"Can't do it. Come back in the morning," the man said as he started to pull the door shut.

Now it was Toler's turn to talk. He shoved a boot in the way, keeping the door from closing.

"Wake your ass up and take care of our horses. I don't take kindly to someone denying my horse a place out of the weather."

If the hostler wasn't awake before he was surely awake now. "I own this livery free and clear, and I say you can come back in the morning. I don't take orders from no strangers."

There was an unwritten rule in the west that anyone that cared for horses was never really closed for business. That went for blacksmith shops, feed stores, and last but definitely not least, livery's. This was the first time that any of the three had ever been denied food and shelter for their horses.

Toler still had his boot blocking the door. He forced the door open and stepped inside. The place was a mess, it looked like it hadn't been cleaned out in weeks.

"I don't think I want to keep my horse here. This bastard wouldn't feed or water the animals anyway. You just go back to sleep you lazy bastard, I'm leaving." With that Toler turned and exited the livery. As he led his horse up the street Bishop and Warrix soon fell in behind him.

"We could have still left the horses there. I don't mind stripping off the saddle and shoveling a little grain or forking some hay," Bishop said.

"It's more than that. There wasn't another horse in that barn and by the looks of it there hadn't been one there for a long time. I don't trust a man that refuses a horse on a night like this. Hell, he might have roasted and ate my horse before morning." The horse Toler led snorted as if in agreement.

"I knew a man back in my younger days that ate horse. He said after you get used to it you'll like it more than beef or pork. I never sat at that man's table after that,'" Bishop said.

"Good to know. But now what are we going to do with our horses? This is looking to be a stormy night, a storm in the way of snow. I'd at least like to get some feed for the three animals," Toler said.

All three men were leading horses that none of them had ever seen prior to the last day or two. Toler and Warrix rode horses they'd taken from two of the men that rode against the ranch. Bishop was pulling a horse he'd taken that very morning. Funny how a man will bond to a horse only a few hours after being introduced.

"Let's head to the general store and hope they ain't closed. If they're anything like that bastard back at the livery then I say we're stuck sleeping on the floor in Last Stop Saloon. I doubt Bradley will mind, especially after we defused that little situation with Chaney," Bishop said.

With the onset of night it seemed the weather had worsened. The wind had picked up and what had once been considered flurries was now nearly a snowstorm. All three men began to worry about the horses.

"If worse comes to worse I say we head back to that half-assed livery and demand he stable our horses," Toler said. He didn't like leaving an animal out in this kind of weather. Sure, he'd camped in bad weather before but even then he made sure his horse had the protection of either fir or pine trees. He also made sure to strip the gear and feed a little grain to the animal. It was looking like they had none of this in the town of Elkton.

It only took a minute to walk back past the Last Stop Saloon on the way to the general store. There wasn't any shouting or fighting to be heard so it appeared that Chaney and his band of merry men were behaving themselves.

The general store was about a hundred feet past the saloon and light could be seen from outside. At least if the man that ran the place was as belligerent as the one at the livery he would be awake. The three tied their horses, tired horses, to a hitch rail and then went inside.

The atmosphere was a welcome change from the rowdies at the saloon and the bastard at the livery. A pleasant looking older couple were at the counter. The woman was working in a journal as the man sorted nails. They both looked up when the door opened to see three men hurry in, the men had snow sticking to their clothes.

"Evening men. Looks like the weather has turned," the man said. He was pleasant and the place seemed prosperous. A man that treated folks with kindness and respect usually prospered.

"Evening, it has at that," Bishop said. He, being the oldest and also Toler's boss, liked to take the lead in every situation. This suited the marshal just fine.

"What can I do for you this evening?" the man asked.

"Quite a lot we hope, but first off can you tell us where we can stable our horses," Bishop said.

"Out back. I got a small barn that will hold a few horses. Got six stalls and plenty of dry hay, even grain if it suits you."

"Well I don't know about suiting me but I'm sure my horse will like it," Bishop said with a smile. The store owner's wife started laughing, soon everyone laughed.

"Just lead them around back, the door's not latched but you better latch it tight before you come back in. As a matter of fact I got a fair sized rock you might put against the door. Windy nights makes that door rattle something awful."

Now it was the store owner's wife that spoke. "You look like you might need some food. I got a big stew on in the back. It's elk, do any of you like elk?"

Of the three, all had experienced elk. Anyone that lived in this part of the territory had eaten elk. "Yes ma'am, we all like elk stew. After we get the horses stabled we'll be back. We also heard you might have accommodations available. We were told at the saloon that the town doesn't have a hotel," Bishop said. He was graceful in the way he conversed with the storeowner and his wife.

"Well, you've come to the right place. The horses are fifty cents apiece for a stall. A bunk will also cost you fifty cents. We charge the same for either a horse or a man," the storeowner said. Again everyone laughed. Warrix was starting to like these two. If the stew was as good as the hospitality then he was going to enjoy his time in Elkton.

"You three take them animals out back to the barn. Once you get inside you can figure everything out. My barn is neat and orderly, try to keep it that way," the man said. Even when he was blunt it was in a friendly manner. He was the type that deserved respect in the way he operated his store and barn.

"We'll be back as soon as we get the horses situated," Bishop said.

The three men exited the store and grabbed the reins of their horses. After being in the warm store it made the outside temperature seem that much colder, it probably was. They headed down an alley and to the back where they were told the barn was. It was out back but not close, it looked about a couple hundred feet away.

The barn was more of a one story affair with little in the way of a hay loft. It was tight and compact. There were six stalls, but each was small. One horse would do fine in each, but it would be nearly impossible to fit two. Three of the stalls already had occupants, these horses probably belonged to the storeowner and his wife. Then again maybe someone else was staying at the bunkhouse.

All three horses seemed satisfied with their new accommodations. The barn seemed tight, very little air stirred inside. It only took ten minutes to get all three horses in a stall. Hay was forked, grain was scooped, and water was poured. After being tied in front of the saloon, and then the general store for so long the three horses were glad for the attention.

Bishop led the two men out of the barn. He stopped long enough to roll some tobacco and paper. He wasn't much of a smoker but when the craving hit it had to be satisfied. "We were lucky to find this place. A night out in the open would have been hard on the three of us, not to mention the horses.

None of us has anything in the way of supplies," Bishop told the two as he struck a match. He put fire to the end of his smoke and drew mightily. He only took the one puff and then crushed out the remains on the ground. That's all he needed, one long puff and his craving was satisfied.

The three men hurried back to the front of the store. There were four horses tied to the hitch rail, the same hitch rail they had just vacated when they took their own horses to the barn. Neither of the three thought anything of the horses. The general store was doing a booming business tonight.

Bishop opened the door and walked in followed closely by Toler and Warrix. All three were in a hurry to try out the stew. What they saw was not what they expected. There were four men at the counter, and one had a hand full of the storeowners shirt. He was nearly shouting; it was so loud that none of the four heard the door open and three men walk in.

"Where did they go? They ain't staying here because we saw them heading out back of the store as we rode in. Tell me damn you," the man shouted as he drew back a hand.

"Release that man and I mean right now," Warrix shouted.

All four, as if in unison, spun around and went for their guns. They were two late, Warrix and his two companions were standing there holding three Colts, each was pointed at a man.

"Don't try it or I promise to shoot the first man that draws his gun," Warrix said. The warning worked, all four men froze, each looking at a gun that was looking at them.

"Toler, how about you and Bishop relieving them of their guns?" Warrix said.

"Now wait just a minute. I ain't giving up my gun. Any man that tries to take it will find himself dead," one of the four said.

Warrix put his gun back in its holster. He marched over and struck the man hard in the stomach. He would have hit him in the face but didn't want to take a chance on hurting his hand. Any other time he would have flattened the man's nose. The man gave up his gun as he tried to catch a breath. Once the four had their teeth pulled they were much easier to get along with. Each of the four carried a handgun but one had a hideaway, a two shot derringer. Not a powerful weapon but at close range could kill just like any other gun. The guns were given to the man and woman behind the counter for safe keeping.

"It sounded like you were looking for us. Now why would that be?" Bishop asked as he held his gun at the ready.

"We ain't saying," another of the four said. Warrix stomped over and did the same as before, he hit the man hard in the stomach. That man did the same as the first, he doubled over in pain.

Now it was Warrix that spoke. "That's two. The next man that speaks and doesn't answer the question will get the living hell beat out of him. Now we just walked in here and found the four of you mistreating the couple that own's this place. I can promise that I'm going to find out why or promise to make your lives a misery. Now why did you come in here and act the way you did?"

"You wouldn't be so brave if you weren't holding guns on us," a third man said.

Again Warrix went to that man and knocked the wind out of him. That left one of the four that hadn't been hit. Warrix grabbed that man and hit him across the face with the back of his hand.

"Who are you and why are you here?"

"Go to hell," the man yelled as he grimaced in anticipation of his next beating.

Just as Warrix was preparing to continue his assault Bishop put a hand on his shoulder. "He ain't going to talk. None of these men are going to answer our questions. They are afraid, they're afraid of whoever hired them to hunt us."

Warrix backed away but as he did he pulled his Colt. He didn't want to give the four a chance to charge and overpower them. "So now what do we do?"

Before Warrix could answer the door opened and Chaney walked in. It might have been hard to believe but Warrix was glad.

"Looks like a standoff in here. What happened?" Chaney asked as he looked at the four strangers.

"Not sure. These four were trying to rough up the man that owns this place. Do you know any of these men?" Bishop asked.

"Naw, I don't know 'em, but I've seen them before. They were with the men that rode in and ran us off Brewer's ranch."

"You're crazy, mister. I ain't seen you before in my life. We didn't kill nobody named Brewer," one of the four said.

"Well that says a lot. No one said Brewer was dead, but he is. You just admitted to a killing. I say we take the four of you out and make use of that big tree down by the livery. It's got a limb that would look real good with four bodies hanging from it," Chaney said.

Warrix could tell the man was upset. He must have held his previous boss in high regard. Now he confronted four men that had a part in his killing. Warrix wouldn't allow a hanging, but he wasn't above letting Chaney have some fun at the four bushwhacker's expense.

"Now you just wait a minute. We didn't kill nobody. I misspoke when I said the man named Brewer was dead. I swear it," one of the four said. His voice indicated that he was afraid that the mention of a hanging might just turn into a real hanging.

Chaney looked at the couple that owned the store. "You wouldn't have a spool of three-quarter inch rope around here would you? I need four lengths of about fifteen feet. I won't need it for longer than thirty minutes."

The four rowdies looked ready to pass out. One actually did. He went down and in the process smacked his head on a shelf. The other three looked ready to make a run for it, the three Colt revolvers being pointed at them was all that was keeping them in place.

"The rope might just come in handy after all, but it won't be used for a hanging, at least not yet. We'll use it to tie you four up until we figure out what to do with you," Bishop said.

Warrix didn't know how they were going to handle these four. The town of Elkton didn't have a town marshal or a jail for that matter. One thing he did know was that they just couldn't ride off knowing the men were still in town to cause trouble. But would they cause more trouble since they'd found the men they were looking for?

That brought up a whole new set of questions. How on earth had they managed to track Warrix, Toler and Bishop to Elkton? And why were they following them anyway? Questions were more numerous at the moment than answers. What the three did know was that they were tired, they were hungry, and they were a long way from home.

Warrix turned to who he figured was the leader of this four-man rabble. "What's your name?"

The man took his eyes off the dangerous looking Chaney and turned toward Warrix. "Names Raymond Ward." That was it, no other details were given. The name came slow, maybe he figured they needed it for his marker after they hung him. He glanced back at Chaney; the man was sporting an evil grin. It was the type of look that preceded mischief.

Two minutes later and the store owner appeared with a spool of rope. Not the thick hanging rope, this was thinner and more manageable. He reached it to Warrix but as he did he thought he recognized him.

"Say, I believe I know you." After a few more seconds he added, "Yeah, now it's coming to me. I was in Dakota City about a month ago. You're the marshal over there."

"Yep, that's me. Name's Joshua Warrix."

"Well, Marshal, I'm glad to make your acquaintance, especially on a day like today," the man said as he looked at the four no-goods.

"Well I feel a bit guilty; it was me and my friends that these men were following. I believe we led them here."

"Think nothing of it, Marshal. My name's Ed Maddox and this is my wife, Becky. We've been in Elkton for going on fifteen years. Had this store nearly that long. I can safely say that what happened here today has never happened before. Had a drunk or two try to cause a little trouble but I took care of it," Ed said. He looked at the man that had tried to rough him up earlier. Ed walked over and kicked the man in the shin. It wasn't a hard kick, but the shin is a tender spot. The man yelped in pain.

"You say you're a marshal. Well what are you going to do about that man attacking me?" the victim of Ed's kick shouted once he caught his breath.

"I'm thinking of telling him to kick you again if you don't shut your damn mouth," Warrix said forgetting there was a lady present. He looked her way and said, "Sorry, ma'am."

"That is quite alright, Marshal. My Ed has been known to use a word or two like that from time to time. I'm just glad you three came in when you did."

Five minutes later and all four had their hands tied firmly behind their backs.

"Now what are we going to do? We got no jail cell to put them in and no way of transporting them to the next town," Bishop said.

Chaney now spoke up. "Bradley's got a room in the back of the saloon. He uses it for junk and such. It's stout and got a good door. I say we put 'em in there until first light."

Bishop smiled; he liked the sound of that. What he really liked was a trip back to the saloon for another beer. The man liked his beer. Warrix though was skeptical. He didn't know whether to trust Chaney and his men. They might just take the four to that tree he mentioned earlier.

"Alright, Chaney, let's say we use your plan and lock these four up at the saloon. What guarantee do I have that you won't hang them while I'm gone?" Warrix asked.

Chaney smiled at Ward and the other three before turning back to the marshal. "Can I talk to you outside, Marshal? What I got to say don't need to be shared with these four bastards."

"We can do that. Toler, you, and Bishop keep a close watch on these four," Warrix said as he and Chaney stepped outside.

"Alright, Chaney, start talking. It's cold out here."

"Marshal, I know you don't know me or the other four Brewer men over at the saloon, but I can assure you we would never hurt anyone unless it was self-defense. Why do you think Brewer kept us on for as long as he did. You're right, we got a grudge against those men in there but that's a matter for a judge. If you put them in that storage room at the saloon then the five of us will see that they don't escape. And you can bet they will be just as healthy in the morning as they are right now."

Warrix listened to the man. It was true that he didn't know the five Brewer men, but he'd heard of Brewer. The man had a good reputation and if he was okay with Chaney and the other four then that said a lot.

"What about Samson Bradley? What'll he say about having four men locked up in his storage room?"

"Bradley will be okay with it. Me and him don't see eye to eye on many things but this is a matter of the law. Bradley and Bishop might have had a falling out but the man's solid. He'll help, I'm sure of it."

There was a gust of wind, and a little snow. That was a sign that this conversation was over, at least the talking outside part was over anyway.

"Let's step back inside and see what Bishop and Toler think of your plan," Warrix said.

The two stepped back inside to find everything about the way they'd left it. The only change was that Ed Maddox was now holding a shotgun, just in case.

Warrix explained Chaney's plan to Bishop and Toler. The two were hesitant at first but considering there were no other options they soon agreed.

"Alright then, let's escort these four over to the saloon and see if Bradley is going to cooperate," Warrix said.

Before leaving Bishop told Ed and Becky that they'd be back as soon as they could. He also said how anxious he was to sample that stew. Warrix noticed Chaney look toward the back of the store where the smell of stew was strong. He wondered when the man had last eaten?

Five minutes later the four troublemakers were marched inside the Last Stop Saloon. Bradley was behind the bar polishing. The man must polish the entire time he's there. He looked at the eight men as they came in, he stopped polishing.

"Chaney, could you and your men take this bunch to a table and watch over them while we talk to the barkeep?" Warrix asked.

"Be glad to, Marshal. It'll give me a chance to fill the others in on the plan."

Bradley was standing and watching the show as Chaney led the four men, men that had their hands tied, to a table in the back. "Well it looks like the three of you managed to get into a little trouble after you left here. I gave you directions to the general store and you show back up with prisoners. I sure hope at least one of you is a lawman. If not that might be considered false imprisonment, or whatever it's called."

"That's a big word for you, Bradley. We got a favor to ask. We need that storage room of yours," Warrix said.

Bradley went back to wiping the bar. "What do you need it for?"

Warrix leaned in closer. "They might have something to do with a murder. We got no other options right now. The three of us are hungry and tired. We can think better in the morning. Now how about it?"

"Well, if they are suspected of committing a murder then what would keep them from murdering me during the night?"

"Because Chaney and the four men with him are going to take turns standing guard," Bishop said. He was getting grouchy; an empty stomach will do that to a man.

The barkeep looked in the direction of Chaney and his men. "I don't know. None of you are lawmen and I feel like I'm breaking the law myself if I lock them men in the back."

Warrix reached in a pocket and pulled out his badge. He didn't pin it on, but he did show it to Bradley. "Does this help. I'm the marshal over in Dakota City. The bank over there was robbed a few days back and I've been chasing the men that did it ever since. I think those four had something to do with it. Maybe they didn't hold up the bank, but they are associated with the men that did. Now what's it gonna be?"

"Chaney and his men might do as they say. The only thing is they ain't ate and I sure can't furnish beer for that bunch, or food for that matter."

"What's eating got to do with watching that storage room all night?" Toler asked.

205

"After you three left Chaney came over and asked if I had any food. He said the four of them ain't had a bite since early yesterday. Said they would be willing to work for it. I got no work, and this is a saloon, not a diner. I couldn't help the four, even if I wanted to. Then Chaney said he was going to go to the general store and see if they had some scraps or something they were going to throw out. I wouldn't mention it, but I do have a soft spot for a man that's hungry. To ask them to guard those four all night knowing they ain't had a bite in over a day and a half seems unkind if you ask me."

Bishop looked at the five, Chaney and the men with him did look ready to start chewing on a chair. "You loan us the storage room for the prisoners, and I'll see that they get fed. By the way, is that their horses outside?"

"They are. I figure if they ain't got money for food then the horses are out of luck too. It's a shame to leave horses out of doors in weather like this," Bradley told the three.

Bishop motioned for Chaney to come over, he had a plan.

"You get everything figured out?" Chaney asked.

"We're working on it. When's the last time you and your friends have had anything to eat?" Bishop asked.

"Early yesterday. We're all flat broke. We ain't even got money to stable our horses," Chaney said.

"Tell you what. We'll see that you get food from the general store. We'll also send something over for the four prisoners, but it'll have to be something they can eat with their fingers, no forks and definitely no knives. You can untie them once they are safely in the storage room but keep a close watch.

"There's a livery at the end of the street that's not being used. The man that runs it is a real ass so you might have an argument, but I don't care. Tell him to wake his sorry ass up and take care of the horses. One of you might want to stay there tonight to make sure the horses are seen to. Tell him we'll settle up in the morning. Also, better take the four horses those men rode in on down there too. Can you see to all that?" Bishop asked. Warrix and Toler were impressed with the old man's organizational skills.

"I sure will. Won't take long at all to have all that done. You did say something about food being sent over."

"I did, now if you got everything under control then we're heading back to the store. We'll see to the food within the hour," Bishop said

With everything taken care of in the saloon the three headed back to the general store for their own supper. As they passed the hitch rail Bishop had another idea.

"Let's take the saddlebags and rifles from those four men's horses with us. No need to let that get taken to the livery. That sleepy bastard might go through the stuff and keep anything he likes," Bishop said. Again Warrix and Toler were impressed. The old man was a good manager, he seemed to always be thinking ahead.

Once inside all three were assaulted by the smell of elk stew. The smell was stronger than before. No doubt Becky Maddox was in the back heating everything up.

"Let's head back and see what we're having," Bishop said. The three each carried the saddlebags and Winchesters taken from the four horses tied up outside the general store.

The back of the general store had a flattop cook stove with an oven. There were five tables, each had four chairs. This looked like a regular restaurant, although smaller. There was even another lady back there. She was helping Becky cut up what looked like beef but was probably elk meat.

"Well I hope the three of you are hungry. This is the busy time of day for us, so we always have plenty. Just take a seat and we'll bring you a plate," Becky said.

Three of the five tables were occupied. In such a small town as Elkton this was probably as busy as it got. The three men took a spot nearest the stove hoping to warm a bit. They had spent most of the afternoon out of doors and the wind and cold was having an effect.

No sooner had they sat down than the two women brought three cups of coffee. "Got milk and sugar if you like that sort of thing," Becky said. She didn't hang around for an answer, she just went and got a small mug of milk and a small bowl of sugar.

No sooner had the three got their coffee the way they liked than three plates were put in front of them. "We serve the same thing to everyone. No one ever complains," Becky said as she hurried over and got a plate of cornbread.

"Does that look alright?" she asked as she stood back and looked the table over.

"This looks just fine. By the way, there's a bunch of men over at the saloon that need food. I believe there's about nine or ten. I'll be glad to pay if you could arrange to have it sent over," Bishop said.

"Be glad to, which saloon?"

"The Last Stop."

"It might be a while, but I think we can handle it. I'll get it ready and then Ed can take it over. Probably cornbread and smoked ham if you think that will do?"

"That will work just fine, but I'll warn you, those are some big men, and they haven't ate in a while. If you send extra I'm sure they won't mind."

Becky smiled. This was turning out to be a good day for business.

"Do you have enough money on you to cover that?" Toler asked. Even Warrix was starting to wonder how much cash the old man carried.

"I think I do but that will probably be the last of it. I can cover the food, stabling the horses, and a bunk for each of us, but that will probably do me in. I don't know how we'll survive until I make it back to the ranch," Bishop said.

The food sitting before them, and the aroma, soon brought the three back to the here and now. No one spoke as they ate. The meal consisted of the stew and cornbread, nothing more. The food was good and the coffee better. Hot coffee on a cold night really hit the spot. Once finished the three continued the conversation.

"How much money do you have, Toler?" Bishop asked.

"Only a dollar. I never carry more than a dollar because I never leave the ranch. What about you, Marshal?"

Warrix reached into a pocket and pulled out a crumpled bill and a few coins. "Looks like a buck fifty, that's it." The five twenty-dollar bills the mayor had given him was not in his pocket. It must have fallen out when he fell into the creek. A rifle and a hundred dollars, that was an expensive fall. Considering it could have cost him his life he figured he'd gotten off cheap.

The three sat in silence as they finished their coffee. Neither man knew how they were going to survive for the next few days until they made it back to the ranch. That was assuming they made it back at all. Finally Toler reached over and picked up one of the pairs of saddlebags.

He began going through the first bag as Bishop worked on making another smoke. The man usually only took one puff of a single cigarette a week, this was his second one tonight. Stress just seemed to have a way with a man's usual habits.

"What's this?" Toler said as he pulled a letter from the bag. He opened it and read. The look on his face was one of surprise. Once he finished he reached it to Bishop.

After finishing he looked at Warrix. "Looks like you got a price on your head, Marshal."

Warrix took the letter and quickly read what the other two already knew. Once finished he refolded the letter and put it back on the table.

"I need a drink. Maybe if Becky has that food ready I'll carry it to the saloon. Maybe the two of you would want to come along?"

"By the tone of that letter we better both come along if for nothing more than being bodyguards. Now why would somebody want you dead, Marshal?" Bishop asked.

Warrix took a last sip of his coffee before answering. "I left Dakota City a few days ago looking for some men that robbed the bank and killed a few people, one of them being my sister. I doubt anyone wants me dead because they fear I'll avenge her death. This has to be something to do with the attack on your ranch, Bishop. What I can't figure out is I'm just a small town marshal. Your ranch isn't even in my jurisdiction," Warrix said.

"Well, I don't know anything about that, but I do know any man who is worth a thousand dollars dead must have made someone mad. And that someone has some money to throw around. A thousand dollars ain't just walking around money," Bishop told the two.

As Bishop and Warrix debated the merits of the letter Toler was busy going through a second set of saddlebags. This pair didn't contain a letter but did contain something the three men had in short supply, money. Toler reached in and pulled out a wad of folded paper money. He tossed the cash in the center of the table as he looked at Bishop and Warrix.

Bishop, the man that would soon be out of cash quickly grabbed the loot and began to count. When finished he looked at the other two men.

"There's a little over four-hundred dollars here. Now why would those men be carrying that kind of money?" Bishop asked.

"My guess is they got paid half of the bounty on me up front. That would be five-hundred dollars. They probably spent a little along the way."

"Sounds about right. Sure wish we could use it for our own needs, but we can't, it doesn't belong to us and anyway, it's evidence," Warrix said.

"The hell it is. This is ill-gotten gains. Lest you forget, this is blood money meant to assure you get killed. We are going to use this money to help us get back to my ranch. And I'll tell you something else we're going to use, their guns," Bishop added.

"Why do we need their weapons? We all got guns," Toler asked.

"Because Chaney and his men don't have guns. He had four men with him, that makes five men that need weapons. The four men they are holding at the saloon forfeited their guns and cash if you ask me?" Bishop said. It was apparent the ranch owner was going to use everything the killers had if it helped him get back to his own ranch.

"I agree. Everything those four men own was going to be used in the process of committing a murder. And the murder was going to be personal for me," Warrix said with a slight chuckle.

"I got the food ready for the men at the saloon. Ed is ready to head that way now," Becky said.

"How much do we owe you, ma'am? I'd like to settle up for what we've had plus the food we're taking to the saloon. Ed won't need to go," Bishop said.

The woman quickly added the total on a sheet of paper. It was eight dollars and fifty cents. Bishop pealed ten dollars out of the wad of folded money and reached it to her. He felt the price was cheap, not much more than fifty cents apiece for the twelve men that benefited. Then again maybe Ed liked hunting elk. If that were the case then the general store was making a good profit. At least that's what he hoped.

"We'll need those guns we took off the four men earlier," Warrix told Ed as they were leaving.

With the food in a big pasteboard box, along with four Colts, a Derringer and four pairs of saddlebags the men headed for the Last Stop Saloon. The four horses were gone from the front of the general store, Chaney must be as good at management as Bishop, Warrix thought.

The three hurried to the saloon. Partly because they had a lot to carry and partly because of the weather. They found Chaney and two of his men sitting at a table.

"Where are your other men?" Bishop asked.

"They're tending to the horses. Nine horses are down at the livery. Cecil came back and said they would be down there for a spell. Said that old bastard at first wouldn't open the door. Told them to come back in the morning. Can you believe a man that runs a livery would turn down the business of nine horses?"

"We can believe it. You better keep at least one man down there tonight. If you don't that ornery bastard might just turn your horses loose," Toler said.

Warrix sat the big box on a table. "We brought the food we promised. There should be plenty. I'd have the man that's staying with the horses to eat at the livery. Don't turn your back on that liveryman."

"Thank you for the food. Me and the boys were starting to wonder if we'd ever eat again. One other thing, you know not a one of us has a gun. Old man Brewer didn't like firearms and wouldn't allow a man to carry one at the ranch. He had several in the house but that doesn't help us now."

Warrix reached into the box and removed the four Colts they'd confiscated from the prisoners back at the general store. He also took out the Derringer. He never considered the hideaway before but had to admit, it would be better than nothing.

"Here's five guns. Take the gun belts from the four men in the back. There should be extra ammunition in the loops. You and your men are welcome to wear their belts and carry their guns, but you'll have to give them back when this is over," Warrix told Chaney.

"That won't be a problem. We'll gladly turn them back over to you. If we make it back to Brewer's ranch then we can gather our gear. We all own guns but kept them locked up in a closet in the bunkhouse. I suppose the five of us will be looking for work now since they killed Brewer. For the life of me I can't figure out why they did it, Brewer was a good man. He always treated us kindly."

"Why don't you and the rest of your men eat first. Then you can feed the prisoners," Bishop told Chaney. Once this was all over, assuming they lived through it, he might consider hiring Chaney and his four men to replace some of the wranglers he'd lost to Rumford. Time would tell.

"I'm going for that beer I promised myself. I reckon you're buying," Warrix said as he looked at Bishop.

As they headed for the bar they noticed that the three cardplayers had vacated the place. Now where could they have gone? The only place in Elkton with a spare bed was over at the general store. No matter, if they froze then it was their own fault.

Bradley served what the men wanted to drink. He was a bit surprised to see them again this late in the evening. "Did you get situated over at the general store?"

"We did. Ed and Becky seem to be real nice people. Are you going to be alright staying here all night?" Warrix asked.

"Yep, I've stayed all night before. As a matter of fact I stay here every night. I got a room off to the end of the bar with my gear. Got a nice bunk in there too. It gets a little chilly, but I don't mind. I sleep better when it's cold. Just so long as Chaney don't drink me out of business I should be alright. What do you three plan on doing come morning?"

"Don't know really. We got men after us, men with guns and probably a rope with a noose on the end. We got men between here and where we need to be too. Between the ones chasing us and the ones blocking our way I don't know what to do," Bishop said. He took a long pull on his beer as he considered what he'd just said. The beer might help numb his already tired brain.

"You're more than welcome to stay in Elkton," Bradley said.

"That's a nice offer but we can't stay. Whoever's chasing us will be here before long. The four you got in your storage room are proof of that. Naw, I reckon we'll be heading out first thing in the morning. We got business to tend to," Bishop said before finishing his beer.

"If you pull out in the morning then what happens to the men you got locked up in my storage room?" Bradley asked.

"We're taking them with us. Wouldn't be right to leave the four here in Elkton," Warrix said.

Just then Chaney walked over. He'd finished his food and looked like a new man although the smell was still the same.

"What do we do with them in the morning?" he asked as he pointed at the storage room.

"We're taking them with us," Toler said.

"No offence, but I don't think that would be a good idea. There's only three of you and as a rule of thumb you never transport when outnumbered."

"Now how did you know that?" Warrix asked.

"I used to be a small town deputy a few years back. Had that job for three years. I'd still be there but they appointed a new marshal and the new one wanted one of his brothers to have my job. After that I wandered a bit before landing at the Brewer place."

The fact that Chaney had once been a lawman went a long way with the marshal. "Since you brought it up how would you and your men like to come along. We could use the help. I can't promise any pay, but I can promise food."

"Food will suit the five of us just fine. What time do you want to head out?" Chaney asked.

"Sort of depends on the weather. We'll know more at first light," Warrix told him.

"Which way we heading?"

"Again, I'd rather wait until first light to make that decision. Right now we're at the mercy of the weather and the men who killed Brewer. We don't know how many are involved in this but I'm sure we'll find out," Warrix said. He had shared more than he wanted to. He still needed to trust Chaney and his men. He didn't know the five, but it looked like they would be working together until something changed. If trouble was out there waiting then the extra manpower would come in handy.

"Alright then, me and the boys will try to get some rest. Whenever you're ready in the morning we'll be ready. I better head down to the livery and take those two some grub. See you in the morning," Chaney said as he picked up what food was left and headed out the door.

"That only leaves two men here to guard the prisoners," Toler said.

"Three," Bradley said as he held up his shotgun. "As long as I got this I don't think there's anything to worry about."

Bishop paid for the beer and the three headed back to the general store.

Ed came over after the three walked in and asked if they needed anything else from the store. He said he and Becky were ready to close.

"Just show us where the bunk room is," Bishop said.

"You've already been there, it's the stable out back."

All three men just looked at each other. None of the three expected to be staying in a barn but that's what it was now looking like.

Ed could tell they were confused. "Before you go getting the wrong idea let me explain. Once inside the barn there's a door to the left. Inside you'll find a potbellied stove and bunks. No one else is staying there tonight so you'll have to light the stove. There's two lanterns for light. It sounds rough but it ain't that bad. I know that for a fact because a few months back Becky took a fit on me. I spent three nights out there myself." Ed leaned in as to not be heard by his wife. "To tell you the truth I felt it was an upgrade," he said as he turned and walked away, laughing as he went.

The three went out the front door and down the alley beside the store. All three felt like they'd been misled. Suddenly they found themselves heading for a barn, it was quite a letdown. Each would have preferred a hotel, but it was what it was. Still though it was better than camping out in the open on a night like this, but not by much.

After entering the main hall of the barn they latched the door from the inside, no need for the rock they'd been told to use earlier. Once inside the barn they found the door Ed spoke of. They opened it and stepped inside. It was really dark in the stable, so a match had to be used. The bunkroom was just as Ed described. In the center of the room was a potbellied stove and along two walls were bunks. Once the two lanterns were lit the men got a better look at their new lodgings.

The room was tight, no drafts could be felt and as windy as it was outside any opening would have made the room breezy. The bunks looked solid, and each had a neat stack of two blankets along with a pillow. The room was as clean as any hotel room the three had ever stayed in. By the looks of things Becky kept the bunkroom neat and orderly. It was a pleasant surprise.

There was a crate of kindling and a stack of freshly split firewood nearby. Ten minutes later and the fire was lit and starting to chase away the chill. All three men quickly turned in. It had been a long day, a hard day.

Bishop was the first up the next morning. He was an early riser, a habit he'd practiced all his life. He checked his pocket watch, it was five-fifteen. The room was probably as cold as it was outside. All three men had been so tired that no one woke during the night to fuel the fire. Bishop quickly relit the stove and looked around. On a shelf nearby was a coffeepot and a bag of Arbuckle coffee. The only problem was water but when he checked the pot he found it to be full. Apparently Ed and Becky filled it each evening when they had men staying. When he opened the lid and dumped in the coffee it landed on ice, the water was frozen solid. At least now he knew the temperature in the room was below freezing.

Once on the stove the heat did its job. It took longer than normal to get the coffee boiling. The aroma took to the air even before all the ice had melted. Bishop didn't mind the wait. He was happy that they had the bunkroom and just as happy with the coffeepot.

The smell of fresh coffee soon brought Toler and Warrix back to life. Both men grabbed a tin cup, and each filled it to the brim. One pleasant surprise was a covered porcelain bowl that contained sugar. There was no cream but still, coffee and sugar was better than a drink of ice water.

"You're up early," Toler told his boss.

"This is late for me, you know that. Back at the ranch did you ever know me to sleep past five?"

"I don't really know but I would suppose not. One thing I do know is when I walked out of the bunkroom every morning you were nowhere to be seen. I suppose work starts earlier on the ranch than in the ranch house," Toler said with a grin. He wasn't above jousting with his boss from time to time.

"You know, Toler, I'd say you're right. But I still get up before everyone else. We make it back to the ranch I promise to start banging on the bunkhouse door at five every morning," Bishop said. Toler regretted the challenge, he liked to sleep until six each morning. Maybe his boss would forget this conversation once they made it back to the ranch.

"Let's grab our stuff and see if the store is open. Maybe Becky gets up early and serves breakfast," Warrix said. He was steering the conversation away from who woke first before the two men started swinging fists at each other.

Warrix was deep in thought as his two companions bantered between each other. Only a few days earlier he'd been a small town marshal living and working day to day for the benefit of Dakota City and its inhabitants.

Now he was miles from home dealing with one problem after another. He'd started out looking for the men that had robbed the town's bank and killed four innocent people, one of which was his sister Mae.

He hated to admit it to himself, but his main concern was bringing the men to justice for the murders they'd committed. The robbery of the bank might just put that institution out of business and that would be bad for the town, but the crime of murder made anything to do with a bank fall to a distant second. If for no reason other than to avenge his sister's death he would bring the men responsible to justice, and hopefully a rope.

The three wondered if the general store would even be open at such an early hour? When Bishop turned the doorknob his question was answered. The smell inside the store told the three that Becky and the other woman that helped her were busy at the cookstove. The smell didn't really say breakfast though. It smelled more of stew again.

"Good morning. How did the bunkroom suit the three of you?" Ed asked. He was behind the counter counting what looked like bolts and nuts. His fingers were oily black from the film that covered the bolts.

"It was way better than we expected. You have to admit that anything attached to a barn don't give a very good first impression. But it was nicer than some of the other places I've stayed while traveling," Bishop said. Again the man was being diplomatic. Nicer than a bunk in a barn left a lot of leeway.

"Glad you liked it. Becky keeps it clean and fills the coffee pot with water each day."

"Thanks for that. I always like coffee when I get up. I like breakfast too if that's available?" Bishop said.

"The gals serve breakfast every morning. That is if you like stew for breakfast. Elk stew today," Ed said. After a moment's thought he added, "It's actually Elk stew every day. I never really thought of it that way before. Hope you like stew."

"Stew will do just fine. If it's the same recipe as last night then that'll be great," Bishop said. The man must really like stew.

"Just head on back and grab a table. Stew should be about ready. The only difference with the morning meal is instead of cornbread they have cathead biscuits," Ed told the three.

The mention of biscuits almost made Bishop run to the back. The man was hungry. All three took a seat at the same table.

"Good to see you three back this morning. Are you interested in some breakfast or just coffee?" Becky asked the men as she checked the coffeepot.

"We'll have both if that's alright. And would it be possible to fix another box of food for the men at the saloon? After we eat I can walk it over to save your husband the trouble," Bishop said. Toler knew when his boss said he would walk it over he really meant Toler would walk it over.

"Be glad to. It'll be smoked ham and biscuits if that works? How many are we preparing for?"

"Same as last night, nine."

The three quickly ate and Bishop paid. The box for the saloon was ready by the time they were finished eating. Before leaving Bishop bought two boxes of forty-four Colt and two boxes of Winchester cartridges. The money they'd found in the saddlebags was coming in real handy.

As the three exited the general store they saw two riders coming into town from the north. The two looked well suited for traveling in such frigid weather. They both wore robes of what looked like buffalo hide. The only thing showing was their eyes.

"Looks like those two got an early start. It's only been daylight for a few minutes. I believe if I was this close to a town I'd have come on in last night," Bishop said.

Toler and Warrix were wary. Arriving in town this early on such a morning wasn't a normal occurrence. They were across the street and ready to enter the Last Chance Saloon when one of the two riders gave a shout.

"You there, stop and give us some information," the man shouted.

Both Warrix and Toler felt this wasn't going to be just a question about directions. Toler reached the box he'd been carrying to Bishop.

"Take this on in, boss. I'll stay out here with the marshal until we figure out what these two want," Toler said.

Bishop was glad to oblige. The wind and snow made him crave another beer; it wasn't even eight in the morning.

Warrix and Toler turned to face the two riders. As they waited they took in the sight. The two men rode stout looking horses but didn't have a packhorse which meant they were traveling from town to town. Both had rifles, probably Winchesters, slung across their saddle horns. This hadn't been evident from a distance because the buffalo robes the two wore hid most of the guns from view. It was evident the two weren't trappers, they were nearly clean shaven. Warrix and Toler had a bad feeling about this. All they could do was wait.

"What's the matter, your friend need a drink so bad that he couldn't hang around to answer a few questions?" one of the riders asked.

Warrix had his hand near his gun, as did Toler.

"We stopped because we thought you might need to know something like where the town marshal is or maybe the county sheriff," Toler said. He could be a real smartass when he wanted to be. This was one of those times.

"Naw friend, we ain't looking for the law. We're looking for four of our friends that said they'd be in Elkton waiting for us. You seen 'em around?"

"Nope," Warrix said.

"Well if you ain't a man of few words. If you ain't seen 'em then what have you seen?"

"If you ain't got anything of importance to ask then we're going inside. You two have a good day," Toler said.

Before either man could take a step both riders quickly raised their Winchesters. "We ain't done talking to you. Now stay put until we're finished. You look smart enough to know what a Winchester will do to a man at this distance."

Warrix and Toler didn't expect such treatment from two complete strangers. Neither man was prepared for this. The look on the two rider's faces told the story that they had the advantage and wouldn't hesitate to pull the trigger on their rifles if pushed. The marshal wondered if the two knew who he was? He wasn't wearing his badge and it probably saved his life. If these two were with the four men they had locked up in the saloon's storage room then they were probably after the bounty too.

"Hold your hands up where we can see 'em. Don't try anything. We know this town ain't got no law, right now me and Slick are the law."

Warrix and Toler did as they were told, both raised their arms slowly knowing any chance of a quick shot in self-defense was now out of the question.

"That one on the right looks like the one that's got the bounty on his head. You remember what the boss told us?"

The one named Slick looked at Warrix. He did fit the description. "What's your name, mister?"

Warrix knew if he gave his name then he was a dead man. As he was trying to think of an alias the front window of the saloon came crashing out, glass flying in every direction. One of the two riders, the one called Slick, raised his gun but before he could fire there was a gunshot. The man was knocked from his horse and in doing so he spooked the second horse. Either from the first man falling or from the gunshot the other horse reared, the rider falling to the ground.

Warrix and Toler had their guns out and were ready to shoot at either man if needed. The first man that was shot lay still. The second rolled to his feet and looked for his Winchester. He didn't find his gun, but he did find two Colts being aimed at him. Now he was the one raising his hands.

"Better check both and see if they got handguns, Toler. I'll keep them covered, just in case," Warrix said.

Toler quickly searched the two men. He found a Colt on the one named Slick and an old Remington on the other man. While searching he noticed the wounded man wasn't dead, he moaned but didn't seem to have enough steam to get to his feet.

As Toler was searching Chaney stuck his head through the broken window. "Did I get him?"

Warrix figured the man had probably saved his life. "You did, Chaney. You did at that. Can a couple of you come out here and lend us a hand?"

Chaney and one of his friends stepped out, both looked to be eating a biscuit. "You know these two, Marshal?"

When Chaney called Warrix by the title of marshal it got the full attention of the rider that hadn't been shot. He didn't say anything but the look on his face told the story, he was looking for the marshal.

"Let's get these two inside. That one you shot don't look so good," Warrix said.

"I reckon not, Marshal. I was going to shoot him in the head but decided you might want some information from him before we hang him," Chaney said. What was it with Chaney, did he just like torturing people with talk of hanging?

When the wounded man heard what Chaney said he came alive. He wasn't hurt all that bad but had been faking it in order to maybe get the drop on someone.

"Why you done shot me and now you say you're going to hang me. I want to see a lawman, and I mean right now. You bastards try to hang me then the law will avenge my death," the man named Slick shouted. He was on his feet now and for all intents and purposes didn't look hurt at all.

"Shut your damn mouth before I introduce you to that big tree down by the livery," Chaney said. The man had a mean streak, at least when it came to lawbreakers.

With the help of Chaney and another of his men the two riders were soon seated inside the saloon. The air had grown crisp due to the missing window. Bradley was at the saloon, which was to be expected, after all the man said he had a side room where he stayed.

"Sorry about your window, Bradley. You got anything around to seal it up with?" Bishop asked.

"Sure do, got a brand new piece of glass out back. Damn thing gets broken out at least every other month. The man that owns this place said it's easier to keep a spare than to have to shut down until another pane is delivered. If I can get someone to help me clear the broken shards and remove the stops I'll have it fixed in no time."

Chaney had the same man that helped bring the two riders in to help Bradley. If Chaney felt bad about knocking the window out he didn't show it. He did say he was a little upset about having to throw his mug of beer out though. Warrix promised to buy him another, that seemed to cheer the man up. The marshal figured since Chaney had probably saved his life the least he could do was buy him another beer, even if it was only eight-thirty in the morning.

With Chaney holding a fresh beer and Bradley busy repairing the window Warrix figured it was time to get some information out of these two. Before he could ask anything though the wounded man started complaining.

"Has this piece of shit town got a doctor? That bastard drinking beer done shot me. I want to see a marshal too. He shot me for no reason," Slick protested.

Warrix stomped over and grabbed the man by the collar of his buffalo robe and nearly raised him out of his chair. "Let me tell you something you drygulching bastard. You and your friend were going to shoot me if you thought I was the man you're looking for. Now anymore talk of your innocence will affect whether you see a doctor or not. Now keep your mouth shut unless you're told to speak." The man decided he wanted to be quiet.

Bishop had sat watching everything since bringing in the box of food. He was considering the situation at hand. There were now six men that needed to be guarded and at some point taken to a town with a jail. He knew a jail was at least a couple days ride from Elkton. Not a pleasant thought of trying to guard six men while traveling, especially when you considered at least one overnight stay.

"Chaney, can you keep an eye on our two newest friends while me and the marshal step outside?" Bishop asked. Chaney quickly agreed as the marshal and Bishop headed toward the door. Toler went too.

Once outside they quickly collected the reins of the two horses. It was seven wonders both hadn't taken off. They looked like they wanted a stall and possibly some feed. Maybe that's why they were hanging around.

"What do you plan to do, Marshal? I don't fancy our chances trying to escort that many men to a town with a proper jail. I also know we can't stay here and guard them," Bishop said.

Warrix had been wondering the same thing. "I agree. We need to be getting back to that ranch of yours. At least we'll be better protected there. You got a few men left that still ride for the brand. The problem is getting there in one piece."

"How many men can we still trust?" Bishop asked Toler.

"Four I know of. One man is injured and might even be dead by now. Plus I'd count your sister and sister in law. They got spunk. Anyone that attacks the ranch house will be met with hot lead and cold hearts."

"Do you think we can trust Chaney and his four men to stay and guard the six prisoners? It know it's asking a lot to be that trusting of a complete stranger, but our options are limited," Bishop asked the marshal.

Warrix considered the question. One thing that put his mind at ease was the fact that Chaney had just saved his life. If you are going to trust someone then a man like that is a good place to start.

"What arrangements can we make for feeding that bunch? And I really don't trust that storage room to hold that many men. Plus they will need to be led one at a time to the privy. If they get the jump on Chaney or any of his men then there could be a lot of killing before things are got under control," Warrix said as much to himself as to the other two men.

"You think there's another building in this town that's made of stone or something a little more sturdy than clapboard?" Toler asked.

That gave Warrix an idea. "Tell you what. Can you take these two horses down to the livery and turn them over to Chaney's men. Me and Bishop are going to the general store and see if Ed has any ideas. He's been here long enough, he'll know this town inside out," Warrix said.

As Toler started toward the livery leading the two horses he thought of something. "Say, Marshal, you think I should bring back these saddlebags? There might be something in there similar to what we found last night."

"That's good thinking. We'll meet you back here in fifteen or twenty minutes."

Bernard Rumford arrived at the Brewer Ranch only a couple of hours after the dramatic rescue of Ralph Bishop. The men that managed to allow his escape weren't all that worried, they'd have him back by evening. They knew which way they were heading; it was toward a town called Elkton.

One of the men that guarded the ranch had been scouting about three miles away that morning when three riders came past. They didn't see him as they rode by. Donald Clark watched from the tree line, taking in everything about the three riders. Clark thought nothing of three strangers heading toward Elkton, at least not at first.

As Clark rode back to the Brewer Ranch he kept thinking. The horses the men rode looked familiar, but the markings of any particular horse weren't exclusive. Hundreds of horses, if not thousands, might have the same blaze or markings. As he rode he kept playing that scene back in his head.

By the time Clark made it back to the ranch he was almost certain that one of the men he'd seen was Bishop. He kept telling himself though that when he arrived he would hear the news that there was no news. As he tied his horse in front of the house one of the other men came out and told him what happened. Several of the other hands were still trying to round up the horses that had been set loose during the escape.

Clark figured as much. Some of the men that had signed on with Rumford weren't all that capable, or all that smart. As he walked into the kitchen he found four men sitting at the table drinking coffee. When the four saw Clark each knew trouble was about to visit, Clark was the man in charge of this bunch of hired killers.

"So you managed to let Bishop escape," Clark said to no one in particular as he headed for the coffeepot.

"Not exactly, he had help," one of the men at the table said.

"The way you say that must mean that because he had help then it don't count. When Mr. Rumford gets here in a few hours maybe you would like to share that little piece of information with him," Clark said as he sat the empty coffeepot back on the stove.

"I ride scout this morning and come back to find the prisoner gone and the coffeepot empty," Clark said. He turned from the stove and looked at the men sitting at the table. "And you four sitting here drinking coffee and too stupid to even refill the pot."

The four men in the kitchen weren't stupid, they were lazy. Most killers were. They lived by the gun and would most likely die by the gun. One thing that was certain about the four, none were cowards. One stood and sat his cup on the table.

"I don't have to listen to your mouth this morning, Clark. You been ramrodding this outfit for what, three days now. Don't come in here insulting me or you might find yourself facing a gun," the man said.

Clark held his empty coffeecup in his right hand and every man in the room knew he was right handed, that's the side he wore his gun on. As the four watched they fully expecting Clark to back down, he didn't. Clark, without ever releasing his grip on the coffeecup, reached across with his left hand and drew his gun. As it cleared the holster he flipped it around to face the man standing in front of him. It all happened so fast that no one moved, they didn't take a breath either.

"You were saying?" Clark asked the man who had initially gone for his gun but was outdrawn by a man using his left hand.

The would-be shootist slowly eased his hand farther away from his holstered gun. He didn't want anything to do with Clark after what he just witnessed.

"I still mean what I said. Just because you pulled some fancy circus stunt don't mean I'm afraid of you," the man said, his voice a bit unsteady.

Clark walked over and took the man's gun. After what he'd just heard he didn't want to be the victim of a backshooting.

"You got exactly ten minutes to get off the ranch. If I find you here after the ten minutes are up then I'll give you back your gun and we can finish this little conversation, man to man," Clark told him.

"And if I do leave how do I get my gun back?"

"You don't. If you want this gun back then my offer still stands. At the ten minute mark if you're still around I'll give you your gun, but you know what happens after that."

The man didn't need to think about this offer very long. He would leave. As he turned to walk out of the kitchen one of the other men at the table laughed at him. This was more than the gunman could stand. He reached down and pulled the gun from the laughing man's holster and turned on Clark. This was expected because Clark drew at the same time, maybe just a little faster because the gunshot everyone heard came from Clark's gun.

"Carry him out of here. You can bury him now and then come back for breakfast," Clark said as he holstered his gun.

"And someone fill that coffeepot. Rumford is supposed to be here this morning and he might like a cup."

The three men seated at the table got to their feet. No one wanted to mess with Clark after the exhibition he'd just put on. As for Clark, he really didn't want to kill the man. If he'd simply walked out and rode off then he would have still been alive. As it was Clark was now short a man. He still had plenty more but that did little to soothe his conscious.

Clark had killed before but never murdered. Every man he'd shot had given him no choice. It was either *kill or be killed* as the old saying goes. Clark didn't consider himself a killer. Killers did just that, killed regardless of the reason. That was the difference. Clark only killed to keep from being killed himself. This thought did little to take away from the fact that his abilities with a Colt had again resulted in the need for another grave to be dug.

With all three men in the process of taking care of the burial, Clark decided to tend to the coffeepot himself. He liked coffee, he also liked it heavily medicated. The recipe he liked was one half cup of coffee filled on up with cream and sugar. He liked it sweet, and he liked it milky. Instead of black the brew actually looked like weak hot chocolate.

Once his cup was filled he walked to the front door and took a seat on the big front porch. The man Rumford was coming to see had managed to escape this very morning. That wasn't going to go over well. Maybe Clark would lay the blame at the feet of the man that was being buried at that very moment. That might work. Easy to blame someone dead, they rarely protested their innocence. Clark drained his cup and stood. In the distance he heard a horse, several horses. He assumed it would be Rumford, he was correct.

Bernard Rumford had arrived on the train that very morning. The nearest depot, the one he always used, was in Fenton. Rumford was tired and a bit grouchy due to being cooped up in a passenger car for the past twelve hours. Prior to that he'd used Pullmans, that service ended earlier, and he was reduced to traveling like everyone else, in a regular passenger car.

Waiting for him at the depot was a horse and buggy driven by one of the few men he trusted, Eugene Beckett. The two had known each other for years. Beckett had been in the employment of Rumford for nearly as long as the two had known each other. Beckett was a little embarrassed to be driving a buggy but it's what his boss wanted. He supposed if he'd been traveling by train as long as his boss then he would have wanted something other than a horse himself.

After gathering Rumford's luggage and stowing in in the back the two climbed aboard and headed toward the Brewer Ranch. The ride would take a good five hours. Five hours would be about the limit of the horse's endurance without a good rest. It was a light buggy but still quite a chore for a single horse.

The only thing on Rumford's mind at the moment was making it to his final destination and getting some rest. He'd kept up with events by way of the telegraph but still his news wasn't as fresh as he preferred. Once at the ranch he wanted to be brought up to date on everything since the bank holdup in Dakota City. If all had gone according to plan then he'd force Ralph Bishop to transfer ownership of the Box W over to him.

The deal would be something Bishop could hardly refuse. He'd be paid with his own money, money that Rumford had been stealing for years by shorting the proceeds from the cattle drives. Also from the stock his men had been rustling from the

Box W. After so many years of scheming and planning Rumford's plans were nearly complete.

The strange thing about what Rumford was planning was that he really didn't consider himself a thief and surely not a murderer. He was buying a ranch that the old man was probably going to lose in a few years anyway. Bishop was even going to come out of this with a little money to boot. Now who could argue that this wasn't a sweet deal for the ranch owner. He could move and take his sister and sister in law away from the harshness of the territory.

As Rumford and Beckett rode he kept telling himself that he was doing Bishop a favor. The old man could travel south and enjoy the remainder of his days in a milder climate. He'd have enough money to buy a small ranch and continue what he'd been doing without any worries.

As far as the men that had been killed that was just part of doing business. He would have considered the men, and the woman, that had been killed but he was unaware of the death of Mae Fuller. He was also unaware of the fact that she was the marshal's sister.

Rumford considered his station in life was about to get a substantial boast with the acquisition of the Box W Ranch. Once he was owner the rustling could be stopped. With no more rustling and no more skimming of cattle drive proceeds the ranch was going to be a gold mine. Bishop had only been scrapping by because of the theft of a portion of his cash from each drive and also the rustling that was taking place. The ranch would now be profitable beyond belief.

The ride to the Brewer Ranch was mostly a quiet one, neither man said more than they had too. Beckett was naturally a quiet man; Rumford had a lot on his mind. When the journey first started Beckett filled Rumford in on what he knew, which wasn't much.

One of the two men Rumford needed to talk to was Heith Bryson, the leader of the men that had killed the miners and robbed the bank in Dakota City. The other was Bradley Allen, the man that recruited the ranch hands away from the Bishop Ranch. Both men had valuable information on how things were going. The few telegrams Rumford received during his journey west were nothing more than morsels of information.

By noon the buggy was within a mile of the ranch. Two riders on horseback challenged Rumford and Beckett, not knowing who either man was. Rather than explain himself to these two underlings Rumford asked to be escorted to the main ranch house where his identity could be verified. That was allowed by the two men on horseback. Rumford didn't know whether to cut the two down a notch or complement them on their caution. He decided to do neither, why heap scorn, or praise, on men he didn't know.

Once at the house the two men were met by Donald Clark. He and Beckett unloaded the buggy while Rumford looked the place over. The house was nice, at least nice in a backwoods sort of way. The Bishop place was much nicer. Rumford had been to the Bishop Ranch, but this was his first visit to the Brewer place.

"Any problems?" Rumford asked fully expecting to hear of none. He was anxious to have his talk with Heith Bryson and learn how much money had been taken from the bank at Dakota City. He was also anxious to talk to Ralph Bishop to tell him how his ranch was about to be taken over.

"We've heard nothing from Bryson, not a word. But that's not the worst of it. Some men came here at first light and managed to release Ralph Bishop. We know where they're heading. I've sent men there to take care of the two interlopers and bring Bishop back," Clark said.

Rumford was stunned. The man he needed to deal with was gone and the money he intended to use was also gone.

"Bryson should have been here days ago. What about the three men with him, have any of them showed up?"

"Not a one," Clark said.

"What about Bishop, how did you and your men allow him to escape?"

Clark expected as much. The men he had were dependable, but no one expected anyone to show up and rescue Bishop from the barn. How the two slipped in unnoticed was anyone's guess, probably just luck was Clark's hunch.

"We had him secured in the barn. The problem was that barn is old and they managed to pry off a few boards. I should have anticipated that but didn't. I've sent six men toward a town called Elkton. They should find him there and bring him back. In this weather I doubt he'd make it far." Clark didn't mention that he was the one that saw the three as they rode toward Elkton. That little bit of information would never be shared.

"Well, he better be brought back. Everything depends on him seeing the wisdom of signing over the deed to the Box W to me. All I've worked for these past few years is in jeopardy because someone pried off a few boards. What are you doing about Heith Bryson? He's got my money. If he has plans of double crossing me then he's a dead man."

"I've got eight men out looking for him. That's one of the reasons Bishop was able to get away, we just didn't have enough men. When we find him what do you want done?" Clark asked.

Rumford had to think that one through. If Bryson had stashed the money somewhere and one of Clark's men killed him then the money might never be found. There were thousands of acres where he could have stashed it.

"No harm comes to Bryson, bring him to me," Rumford said.

"I'll get the word out. Why don't you get situated in the house, we saved the master bedroom for you. It was old man Brewer's room," Clark said. He hoped if Rumford got a little rest he might be able to think straight. Right now the way things were going everyone needed to think straight.

"How far away is this town you called Elkton?" Rumford asked.

"Maybe fifteen miles."

"And how many men have you got here?"

Clark thought of the man they had shot and buried earlier; he could probably use that man about now. "Six counting me."

"Pick out three and send them to Elkton. I need Bishop brought back safely. That will still leave four of us here. With no one to guard surely the four of us will be safe," Rumford said.

"I'll have three men saddle horses and head out. This late in the day it'll probably be dark by the time they get there. If they find him I strongly suggest they don't try coming back tonight. The weather's bad and who knows if Bishop has other friends out looking for him."

Rumford knew Clark was right. "That will work. Once they find him keep him safe and head back at first light."

Rumford turned and headed inside. The man was tired, too tired to think of food or even coffee for that matter.

Warrix went to the general store. He wanted to talk to Ed and Becky. Maybe they knew of a better place in town where the prisoners could be kept.

"Well howdy, Marshal. We figured you would be gone by now," Ed said when Warrix walked in.

"We've had a development. A couple of men came to town and started a little trouble. I think they are associated with the four we tangled with in here last night."

"I heard a couple of gunshots but didn't think much of it. That saloon manages to have a gun go off every couple of days. Mostly it's men firing off a round just for the fun of it. Did anyone get hurt?"

"One man caught a bullet. I think he'll be alright. Say, that old storage room in the back of the Last Stop isn't very sturdy. You wouldn't know of a building in town that's made of stone or some sort of masonry?"

It only took Ed a second to give an answer. "The old post office. It's made of stone and still got a good roof. The government saw fit to build a new post office a couple of years ago, it's stone too. The old one was too small, not that it wasn't big enough for Elkton. The problem was that the mail for the surrounding territory comes through Elkton and the old building was just too cramped."

"Anyway I can see it?" Warrix asked.

"You sure can, it belongs to me. I bought it just after they opened the new one. Got it for a song. Still don't know what I'm going to do with it."

Ed grabbed his coat and a key from the back of the counter. "Let's go, Marshal. I've been meaning to check on it for a day or two now, this will give me a reason."

Ed and Warrix turned right after leaving the general store. The old post office was only a couple hundred feet down the street, but it sat back a ways. The building looked sturdy; it didn't even look that old. Once inside Warrix was impressed. There was a foyer type area where folks waited. The counter was small and just behind that was where the mail was brought in and sorted. This room was separate from the rest of the space. There wasn't a back door, all the mail must have been brought through the front. The door that led from the sorting room was separated from the counter and foyer by a solid door, it was actually a metal door.

"This would work a lot better than that storage room. Would you let us use it for a few days until we can make arrangements to have those men escorted to the nearest town that has a jail and a courthouse? The territory has a wagon they use to transport prisoners. I believe it's simply called the prison wagon. I don't know for sure, but I believe you can be reimbursed by the territory for your troubles."

"Marshal, whether I get paid or not is a matter for another day. If you can use this to keep folks safe then by all means you can use the building. I'm not turning down any compensation for the use of it but whether I see any money or not won't stop you from having use of this old building," Ed told him.

"There's another thing. We now have six men that need to be housed here. Chaney and his four men, the ones that'll be doing the guarding, make eleven men. They will all need to be fed. Bishop has some money and will pay what he can. Once this is all over he can see to it that the tab is paid for the food. Will that be alright with you?"

Again Ed said he didn't mind. He was a law and order man and would do his part to see that justice was served. He reached the key for the old post office to Warrix, and the two men left.

The saloon was just the way the marshal had left it. The two newcomers were still seated near the broken window, a window that had now been repaired. Bishop stood and met the marshal halfway across the room.

"Has either of them said anything useful?" Warrix asked.

"Said they're working for a man by the name of Donald Clark. Said they were sent from the Brewer Ranch to apprehend me and bring me back," Bishop said.

"That was a lot of information to give up without a fight," Warrix said as he looked at the two, they were looking back at him.

"The man that got shot by Chaney seems to be in a talkative mood. He wants a doctor and probably needs one. That other one told him to shut up or Clark would see him killed. The injured one, I believe his name is Slick, didn't stop talking. He's in pain."

"Does this town even have a doctor? If there is a doctor in Elkton then he should probably be sent for. While I was gone I found us a building much better suited for holding prisoners. It's the old post office building. The couple over at the general store own it. Ed said for us to use it, the man wants to do his part."

"Well, I believe anything is better than the store room we're using now. It's one step above a tent if you ask me," Bishop said.

"Let's get everyone ready. I want all six moved before anything else happens," Warrix said. "Tie the hands of all six behind their backs. There'll be eight of us guarding them along the way. Chaney and his four men can lead and the three of us will follow. We'll carry as many Winchesters as we've got. Maybe one of you could also borrow that Greener from Bradley."

An hour later and all six men had been safely moved to the other building. Slick complained the entire time. A doctor had been sent for; he wasn't really a doctor, but Slick would never know it. The man worked on horses and cows. This, he said, was his first human. Warrix thought giving a couple of the men that designation was being generous.

"This will work nicely," Bishop said as he scouted the small building. "That metal door was a stroke of luck, and the building only has those two small windows back where the prisoners will be kept. The only drawback is the two windows in that front room. They would give anyone outside with a rifle a clear line of sight. The front door is the only door in the building, that's both good and bad. Only one door to defend is the good part, the only way out is the bad part. All in all though it's a welcome improvement over the storage room in the back of the Last Stop Saloon."

Chaney came from the back after seeing to the prisoners. "I don't think we ought to start a fire in that stove back there. I don't know what kind of mischief those men could cause with a lit stove but I'm sure they would try something. We'll keep the fire out front going and maybe a little heat will make it back there, I really don't care. What I do care about is coffee and that old flattop stove in the front room can supply that, as long as we get our hands on a pot, and some coffee, and maybe some cream."

"Ed over at the general store is going to run a tab on the food and what few supplies you might need while we're gone. Head over there now and grab the fixings for coffee. You and your men will be given two meals a day, same goes for the six prisoners. Try to keep it light though, I'm not sure where the money's coming from to cover all this," Warrix told the man.

After leaving the town of Elkton's newest jail Warrix headed for the barn behind the store. He and Toler saddled the three horses while Bishop reached over two-hundred dollars of the money he'd found in the saddlebags the night before.

"Here you go, Ed. This might seem like I'm shorting you on the payment, but I promise I'm good for it. As soon as I get this business settled with the bastards that are causing all the trouble I promise to be back and settle in full. You got eleven men that need food twice a day. We are leaving Chaney in charge, whatever he needs, within reason, I'd like you to see to it," Bishop said. It dawned on him that he'd used bad language in the presence of Becky. "My apologies ma'am."

Becky chuckled, "No apologies needed Mr. Bishop. That's the same bastards that tried to rough up Ed." All three laughed.

"Do you think it's wise to be heading out this late in the day. You won't have much daylight left to travel in," Ed said.

"Me and the marshal discussed it. The problem is we are running out of time. If anyone comes in here asking about me or the other two I'd appreciate it if you didn't say anything."

"Don't you worry, Mr. Bishop. Me and Ed will be as quiet as church mice," Becky said.

Bishop said his thanks and then headed out back to the barn. He found the marshal and Toler leading the three horses from the barn, all three were saddled and looked ready to hit the trail.

"I got everything squared away with Ed and Becky. I gave them two-hundred dollars. I figure that will last five or six days considering the needs of eleven men. If all eleven were out in the wild it wouldn't cost two or three dollars a day but in a town and eating town food it's a bit more," Bishop said.

"Now, Boss, you ain't pleading poverty on us are you?" Toler said with a wide grin on his face.

Bishop looked at his foreman. "I believe I am. I'm seventy or eighty miles from the Box W and got who knows how many men after me. We are operating on money we confiscated from some of those very same men. If we aren't careful, and lucky, then none of us are making it out of this alive."

Warrix just stood there as he listened to the ranch owner vent his frustration. Everything the man said was true, and then some.

Once finished Bishop climbed in the saddle. "You know something. We stole this horse yesterday and by the looks of the two you're riding I'd say those belong to someone else too. That would make the three of us horse thieves." After a moment's thought Bishop added, "After this is over I'm keeping this one and I'm going to name her Trouble because that's all the three of us are good at, finding trouble."

The name seemed appropriate. It was nearly three in the afternoon when they rode out of town. None of the men had any idea where they were going but knew in the next couple of days they would need to either be at the Brewer Ranch or the Box W to settle things. Settling meant killing, all three were in agreement on that.

The trail the three used was through an empty land crowded with timber. No man or horse had used this particular path in ages. It was covered with tracks of unshod animals. Elk and deer, even an occasional buffalo track covered the trail. If that many animals found use for this particular trail then it was doubtful that men were about, at least not close.

"Do any of you have a destination in mind? We got two good hours of daylight left and after that we're lost," Bishop said.

"I know where we're going, and we should be there right about dark. It's an old trapper's cabin, must be thirty years old. I found it a couple of years back while hunting. You remember that week I take off every December to scout around and see what I can see. It's the same trip where you make me take along a tally book. Even on my time off I got to work counting your cattle," Toler said half-jokingly.

"I know very well that week you take off every winter. Always wondered what kept you from freezing to death," Bishop said.

"If this cabin is that old then does it still have a roof?" the marshal asked.

"It does at that. Every time I visit I bring a pack horse to carry my supplies. Part of those supplies last year was a roll of that new tarpaper folks are now using on their roofs. It ain't the prettiest sight but it does shed the rain and snow. Got to be real careful about putting that stuff close to a hot flue though. 'Bout near burned the cabin down last year," Toler said.

"This cabin you speak of, is it out of the way enough that no one knows it exists?" Warrix asked.

"Funny thing about that place, even if you were looking I doubt you could find it. It's tucked tight in a narrow little gorge where the water runs cold, and the timber grows tall. There's enough game there to feed a man for the rest of his life.

"Last year while I was looking around I nearly got ambushed by a big bear. Tried to shoot the damn thing but wouldn't you know it, I dropped my rifle. All I could do was climb a big cedar tree. That big brown bastard kept me up in that tree all evening. By the time he left it was nearly dark. When I finally got the nerve to climb down I grabbed my rifle and ran to the cabin. The stock of that gun was cracked. All I can figure is the bear stood on it and ruined it. Lucky he didn't bend the barrel," Toler said. He didn't seem ashamed or embarrassed of the fact that he'd dropped his gun. He actually told the story as if it was one of his fondest memories.

"How on earth did you manage to let a big grizzly sneak up on you? I've only encountered a grizzly once in my life and I heard him coming from a thousand yards away. He was grunting and snorting and making no effort to be quiet," Warrix said.

"You know that's the strangest part, he didn't make a sound. I believe that bear was stalking me. He was hunting. If I hadn't turned around when I did he would've had me," Toler said. He grew quiet as he replayed the event in his mind.

"Sounds like a man killer. I've heard of grizzlies that developed a liking for human flesh. Had one near the ranch when I first came here. He took two men before we finally hunted him down and put an end to it. Some of the men at the ranch wanted to carve him up and roast some of the steaks, said bear meat was as good as beef. When I reminded them that the bear had eaten two of the wranglers they couldn't stomach any bear meat, neither could I," Bishop told the two.

This definitely looked like bear country. The men had passed rocky outcroppings everywhere. A bear could live here and possibly never see a man, but then again the territory was getting crowded. It was hard to travel five miles in any direction and not see the track of a shod horse.

One thing the men wished they had was a coffeepot and maybe a skillet. Some coffee and something to put in the skillet would be nice too. In all the preparations of seeing to the needs of the prisoners and Chaney's men they had neglected themselves. They had pulled out of Elkton in a hurry and done something stupid, left without provisions. It wouldn't be the first time the three had gone without supper.

Just about dark the men entered the small gorge where Toler said the cabin was located. As they drew closer they smelled woodsmoke. All three men stopped as they looked around.

"Does anyone own that cabin, Toler?" Bishop asked.

"Nope, I checked with old man Brewer two years ago. He knew of the cabin, said it lay about five miles from his northern most boundary. When he acquired the land for his spread he scouted the area and found the cabin. Didn't want nothing to do that that land, too rocky and gnarled for cattle. When he did his boundaries and filed he made sure to check. No one ever filed for this area, it's unwanted."

"How do you want to handle this, Marshal? We can't just walk up and knock on the door," Bishop asked.

"How much farther?"

Toler thought a minute as he looked around. "Quarter mile, maybe a half at the most."

"Let's tie our horses here and go the rest of the way on foot. We each take a Winchester. We'll get as close as we can and then see what our best option is," Warrix said.

After getting the three horses situated Toler led the way. As they approached the smell of woodsmoke grew stronger, but the cabin was still not in view. Toler's description was right, you needed to be nearly right at the cabin to find it. When it was in view the men knew they had a problem. There was only one way to approach without being seen if someone inside was actually looking.

"What do you think, Marshal? If we go marching up there then we'd be sitting ducks," Toler said.

"I'd bet that whoever's in there feels safe. Like I said this place is damn near impossible to find. Whoever is in there don't suspect anyone is outside. You think it might be some of the men that's been after us?" Bishop asked.

"I'd doubt it. Why would anyone be this far off the beaten trail if they were looking for us? Might just be a trapper or a hunter. Maybe someone that's hiding out for reasons other than hunting us," Toler added.

It took Warrix to point out the obvious. "Then where's his horse? If I was just out hunting I sure wouldn't be suspecting someone was looking for me."

It was a good point. A man that took precautions with his horse was probably either on the run or chasing someone himself. As the three talked they made sure to stay hidden.

Until they figured out who was in the cabin and why he was here they weren't taking any chances.

As the three considered their options the door to the cabin opened and a man walked out carrying a bucket. It was Heith Bryson. Bishop and Toler knew the man, he used to work at the Box W Ranch. Warrix could tell the two might know Bryson by the look on their faces.

"Either of you know that man?"

"Yeah, I know him. We think he might have had something to do with that bank robbery that happened in Dakota City a few days back," Toler said.

Warrix could feel his anger start to build. This was one of the men that killed his sister, this could be the very man that killed her. He took charge of the situation.

"Toler, go right, Bishop, left. We'll see what he's doing, probably going for water for cooking. If that's the case then we might be able to take him alive, and we really need to take him alive," Warrix stressed.

Bishop and Toler quietly moved in the direction the marshal wanted. They didn't realize it, but Warrix had sent them away in order to keep them safe because as soon as each was far enough away he stood and sprinted toward Bryson.

Bryson had left the safety of the trapper's cabin to fetch water for coffee and cooking. When he heard something to his left he turned to see a man running toward him. He threw down the bucket and went for his gun, but he was too late. Warrix nearly ran over Bryson in his headlong rush to capture the man that had participated in the death of his sister.

When the two men came to a stop Warrix jerked the gun out of Bryson's hand and tossed it to the side. He then pounded the man's face with two savage blows from his right fist. Bryson, who had been trying to regain his footing, went limp and fell to the ground.

The marshal heard running footsteps and turned to find both Bishop and Toler heading his way in a hurry. Both were holding guns, but it wasn't needed, Bryson was out cold.

"Did you just set this up, Marshal?" Bishop asked with a grin.

"I might have. At any rate it worked, and nobody got hurt." There was a groan as Bryson started to move.

"Well nobody got hurt except Bryson," Warrix added.

"We better scout around and make sure he's alone," Toler said as he removed Bryson's gun belt. He quickly wrapped it around the man's forearms and torso about halfway between his wrists and his elbows. He then put a boot on the man's midsection and forced all the air out of his lungs. He then fastened the buckle. When he removed his boot Bryson took in a ragged breath, or at least as much of one as the belt would allow.

"I've never seen that done before. He can't move his arms and he can't undo his belt. Now where did you learn something like that," Bishop asked.

"Oh I don't know, boss. A man just picks up a few things in his life," Toler said with a big grin.

"That should hold him while we check around. Scout out a couple of hundred feet. If we don't find anything then we can bring in the horses. Let's see if we can find Bryson's horse while we're at it."

Fifteen minute later and all four horses were tied up next to the cabin. Bryson's horse had been found upstream of the cabin tied out near water. Warrix and Bishop had to admit, this was an excellent hideout. The only thing missing was grass for the horses. The spot was so remote and shaded by timber that nearly nothing grew at ground level.

"We can tend to the horses after we get Bryson inside and secured to a chair. I don't want him out here shouting his damn head off if some of his friends show up," Warrix said.

Fifteen minutes later and the bank robbing bastard was tied and bound to a rough looking chair inside the cabin. With that taken care of it was time to look around and see what was what. The first thing they found was a pair of saddlebags, a pair of bulging saddlebags. Bryson sat quietly as the search took place. When the saddlebags were found beside a bunk and placed on the table, Bryson looked like he was ready to cry.

Warrix knew by the feel of the saddlebags that they probably contain way more than tobacco and coffee. When he opened the first one it was filled with cash, filled to the point that it was nearly ready to spill out. The second bag held cash and quite a few gold pieces. It wouldn't take many fifty dollar gold pieces to soon add up to a substantial amount of money.

"You mind explaining this?" Warrix asked. He knew it was the money from the bank holdup.

"I don't know anything about that. I just got here right before you."

Warrix resisted the urge to just shoot the man. "So you're saying you walked in and saw this pair of saddlebags and didn't think that was suspicious? You didn't think someone else might be using this cabin? You didn't look in those saddlebags? You just came in here, saw the saddlebags, and then decided to go get a bucket of water for coffee. Is that the way it happened Bryson?"

The man smiled. He was stupid enough to think if he agreed then Warrix would believe that's the way it really happened.

"That's right, Marshal. The way you said it was the way it happened." Bryson didn't know it, but he had just made a serious blunder.

"Now as far as I know me and you have never met, is that right?"

"No, Marshal, we've never met. I'm not a lawbreaker and ain't acquainted with lawmen."

"Then why are you calling me marshal? I'm not wearing a badge," Warrix asked the man.

Bryson knew Warrix was a marshal because he was with the men that shot his horse out from under him a few days back. He actually thought the marshal had been shot but here he was standing before him alive and well. It was time to continue the lie.

"I swear we've never met. I only called you marshal because I figured you was a lawman."

Warrix was growing impatient. "What about all this money? Do you know anything about that?"

"Naw, never seen it before," Bryson said.

Bishop had been going through the contents of the saddlebags when he saw something that would take the wind out of Bryson's sails.

"Would you look at this. The inside flap of these saddlebags has the name Heith Bryson written in ink," Bishop said as he held the bags so everyone could see.

Bryson couldn't continue his argument now. He'd actually forgotten about his name being on his saddlebags, something most men did to prove ownership.

Warrix just stood over the man. If Bishop and Toler weren't around he might just grab a rope and save the territory the expense of a trial.

"Bryson, I only have one more question. Who shot the bank teller?"

"I don't know anything about that. We took some cash from the bank but didn't harm anyone."

# Marshal Warrix

Warrix pulled his Colt and pressed it against the center of Bryson's forehead. "I'll ask again, who shot the bank teller?"

There was a pause as Bryson considered his options, they were few. "No one shot anyone, I'm telling you that everyone was just fine when we left."

Warrix only smiled at the man as he pulled back the hammer on his Colt. The metallic sound was crisp, and ominous.

"Wait, wait. It was..." there was a pause as Bryson tried to think of a name. He was the one that actually killed the teller but to admit to that would mean certain death.

"It was Marcus Rowley. He killed the lady at the bank. I told him not to use violence, I swear I did but he killed her anyway. The man's a murderer."

Warrix knew Bryson was lying, he could just tell but there was no way to prove it. There was still enough evidence against the man to warrant a hanging. The marshal told himself that he'd make sure to witness that event.

While this had been going on Bishop and Toler had been arranging and counting the money. Both men stopped counting when they reached the staggering sum of ten-thousand dollars. All three knew it was the money from the bank in Dakota City. They also knew that the men working with Bryson had all been found dead. That left Bryson to be held accountable for the holdup and also the murders.

"I'm going to go for some water now. It's going to take a while because that dumbass Bryson tied his horse upstream of the cabin. I suppose you like your coffee to taste of horse droppings. If I decide to share a cup I'll make sure to go outside and freshen it up for you," Toler said as he looked at the man. Bryson could only grunt his disapproval.

Warrix had used all the discipline and control he could muster to keep his outrage in check. He was of the calculated personality. He could be harsh at times but only when the situation required. He could be kind at times, which was most of the time. He did have a dark side that most folks that knew him weren't aware of. That dark side had nearly emerged while holding a gun to the head of the man that most likely killed his sister. Now that he had the man in custody he would try to keep his temper in check. One thing he did know, if it appeared Bryson was going to escape or be rescued he wouldn't hesitate to use the Colt.

It took Toler nearly ten minutes to walk to a spot where the water was clear and didn't have the possibility of being contaminated by Bryson's horse. As he was walking back he noticed a trail that came in from the back of the cabin. It was hard packed ground and in places solid rock, so the trail wasn't that noticeable. As he walked he saw something that nearly made his blood run cold.

As Bishop and Warrix repacked the money they noticed the supplies Bryson had brought in. It was more than a pair of saddlebags could hold. But the only saddlebags Bryson had were filled with money. Just as that fact hit home the door burst open and Toler barged in.

"Found two more sets of tracks fifty yards from here. Looks like someone rode in with Bryson and then left. Tracks look fresh and I mean minutes fresh."

Warrix went to the tiny window in the back of the cabin and eased open the shutter. He didn't see anything, but he heard men in the distance talking.

"How many men you got with you Bryson?" Warrix asked. Bryson only smiled.

Warrix knew time was something he didn't have in abundance at the moment. He grabbed his Colt and again pressed it against Bryson's forehead. "Answer me damn you before I put a hole in that head of yours."

"You won't shoot me; it'll give you away."

Bryson had just spoken his first honest words of the day and he was right, Warrix wouldn't shoot. He eased the gun away and turned to go back to the window. He took only a half-step before turning and cracking the butt of the gun against Bryson's skull. The man didn't grunt, he didn't groan, he didn't cry out, he was just knocked unconscious. Warrix might have used a little more force than he intended but really didn't care.

"Bishop, stay here and keep watch on Bryson. Toler, you, and me need to get to a flanking position before those riders get here," Warrix said as he picked up his Winchester and headed for the door.

There were actually three riders, and they weren't using caution as they approached the cabin. Bishop was peeking out the back window, he had his Winchester pointed at the riders. Warrix and Toler also had good positions. They could shoot all day without fear of getting shot themselves.

When the riders got withing range, and also in what could be considered a kill box, Warrix called out.

"Stop right there, we've got you surrounded. Throw down your weapons."

The three riders stopped, each looking in the direction of where they thought the voice came from. None of the men threw down their guns. They each started backing their horses up a bit but in the confines of the trail there wasn't much room for three horses and riders to maneuver.

"Drop your guns, this is your last warning," Warrix shouted.

The three riders seemed to be discussing matters between themselves. Just when it looked like they were going to cooperate all three raised their guns and started blasting away at where Warrix was. He was well protected behind both rock and timber and weathered the storm of lead without a scratch. It was more than could be said for the three riders.

Bishop fired from the cabin window knocking one of the three out of the saddle. Toler did the same, dispatching a second rider with his first shot. The last man turned his attention on the cabin and fired two shots before Toler took care of him with another well placed slug. The man hit the ground joining the other two. It was all over in less than ten seconds.

Once Toler and Warrix were certain none of the three still posed a threat they cautiously came from their firing positions and headed to where the three men lay. It only took a minute to determine that all three were dead. The power and accuracy of a Winchester in the hands of men that knew how to use them was lying there on the ground in full display.

As Toler and Warrix scouted around and also gathered the three horses they were joined by Bishop.

"Shouldn't at least one of us be guarding Bryson?" Warrix asked.

Bishop, who had stooped to get a closer look at the dead men's faces stood. "Won't be any need of that now. He's dead, killed by his own men." It was the shot the last man had fired, he had actually fired two with one hitting Bryson in the head. The man had never regained consciousness after being knocked out by Warrix.

"Well that takes care of that," the marshal said. In a way he was glad to be shed of the murderer but in another way he really wanted to see him hang. Bryson had gotten off easy as far as the marshal was concerned.

It was too dangerous to leave the bodies close to the cabin with the number of bears and wolves in the area. It was decided to tie a rope around the legs of all four and drag them a quarter mile away where a deep ravine had been spotted when they first rode in. All four were rolled as unceremoniously as possible over the side. The bodies rolled and tumbled a hundred feet to the bottom. All four landed in a pile. Partners in crime, partners in death.

"I figure we ought to take turns standing guard tonight. No need to take any chances on more of Bryson's bunch showing up," Warrix said. The other two men readily agreed.

Back at the cabin the men quickly fixed coffee, compliments of Bryson and his killers. They also had bacon and biscuits, also compliments of Bryson.

It had been dark nearly an hour by the time they finished their supper. Warrix decided to stand watch first. He was glad to have justice served on the man that killed Mae. But to have achieved what he had set out to do all those days ago was anti-climactic. His emotions were jumbled at the moment, and he needed time to calm his nerves. He knew if sleep came tonight it wouldn't be for a few hours. His first watch would be four hours. Maybe by the end of that his fatigue would overpower his thoughts, maybe.

The night passed peaceful enough. The horses were a bit skittish, but this might have been expected. With four fresh kills located only a quarter mile away predators were to be expected. The horses sensed the danger but didn't have much to worry about. Anything that came near the mounts would meet a quick end from a Winchester.

Bishop was up first, as usual. He quickly fixed flapjacks, bacon, and coffee. One of the four men they had killed must have really liked flapjacks because he was carrying a quart jar of maple syrup in his saddlebags.

Bishop ate as he cooked so when everything was ready he stepped outside so the other two could eat. Both men had to admit, the ranch owner could really cook but then again, how hard was bacon and flapjacks?

"Where do you think we are?" Warrix asked.

Toler knew exactly where they were. "We're a good five hour ride from the Brewer Ranch. What do you have in mind?"

"Something's been bothering me about those four men from last evening," Bishop said.

Toler and Warrix had been standing outside the cabin when Bishop walked over.

"What's that?" the marshal asked.

"Well let's figure out what we know for sure. Bryson killed the men that helped him with the bank job, we know that for sure. We also know that these other three men were some of Rumford's men, previously men that worked at the Box W Ranch. Now if Rumford was expecting Bryson and the other men that robbed the bank to bring him the money then why did Bryson kill them all unless he was planning on keeping the money for himself?"

Toler and Warrix now understood the question. They waited for Bishop to proceed, which he did.

"Now, the only way this would work is for Bryson to have been working with those three we killed last night. My guess is Rumford sent those three men to find the missing money, and find Bryson too. Rumford didn't know the three men he sent to bring in Bryson were actually working with him. Does that sound about right?" Bishop asked.

"What makes you think the three were working with Bryson? I don't quite follow," Toler asked.

"Because after killing the other men that helped with the bank heist he didn't have a friend in the world. That must have been the plan all along. And if this wasn't put together by all four then how on earth did they find him here? This place is as well-hidden as any I've ever seen. They were all working together. Plus Rumford's men will be looking for a single man, Heith Bryson. Bryson and the other three could split up the money and ride out of here together, no one would ever be the wiser," Bishop said.

Toler and Warrix thought about it. There were a few holes in Bishop's theory but all in all it sounded about right. The one thing that made it all seem plausible was the fact that after Heith Bryson had robbed the bank and was in possession of the money there was no way he was going to turn it over to Rumford. Bryson and his three accomplices would have been out of the territory in a few days and the money would never have been recovered.

Now all Warrix, Toler and Bishop had to do was make it back to the Box W Ranch and see if Rumford's plans could be thwarted. It seemed doubtful. Rumford held all the cards. There was scant evidence that the man had even committed a crime. Everyone that knew what he'd done was either dead or working for him. Unless a witness could be produced all the man had to do was board the next train back to Chicago and that would be that. At least the money he was going to use against Bishop had been recovered.

By four o'clock the next day Rumford was growing anxious. He was still at the Brewer Ranch where he paced the floors. He needed Bryson and the money found and brought back, he also needed Bishop. With the money in hand and Bishop captured he could dictate the terms for the transfer of the ranch. Without either of the two it would be nearly impossible. Even if Bishop was killed the plan would still work. Rumford could forge the signature; it would be hard for a dead man to dispute the handwriting.

The three men Rumford sent looking for Bryson and his money were told once the money was retrieved to kill Bryson but bring the body back to the Brewer Ranch. He was going to turn over the body to the nearest town with a marshal and claim he had killed the notorious bank robber, but hadn't found the money. That money would never be associated to Rumford although he would be in full possession of it.

If they could bring in the body of Marshal Warrix that would just be a bonus. The story would be that the marshal had been trying to apprehend Bryson and in the process had managed to get himself killed. The reason Rumford wanted the marshal killed was he needed to have a marshal in Dakota City that he could control. He'd been the one to put the bounty out on Warrix and once the man was dead he'd have someone sworn in that he could trust to go along with his plans. Dakota City would be a very important part of Rumford's operation.

As Rumford contemplated his plans for the future he was interrupted by Clark.

"Got three riders heading this way. Looks like they're leading two horses, both carrying bodies," Clark said.

Rumford nearly ran to the front door. Sure enough there were three riders leading two horses. The horses each carried a body.

Rumford stepped to the porch and waited. The three riders looked tired; their bodies slumped low in the saddle as they approached. Men that spent two full days hunting down their prey had every reason to be tired.

Rumford couldn't believe it, his dreams of taking over the Box W Ranch were about to come true. Before the riders even made it to the front steps he shouted.

"Did you get the money?"

"Got it, Boss," came the reply.

"I hope those two bodies are Bishop and Warrix. I've lost a lot of men trying to accomplish just that," Rumford said.

The three riders almost in unison raised their heads and also raised their guns. It was the last thing Rumford expected. As soon as he saw their faces he went for his gun, but it was a foolish move. Toler shot him before his gun even cleared leather.

Clark recognized the three as the same three he'd seen two days prior. In his fury at letting the men escape then, and to now be tricked by the same three, he also did something foolish. Even though he had three guns pointed at him he went for his gun anyway. He was hit by three bullets almost simultaneously. His last thoughts would never be known. The force of the three bullets knocked him straight back, slamming against the wall, then sliding to the porch floor.

Three more men came running from the barn but once they saw the three riders holding guns on their boss they quickly threw up their hands.

Rumford stood holding a bloody hand to his side. He looked up at Bishop. "Who have you got tied on the back of those horses?"

Bishop looked at the two horses. "Just two bedrolls with a little brush stuffed inside. We wanted it to look real convincing when we took you into custody."

"Into custody, for what charge. You don't have anyone that can implicate me in a crime," Rumford said.

Now it was Warrix that spoke. "You just admitted that you've been trying to kill both Bishop and me. You also admitted to orchestrating the bank robbery that led to the deaths of four innocent people. I think the three of us are the witnesses that will see you sent to the gallows."

Nathan Wright

Warrix wanted to say the name of his sister but knew her memory was too precious for the ears of the man that had been a participant in her killing. When the trap door opened, and Rumford fell through, he knew Mae would finally be avenged.

# The End

Made in the USA
Monee, IL
20 February 2023

28347658R00152